KINGS OF MAFIA

CRAVING DANGER

USA TODAY BESTSELLING AUTHOR
MICHELLE HEARD

Cover Designer: Okay Creations

Editor: Sheena Taylor

TABLE OF CONTENTS

Dedication

To all the readers who need an escape from reality.

This book is for you.

———————————

Songlist

Click here - *Spotify*

Unsteady – X Ambassadors, Erich Lee

Going Down Fighting – Phlotilla, Andrea Wasse, Topher Mohr

Shadow Preachers – Zella Day

War Of Hearts – Ruelle

The War – SYML

Love In The Dark – Adele

Breathing Underwater – Hot Milk

Take Me To Church – MILCK

I Won't Let You Down – Erin McCarley

Hero – Alan Walker, Sasha Alex Sloan

Everything I Did To Get To You – Ben Platt

Synopsis

At the office, Samantha is mouthy AF and hellbent on testing my patience. So you can imagine my surprise when my new personal assistant walks into my club with a very specific fantasy.

When the man Samantha's paired with doesn't stick to the rules, I step in to take his place. Wearing a mask protects my identity, and soon the little wildcat from the office is telling me all her darkest secrets and fantasies.

During the day, she gives me hell, but at night, she becomes my wounded kitten.

I know I'm playing a dangerous game.
She doesn't know I'm one of the heads of the Cosa Nostra. She doesn't know her boss and her nightly visitor is the same person.

With my enemy on the attack and her past coming to haunt her, our secrets come out in the most explosive way possible, threatening to rip Samantha away from me.

But my wildcat has another thing coming if she thinks I'll ever let go.

Craving Danger

Mafia / Organized Crime / Suspense Romance
STANDALONE in the Kings of Mafia
Book 2

Authors Note:

Franco Vitale in Brutalize Me is not the same person as the main character in this book. I just really loved the name, so I used it twice. Sorry for the confusion.

This book contains subject matter that may be sensitive for some readers.
There is triggering content related to:
Mental and emotional abuse
On-page rape
Attempted murder
Being drugged
Graphic violence & torture
Trauma-related panic attacks

18+ only.
Please read responsibly.

"Reality doesn't impress me. I only believe in intoxication, in ecstasy, and when ordinary life shackles me, I escape, one way or another. No more walls."

—— Anaïs Nin

Chapter 1

Samantha

Franco Vitale; 35. Samantha Blakely; 26.

I've only been Mr. Vitale's personal assistant for two weeks, and I'm already considering quitting.

God, the man is impossible.

Letting out a huff, I suppress the urge to kick the printer. The stupid machine keeps giving me error messages.

I'm starving. I could wolf down an entire pizza on my own right now.

My phone starts ringing for the millionth time today, and I feel like whining like a puppy as I dart to my desk to answer the internal call from Mr. Vitale's office.

"Yes, Sir?"

"Where's the contract?"

I close my eyes and take a deep breath before I explain for the fourth time, "The printer is giving error messages. I'm waiting for Andy from IT to fix it."

"There are hundreds of printers in this building! I want the contract on my desk in five minutes," he barks before hanging up.

Impatient ass.

I've worked at Vitale Pharmaceuticals in the administration department for the past eight months, and until I got promoted to Mr. Vitale's PA, I loved my job.

It's only been two weeks. Give it more time. You just need to get used to how Mr. Vitale wants things done, then it will get better.

I roll my eyes because my gut instinct tells me it won't improve. Mr. Vitale is just one of those people who's never satisfied with anything.

All the employees in the building cower in fear whenever he's near. I should've known I was in trouble when I got promoted and the admin team gave me looks of pity as if I was on death row.

While I worked on the third floor, I didn't see much of Mr. Vitale, but the few times our paths crossed, he always looked like he was a second away from wringing someone's neck.

The past two weeks as his PA have shown me the man is always grumpy, and he loses his temper at the speed of light. He's downright rude and impossible to please.

I quickly email the contract to the admin department's printer, which is still linked to my profile, before hurrying to the elevators.

While heading down to the third floor, I wiggle my toes in the high heels I'm wearing. It gives my tired feet some relief before the doors slide open, and I rush toward the printer. I lose precious time when I have to sift through all the printed documents and ensure I have the whole contract before hurrying back to the elevators.

Who needs to go to a gym when you work for Franco Vitale?

In the elevator, I quickly pull my bra strap back into place. I've lost weight from all the running around and need to get new underwear.

The doors open, and I shoot forward like a bullet, but my heart sinks when my desk comes into view.

Crap.

Mr. Vitale is standing by the printer in all his six-foot-five glory, his arms crossed over his broad chest as he watches the machine spit out page after page.

When I reach him, I hold the papers out to him. "Here's the contract, sir."

His dark brown eyes flick to me, and I feel the punch of his intense gaze in my gut. I swear, whenever this man looks at me, I feel like I'm nothing but a worm.

I've worked with intimidating people in the past, but Mr. Vitale overshadows them all.

The first time I laid eyes on him, I was struck speechless by how handsome he was, but the attraction died a quick death after I watched one PA after another leave the building in tears.

As the printer spits out the last page, his dark gaze remains locked on me while he swipes the contract from the traitorous machine.

His tone is low and filled with a world of warning as he mutters, "If you can't do something as simple as printing a document, we're going to have a problem, Miss Blakely."

I suck in a deep breath as I watch him stalk back to his office, and the moment the door shuts behind him, I glare at the printer. "Sure, for him, you'll print."

"What's the problem?" Andy, one of the IT guys, asks from behind me.

With a tired sigh, I set the now spare copy of the contract down on my desk and gesture at the machine. "It won't print for me. I've checked everything, but it keeps giving me error messages. It printed for Mr. Vitale, though."

"Let me take a quick look."

Andy takes a seat at my desk, and after typing for less than a minute, the stupid machine starts printing.

"I've reinstalled the printer, so you shouldn't have a problem again."

"Thank you." I gather the document and shred it, seeing as it's no longer needed.

"You're welcome."

As Andy walks away, my phone starts to ring, and I quickly pick up the earpiece. "Yes, Sir?"

"Get Mr. Castro on the line," Mr. Vitale orders before hanging up.

Taking a seat in my chair, I dial Mr. Castro's number. The call goes through to voicemail, and as I leave a quick message, the ache in my shoulders intensifies from all the tension.

Checking the time, I notice it's just turned five o'clock. *Thank God.*

I quickly dial Mr. Vitale's extension.

"Hm," he answers.

"Mr. Castro wasn't available. I left a message for him to return your call."

"Hm." The line goes dead, and I suck in a deep breath of air.

My boss has zero manners, and it aggravates me to no end.

Redialing his extension, I wait for him to answer with his usual grunt before I say, "It's five o'clock, sir. I'm going home. Have a good night."

Before he can grunt, I put the earpiece down, feeling a little burst of triumph for getting to hang up on him first.

I switch off my computer and gather my handbag from the bottom drawer where I keep it, but as I rise from my chair, Mr. Vitale's door swings open, and he barks, "My office. Now."

God. What now?

I place my handbag on my desk, and with tension coiling in my stomach, I head into the office, otherwise referred to by me as the chamber of wrath.

Mr. Vitale stands in front of the floor-to-ceiling windows overlooking Manhattan. He looks like a god, and his dress shirt and vest span tightly across his broad shoulders.

At the most random times, I'm struck with thoughts of how handsome the man is, but then he opens his mouth, and the unwelcome attraction disappears.

When he remains silent, I ask, "Sir?"

Without turning to look at me, he grumbles, "Mrs. Ross assured me you're a hard worker."

A confused frown furrows my brow.

Am I supposed to say something or keep quiet?

Keeping his arms crossed over his chest, he turns and levels me with an unforgiving look, instantly making me feel apprehensive and nervous.

"I've given you two weeks to settle into the position." His eyes narrow on me and it makes me feel like I'm a petulant child who's being scolded by the headmaster. "I don't have time to waste, so if I ask you for something, I expect the order to be carried out instantly."

"Andy had to reinstall the printer on my computer," I explain, my tone tight from all the tension.

"I won't tolerate excuses," he snaps. "You're employed as my personal assistant to make my life easier. If a problem arises, I expect you to solve it."

Resisting the urge to cross my arms over my chest, I fist my hands at my sides and say, "Yes, Mr. Vitale." I raise an eyebrow at the insufferable man. "Will that be all, sir?"

He shakes his head. "Your position isn't nine to five."

What?

He nods in the direction of the door, his tone harsh and clearly stating this topic is not up for discussion as he mutters, "If you have a problem putting in extra hours, you're more than welcome to hand in your resignation."

Anger begins to bubble in my chest, but I keep my expression respectful as I say, "I don't mind working late, but I'd appreciate it greatly if you would notify me in the morning so I can cancel any plans I might've made for the evening."

Plans? Ha. I live like a freaking hermit.

Still, it's not something he needs to know. I just want him to show me respect and give me sufficient notice, so I don't get my hopes up I'll get to leave the office at five.

Mr. Vitale's features tighten, and it looks like he's a moment away from losing his temper, but then he gives me a curt nod. "For the unforeseeable future, I expect you at the office from seven a.m. to seven p.m."

Twelve hours? The man is insane!

Turning his attention to the stacks of folders and paperwork on his desk, he mutters, "Don't worry. You'll be compensated for the extra time."

Hearing I'll be paid overtime makes my anger lessen. I could use the extra funds to pay off my credit card. The second-hand fridge I got when I moved to New York gave up the ghost the past weekend, and I was forced to go into debt to buy a new one.

"Do you need me to stay late tonight?" I ask.

Letting out an impatient huff, Mr. Vitale's eyes snap to mine. "Yes. Get back to work."

Leaving his office, I pull the door shut behind me. My stomach rumbles, a reminder I haven't eaten anything today.

You're getting paid overtime.

I take a seat at my desk and switch on my computer. Opening my email folder, I see Mr. Vitale's already sent eight emails, and I get back to work, determined to show him I'm a damn good PA.

Chapter 2

Franco

After ending the call with Salvador Castro, my contact for medical supplies, I get up from behind my desk. I grab my jacket, and while shrugging it on, I head to the door.

When I step out of my office, it's to hear my PA's stomach rumble.

"You can go home," I mutter, and without another word, I stalk toward the elevators.

I hear her mumble something under her breath, and it has me stopping dead in my tracks. Glancing at the woman who's been testing my patience for the past two weeks, I raise an eyebrow at her.

"Do you have something to say, Miss Blakely?"

She grabs her handbag and walks toward me with an unhappy expression tightening her features. "Next time you expect me to work until nine p.m. the least you could do is provide dinner."

My gaze sharpens on her, and my tone is grim as I say, "I wasn't aware you didn't know how to order food."

Her eyebrows draw together. "Of course, I know how to order food."

"Then it's no one's fault but your own for not eating today."

Christ, I'm going to fire her. Why the fuck is it so hard to find competent help?

She walks by me as she says, "I wasn't aware I'm allowed to eat at my desk. It will make things so much easier. Have a good night, Mr. Vitale."

Clenching my jaw, I follow her toward the elevators.

I swear the woman is just a pretty head with no brains. The first time I saw her, the breath was knocked from my lungs by her striking beauty. Her blonde hair is always styled in soft curls, and her green eyes look dark against her pale skin. The freckles scattered over her nose complement her features.

Not to mention, the woman has curves in all the right places and an ass that makes my palm itch. Especially when she fucks up or gives me attitude.

But the attraction has vanished over the past two weeks because she's done nothing but aggravate the living shit out of me.

We step into the elevator, and I catch the soft vanilla scent of her perfume as she stands next to me. The top of her head reaches my chin, and I guess without the high heels she's wearing, she'd reach my shoulder.

She keeps shifting her weight from one foot to the other, giving me the impression her shoes are hurting her.

The silence is thick and filled with a world of tension as we ride down to the ground floor.

As the doors slide open, and she hurries out of the elevator, I say, "Bring comfortable shoes to wear when you're sitting at your desk. Maybe then you'll be less moody."

The sound of heels tapping on the tiles stops, and she swings around to face me with a barely contained glare. "I've been nothing but respectful, Mr. Vitale. Maybe you should take your own suggestion and wear comfortable shoes, seeing as you're the moody one."

She turns around, her hair flying over her shoulders, and hurries toward the exit with her spine stiff and her head held high.

My eyes burn on the woman who has more guts than brains for speaking like that to me because I'm her employer.

But if she knew who I really am – one of the heads of the Cosa Nostra, then she'd know just how brave or stupid she's being.

My employees live in a different world where the closest they ever get to the mafia is when they watch *The Godfather*.

Shaking my head, I walk to the exit, where Lorenzo and Milo are waiting for me. They're my guards, and whenever I'm at Vitale Health, my medical supply company, they work in the security room.

The two men have been with me since I was eighteen, and they've become family.

"You can't fire her," Milo reminds me. "You've already gone through four assistants this year, and a fifth will reflect poorly on you."

Shaking my head, I mutter, "If she doesn't get her shit together in the next two weeks, I'm firing her ass, and you can take over as my assistant."

"Fuck, no," Milo chuckles. "I'd much rather take a bullet than subject myself to that kind of torture."

A frown darkens my forehead. "Are you telling me I'm a nightmare to work for?"

We step out of the air-conditioned building and into the hot evening air.

Christ, I can't wait for winter.

Milo opens the backdoor to the G-Wagon and grins at me. "Only when you're in the office."

I glance at Lorenzo, who's been quiet. "Do you agree with Milo?"

He holds up his hands in the universal sign for I-want-no-part-in-this. "I'm Switzerland."

Climbing into the back of the armored G-Wagon, I let out a huff.

I know I'm not the easiest person to work with, and even though I've tried to ease up on the staff, I find it impossible. Whenever I try to be more easygoing, they fuck up, and I lose my temper. It's an annoying cycle.

After getting in behind the steering wheel, Lorenzo asks, "Where to?"

"Paradiso."

Where the other capos have regular strip joints, nightclubs, and casinos, I own *Paradiso*, an adult club where everything goes as long as participating members sign an agreement.

The club provides members with private rooms and every adult toy on the market at an exorbitant fee.

Even though I own a taboo club, I never partake. I've seen people do some weird shit to each other on the

24

security cameras that are there to make sure no one dies on the premises.

Milo pulls into the secure employee parking area behind the club, and after climbing out of the G-Wagon, I enter the building using the back entrance that's guarded by two of my men.

I don't fuck around when it comes to security and spend a small fortune to make sure all my businesses are well protected.

I head straight to my office so I can change out of my suit. Every employee wears a black uniform that consists of cargo pants and a long-sleeve shirt. They also wear skull-face balaclavas to protect their identities.

Where the word *Paradiso* is printed in a silver font on the employees' shirts, mine is gold. It's the only thing setting me apart from them.

When I'm done changing into my uniform, I pull the balaclava over my head and leave the office to check on the staff.

Few people know I'm the owner of *Paradiso*, and I'd like to keep it that way.

As I walk to the security room, my eyes flick over the gray walls and black tiles. The décor is dark, lending a forbidden ambience to the club.

Stepping into the room, I glance at the security team before turning my attention to the numerous monitors.

"Is everything running smoothly?" I ask while watching Mrs. Gilbert enter a room with two men who are easily half her age. While her husband thinks she's bowling with her friends, she comes here to have her brains fucked out.

I have so much dirt on the elite of New York I can easily bury them all.

"Yes, sir," Brian answers. He gets up from his chair and comes closer with a tablet in his hand. Showing the screen to me, he says, "We have two new members. They've been vetted, and tonight's their first time here. Mr. Dugray's membership was canceled after he tried to start a fight with Mr. Bishop because Mr. Bishop refused to be hogtied during sex."

My eyes flick to the monitors again and stop on a screen showing two members snuggling on a bed. It's something I've been noticing more and more. Sometimes, people just want to be held.

I nod as Brian continues to update me, and when he's done, I leave the security room to take a walk through the rest of the club.

When I first opened *Paradiso*, I vetted all the members myself, but with time, I handed the responsibility to Brian.

I walk to the main floor, where members are able to converse with each other while enjoying a drink. The area is decorated with plush couches, round tables with stools, and ferns to lend some greenery to the otherwise dark décor.

Happy that everything is in order, I head back to my office to get some work done.

Vitale Health and *Paradiso* are my only legitimate businesses. I own a trucking company, which I use to transport weapons in aircon units for Renzo, my closest friend and one of the capos. I'm close with Dario, Angelo, and Damiano, the other heads of the Cosa Nostra, but Renzo is like a brother to me.

Even though my companies pad my bank account, I make the bulk of my fortune by printing counterfeit money for Salvator Castro and Lina Diaz, who supply me with medical equipment.

It's a shit ton of work that keeps me busy from the crack of dawn until midnight. I only take time off to play poker with the other heads of the Cosa Nostra or to attend an event hosted by one of them.

Working long hours is part of the reason I'm still single at the age of thirty-five. That and the fact I can't tolerate most of the women I cross paths with.

While I sit at my desk my thoughts turn to Miss Blakely. It's been a while since I met someone who annoyed me as much as she does.

Honestly, it's not because she takes too long to carry out an order. I just feel there's something off about the woman, and if there's one thing I hate, it's when people pretend to be someone their not.

I had Milo do a check on her, and we came up with nothing. Miss Blakely lived a normal and boring life in Houston before moving to New York. She doesn't even have an outstanding traffic fine.

My gut tells me she's hiding something, though.

Annoyed that I'm thinking of the woman, I shake my head and force myself to focus on my work.

Chapter 3

Samantha

Picking up my third slice of pizza, I eat it while looking at my bank accounts. With all the overtime I'll probably be working, I'll be able to pay the credit card off in no time.

I would've had enough money for the fridge if I hadn't paid the membership fee for *Paradiso*, a taboo club in the heart of Manhattan.

I joined the club because I want to spend time with a man in a secure environment. I'm hoping it will help me work through my issues with men.

Men. God, I've been unlucky when it comes to the opposite species.

With the pizza forgotten in my hand, my thoughts spiral down the dark hole Todd Grant ripped through my life. When I started dating him, I thought I'd struck gold. The neurosurgeon was charming and polite and went out of his way to make me feel special. All the female staff at the hospital envied me.

Then, everything came crashing down around me, and I was forced to flee Houston. I didn't even sell the house I bought with the money I inherited from my grandmother. I just locked the front door and ran like the devil himself was after me.

Todd Grant.

I close my eyes, and even though it's been a year since I ran away from my ex-boyfriend, the trauma is still fresh in my mind.

I tried going to therapy, but it didn't help. I couldn't bring myself to speak about what happened to me. I also haven't told my family, because they'd lose their shit and demand I go to the police.

It was easier to run to New York under the pretense of needing a fresh start after breaking things off with Todd.

If only I could run from the memories.

Unable to move a muscle, I hear him come closer…

I dart up from the couch, letting the magazine fall to the floor. Needing to make sure I'm safe, I check all the windows and doors.

At first, I was scared Todd would follow me to New York, and even though he didn't, I'm unable to shake the fear that he might appear at any moment.

Instead of letting the fear and memories overwhelm me, I think about work and the grumpy asshole I have for a boss.

Would it kill the man to treat his employees with respect?

Switching off the lights in the kitchen and living room, I head to my bedroom and climb into bed. I was beyond exhausted when I got home, but now that it's time to sleep, I'm wide awake.

I can't believe the asshole said I'm moody. Hah.

Turning onto my left side, I punch my pillow and let out a sigh.

I'm going to work hard and show him what I'm capable of. I'll be the best PA the man has ever seen.

I've set my alarm for five so I can be at the office at seven. Even though Mr. Vitale pissed me off, I'm taking the man's advice and have already packed a pair of comfy ballet flats to wear while I'm at my desk. I've also packed snacks, so I'll have something to nibble on whenever I have to skip lunch or dinner.

Unable to fall asleep, I grab my phone and unlock the screen. I Google the printer at the office and read up on troubleshooting the most common errors, which works like a charm because with every sentence I read, my eyelids grow heavy, and before I know it, I drift off to sleep.

I rearranged the folders on my computer so they're easy for me to find, and I've mastered the printer. With the ballet flats on my feet, I'm preparing templates of the contracts and documents Mr. Vitale often uses.

I'm wearing a pantsuit and have my hair pinned up so it's out of my face.

Today, I'm ready for Mr. Vitale.

My phone rings, and seeing it's Charlotte from reception, I quickly press the button to answer. "Is he here?"

"Yes. He's by the elevators," she whispers as if we're sharing state secrets.

I asked Charlotte to give me a heads-up in the mornings so I can get Mr. Vitale's coffee ready.

"Thank you!" I end the call and quickly change the flats for my high heels. Wearing the wireless Bluetooth earpiece I installed this morning, I get up from behind my desk and rush to the kitchenette.

I pour Mr. Vitale a cup of coffee and place two shortbread cookies on the saucer. Carrying the tray to his office, I set it down on the side of his desk and quickly dart to the door. Just as I step out of his office Mr. Vitale comes stalking down the hallway.

Today, he's wearing a gray suit, and I have to admit, he looks hot as hell.

Emphasis on hell.

Smiling the most professional smile I can muster, I say, "Morning, Mr. Vitale."

His eyes sweep over my pantsuit and heels before settling on the wireless earpiece, then he mutters, "Morning."

I wait for him to disappear into his office before taking a seat at my desk. Not even a minute has passed when the emails start coming through.

I'm almost done with all the emails when a new one pops up with a request to print the latest report from the sales department.

I carry out the request and smile from ear to ear when I gather the papers from the printer. Just as I step away from the machine, a call comes through, and I quickly tap the button on the earpiece, "Samantha speaking, how can I help you?"

"Print the report I just emailed," Mr. Vitale's voice rumbles over the line.

I walk to his office, and not bothering knocking, I push the door open. "Here's the report, sir."

His eyes widen slightly with surprise as I place the document on his desk.

Feeling triumphant, I turn around and walk back to my desk.

With a smile on my face, I work until twelve, then dial Mr. Vitale's extension.

"What?" he barks over the line.

"Can I order you something for lunch, sir?"

There's a moment's silence before he says, "Anything but fish."

The line goes dead, and I scrunch my nose while I wonder what to get him to eat.

Something that's not messy and easy to eat.

I check the menus of nearby restaurants and decide to get fried chicken and bacon sandwiches.

After I place the order, I continue compiling a performance report from all the information the department heads sent me.

By the time our food arrives, I've already completed the detailed performance report and send it in an email to Mr.

Vitale. I pay the delivery guy, then walk to the kitchenette so I can place the sandwich on a plate and add a bottle of chilled water to the tray. Feeling quite happy with myself, I head to Mr. Vitale's office.

When I enter the chamber of wrath, Mr. Vitale's head snaps up, and his eyes narrow on me.

I place the tray on the corner of the desk and smile at the insufferable man. "Enjoy your lunch, sir."

His eyes narrow even more, and tilting his head, he says, "Explain to me why it took you two weeks to deliver this standard of work."

Asshole.

Keeping the smile plastered on my face, I answer, "I just needed time to get into the routine."

His gaze flicks to the report, then he mutters, "I see you took the initiative to consolidate all the departments."

"I thought it would be easier for you, sir."

The man only nods before getting back to work.

"I just want to let you know I have an appointment tonight, so I'll only be able to work until six," I advise him.

Without looking up, he makes the sound I'm quickly learning to hate.

"Hm."

I suppress the urge to let out a sigh as I turn around and head back to my desk.

Taking a bite of my sandwich, I continue with my duties because I'm adamant to stay one step ahead of Mr. Vitale. Also, I have to leave work at six because I have my first appointment at *Paradiso* tonight. I'm both nervous and excited.

I really hope everything goes well tonight. I'd hate to have paid the membership fee only to be disappointed.

Chapter 4

Samantha

With my first appointment at *Paradiso* scheduled for seven thirty, I take my time showering and getting ready.

The apprehensive part of me thinks I'm insane for joining the club. People go there to have wild sex, and here I am, just wanting to talk to a man.

Maybe I should cancel.

Checking my reflection in the mirror, I take in the black dress I'm wearing and wonder whether it's too formal. Then again, I don't think jeans would be appropriate.

"You look fine," I whisper before turning away from the mirror.

Just as I gather my keys from the side table near the front door, my phone starts to ring. I answer the call and position the device between my shoulder and ear before opening the front door.

"Samantha speaking."

"Hey, sweetie. It's Mom."

"Oh hey," I say, my tone a little lighter. "How are you?"

"Good. I'm calling to let you know I won the knitting contest. Your mother is a whole two-hundred-and-fifty dollars richer."

A grin spreads over my face while I lock the door, and as I head out of my apartment building, I chuckle, "Wow, I'm so proud of you. What did you knit?"

"Nothing. We just knitted to see who's the fastest." From the chopping sounds, I assume Mom's busy preparing dinner. "How are things in New York?"

"I can't complain. Work has been super busy since I got the promotion."

My eyes keep darting around me as I walk to the nearest subway station. Unless it's for work, I seldom leave the safety of my apartment.

It's uncanny how one person's actions can change your entire perspective about people. I never had trust issues until I met Todd. Now I live in constant fear that everyone is out to hurt me.

"Just don't overdo it," Mom says. I hear sizzling in the background before she asks, "Have you met anyone new?"

Wanting to set her mind at ease, I lie, "Yes. I'm actually on my way to a date."

"Oh, really? I'm so glad to hear that. What's he like?"

Shit.

"I don't know him so well yet." Needing to get off the topic of my love life, I say, "I'm also going to the movies on Saturday with Jenny."

I met Jenny in the admin department. She just kept trying until I gave up and accepted her friendship. It took a while to get used to her bubbly personality, but eight months later, she's my best friend.

"I thought she was on vacation with her boyfriend?"

"She got back today."

There's a moment's silence, then Mom asks, "We're still seeing you for your Dad's birthday party, right?"

"Yes, I wouldn't miss it for the world."

Unless Mr. Vitale cancels the vacation time I requested before getting the promotion.

I'll have to ask him about it tomorrow.

"Thanks for the call, Mom, but I have to go."

"Sure. I'll talk to you next week."

Tucking my phone into my handbag, I take the subway to the heart of Manhattan, and as I near the club, my stomach begins to spin with nerves.

Chill. You're just going to have a conversation with a man.

The club assured me there are security measures to ensure every member's safety.

My steps slow down as I near the entrance to the club. The words *Paradiso* are in large gold letters across the wall, and a red carpet leads up to the door where a bouncer is standing guard.

A Rolls Royce stops in front of the entrance, and I watch as a woman who seems to be in her fifties gets out of the expensive vehicle.

There's an air of wealth surrounding her as she walks into the club.

If she can do it, so can you. If you feel uncomfortable, you can leave at any time.

Lifting my chin, I suck in a deep breath before I walk toward the bouncer. The man's eyes settle on me, and it makes me feel a hundred times more nervous.

His tone makes him sound like a butler when he says, "Evening, Ma'am. Just a moment."

I glance around us while I wait, then the bouncer says, "Welcome, Miss Blakely. Seeing it's your first time visiting *Paradiso*, just follow the hallway to where you'll be met by one of the staff members."

My eyebrow darts up. "How did you know who I am?"

Giving me a smile, he gestures to a camera above the doorway. "The security team notified me."

Wow. Fancy.

Nodding at him, I enter the building. My hands clutch the strap of my handbag as I take in the gray walls and black tiles. Soft yellow light shines from the ceiling, and I see someone dressed in black waiting for me up ahead.

My gaze locks on the black ski mask with a skeleton face the person is wearing, and I consider making a U-turn.

That's not intimidating at all.

I understand the masks are to protect their identities, but damn, they could've gone with something more subtle.

"Evening, Miss Blakely," the woman says. "Would you like to take a seat with me, so we can discuss any questions you might have?"

An awkward smile brushes over my lips. "Please."

"This way," she murmurs.

I follow her to an area that looks comfortable. There are couches and tables where people are seated together and enjoying drinks.

I love the ferns situated between the tables. It gives the couples some privacy.

A bar counter lines the one wall, and servers move between the tables and couches.

The atmosphere feels professional, and it helps ease my apprehensiveness a little.

"Please take a seat," the woman assigned to welcome me says.

Turning my attention to her, I sit down on a black leather couch and place my handbag on my lap.

My eyes lock on her brown ones, and not knowing what to say, I wait for her to talk first.

"Welcome to *Paradiso*."

I can't tell if she's smiling.

"Thank you."

"We want to assure you that your privacy comes first. Whatever you choose to do will remain between you and your partner or partners."

Partners. Hell has a better chance of freezing over.

"You've requested to have a conversation with a man. Is that right?"

"Yes."

"You didn't give any requirements for age, personality, or looks."

"None of that matters." Feeling uncomfortable, I grip my handbag tighter. "I just want a man I can talk to."

"Whatever you want." She gestures for a server to come closer. "Would you like something to drink?"

"Yeah, sure. A martini would be nice."

She places the order before looking at me again. "I want to assure you that this is a safe space where you can explore and live out your fantasies. There are cameras everywhere, and we have a zero-tolerance policy should a member break the rules the other party has put in place."

I nod and glance at the other people, wondering which man I'll be talking to.

"Do you have any questions?" she asks.

"Not at the moment."

"I'll leave you then to enjoy your evening. Should your request change during the course of the evening, just notify any of the staff members, and they'll assist you."

Nodding, I watch as she gets up and leaves, and feeling more anxious, I start to nibble on my bottom lip.

I glance at the other members again and find everything…normal.

I expected a raunchy vibe. People getting it on wherever there's an empty space, but this place is pretty decent.

The server brings me a martini, and I murmur, "Thank you."

Needing all the liquid courage I can get, I take a couple of sips, and just as I pop the olive into my mouth, a man approaches me.

Shit. Here we go.

He seems to be in his forties, his salt and pepper hair graying at his temples.

When he reaches me, I stand up and say, "Hi, I'm Samantha."

A crooked smile tugs at his mouth, and he looks just as nervous as I feel.

"Hi, I'm Doyle. It's nice to meet you."

When I take a seat again, and just stare at each other. When it's clear he's not going to talk first, I clear my throat and let out a nervous chuckle. "This isn't awkward at all."

His smile widens a little. "Yeah. Is this your first time coming here?"

"Yes. I thought I'd give it a try. And you?"

"I'm a virgin as well."

Alrighty then.

We smile awkwardly at each other before I take another sip of my drink.

Doyle relaxes back against the couch and glances around, and I take the moment to stare at him.

He seems harmless. The man has zero body muscle, so there's a good chance I can beat him in a fight.

The thought helps me relax enough to ask, "What do you like to do in your spare time?"

His eyes snap back to me, and he thinks for a moment before he answers, "I never miss a chance to go camping. I love fishing and hunting. Do you like being outdoors?"

No. I don't do bugs and wild animals.

"I'm not much of a camping and fishing gal. I love spending a weekend in a cabin up in the mountains or going to the beach."

"Oh. Okay," he replies, not sounding impressed with me. "So, what do you do for a living?"

"I'm a PA, and you?"

"I'm an accountant."

He glances around us again while I finish the rest of my martini.

I expected to have a panic attack, but instead, I might die of boredom. It's a good thing.

Smiling, my muscles relax, and when Doyle looks at me again, he looks a little bewildered as he stammers, "Y-you're pretty when y-you smile."

His face goes beet red, and it makes me feel sorry for the guy.

"I think we're doing great as first-timers," I say, hoping it will help him relax.

"Yeah?"

Nodding, I chuckle. "We haven't made a run for it yet. I'm totally taking it as a win."

"Right." He waves at a server and orders a beer.

The server picks up my empty glass and asks, "Would you like another martini, Miss Blakely?"

"Please."

When we're alone again, Doyle asks, "Why are you here?"

To regain some of the control I've lost and to learn to trust men again.

My smile wavers as I answer, "Just to have a conversation. And you?"

"Even though we live in a city with a population of eight million, it's hard meeting like-minded people, and dating apps aren't my cup of tea."

I glance to the side and lock eyes with one of the staff members who's standing with his arms crossed over his chest while watching us.

Wow. They really take security seriously here.

Even though he's dressed the same as all the other staff, it's clear as daylight the man spends a lot of time in the gym by the way his clothes fit his body.

I'm still staring at the staff member when he walks away. There's something familiar about how he moves, but then the server pulls my attention away as a martini is placed on the table between Doyle and me.

Chapter 5

Franco

Walking toward the main section of *Paradiso*, my thoughts are filled with Miss Blakely.

The woman actually impressed me today.

From the moment I got to the office until we left, she worked so fast I struggled to keep up. It became a fucking competition, and the pace was relentless.

A smile threatens to tug at the corner of my mouth because today Miss Blakely was the kind of PA I've been looking for since I started the company.

Entering the main room, my eyes drift over the members who are enjoying drinks. I notice a new man talking to a blonde, and as I keep walking, her face starts to come into view.

When I have a direct view of her, my feet come to a halt, and my lips part with shock.

What the fuck?

I watch as my PA smiles awkwardly at her partner.

What the hell is she doing here?

It takes a lot to shock me, but seeing my PA at *Paradiso* has stunned me senseless.

This is the last place I expected to see Miss Blakely.

Suddenly, her eyes meet mine and every muscle in my body freezes.

It's okay. She won't recognize you.

Instead of just glancing at me, Miss Blakely tilts her head and continues to stare.

Turning around, I stalk to the security room and take up position in front of the security monitors for the main floor.

"Zoom in on Samantha Blakely," I order.

A moment later I have a closeup view of my PA and the man she's been paired with.

"Bring me her file," I order to no one specific.

Miss Blakely looks beautiful in the little black dress she's wearing, and when she smiles at her partner, a frown forms on my forehead.

Is she into kinky sex?

The image of Miss Blakely being fucked by the two men Mrs. Gilbert loves so much flits through my mind, and I feel a little nauseous.

"Here's the file, sir," Brian says.

I take the folder, and opening it, my eyes dart over Miss Blakely's personal information. When I get to the section highlighting her choice of partner and preferences, my frown darkens.

It says she only wants to have a conversation with a man. There's no mention of anything sexual or taboo.

Why would she pay such an exorbitant membership fee just to talk to men? Surely the woman has men throwing themselves at her feet?

My gaze returns to the monitor, and I watch as she sips her drink while glancing at the other members. Her partner looks awkward as fuck.

Nothing exciting happens, and they hardly talk to each other.

I check the folder again and see she's paired with Doyle Gleason.

"Give me Mr. Gleason's file," I demand as my eyes return to the monitor.

The awkward pair are talking, but the conversation doesn't last long before they're watching the other members once more.

When Brian hands me Mr. Gleason's file, I check what he wants from a partner. Seeing he's open to conversations but would essentially like to find a sexual partner, I ask, "Who paired Mr. Gleason with Miss Blakely?"

"I did," Brian answers. "They're both new and open to having conversations."

"He's not her type," I mutter.

"Miss Blakely was clear that she didn't care what the man looked like."

Really? Why though?

"Still. The man is fifteen years older than her. Next time, pair her with someone younger."

"Yes, sir."

I drop the files on the nearest desk, and walking out of the security room, I head to my office so I can get some work done.

My thoughts keep returning to my PA, who has managed to impress and shock me all in one day. I can't fathom why someone like her would pay to have a conversation with a man.

Sitting at my desk, I stare at nothing in particular as I try to make sense of the enigma that's my PA.

It can't be because she's lonely. The woman could walk into any bar or club, and she'll have men clamoring to buy her a drink.

Not once has she given me the impression she's shy.

Picking up my phone, I dial the extension for Brian.

"Yes, sir?"

"In the future, let me know when Miss Blakely makes an appointment and what her requests are."

"Will do, sir."

Ending the call, I force my attention back to my work and try to forget about my PA sitting in the main room of my club.

I emailed everything I need Miss Blakely to do first thing this morning because I won't be in the office today.

Which is a good thing. I'm still processing the fact that she's a member at *Paradiso,* and for the life of me, I can't figure out why such a beautiful woman would have a problem talking to men.

I mean, she's fine giving me attitude all day long.

After I laid into her the other day, she came back swinging. Not once has she burst into tears like many of my previous assistants.

The woman is one hell of an enigma, and it's piqued my curiosity.

Pulling up to the truck yard, I see Renzo leaning against the hood of his SUV.

Milo stops the G-Wagon, and when I get out, Renzo mutters playfully, "Is this the time to get here? I've been waiting for over ten minutes."

I place my hand on the hood of the SUV, and feeling how hot the engine is, I mutter, "Bullshit. But kudos to you for managing to be on time for once."

Renzo is known for being late, and usually, I'm the one who's kept waiting.

Grinning at my friend, I ask, "Did you wet the bed?"

He lets out a chuckle. "No, my sister and her kids are in town. The little shits scream at the top of their lungs from morning to evening, so I had to escape the torture."

"How is Valeria?" I ask as we walk toward the entrance of the warehouse.

"She's good. Pregnant again." He shakes his head. "She says it's up to her to keep the family name going, seeing as I won't even consider getting married."

"Well, it takes a load off your shoulders."

Renzo and I have been best friends since middle school, and we're more like brothers than best friends.

I take in the shipment of arms Renzo brought in and let out a low whistle. "Christ. We're going to be here the whole day."

Sucking in a deep breath, he lets it out slowly before he says, "This shipment is important. Nothing can go wrong."

We watch as the men pack the weapons into hollowed-out airconditioning units.

"We'll get the trucks across the border," I assure him.

Walking over to the weapons, I pick up an Uzi and inspect it.

"Good quality, right?" Renzo asks.

"Yeah. There'll always be a market for this submachine gun."

When my phone vibrates in my pocket, I put the weapon down on the pile and answer the call.

"Vitale speaking."

"It's Samantha, sir. Mr. Franks would like to make an appointment with you for Monday morning. I just wanted to check if it's okay with you to schedule the meeting for eight o'clock."

"That's fine," I mutter before hanging up.

Renzo raises an eyebrow at me, then asks, "What's the longest you've managed to keep a PA? Two months?"

I glare at my friend. "It's not my fault they're all incompetent."

"Right." He crosses his arms over his chest and turns his gaze to where the men are hard at work. "You go through assistants like I go through toilet paper. Maybe you should try saying please and thank you once in a while."

I let out a sigh and shake my head. "Miss Blakely has an uncanny way of annoying the living hell out of me."

Renzo's eyebrow pops up. "Yeah? You sure it's not the other way around?"

"Fuck off."

A burst of laughter escapes him. "At least this one is easy on the eyes."

I don't say anything about his comment and just grunt.

My phone vibrates again, and checking it, I see it's a message from Brian. I open it and read that Miss Blakely has requested another meeting. This time, she wants to be alone in a room with a man, but no touching is allowed.

Interesting.

Chapter 6

Samantha

Ugh, I wish Mr. Vitale would stay out of the office. Last Friday was so peaceful when he didn't come in.

I roll my shoulders to ease some of the tension while I put together all the documents that will be needed for a meeting on Thursday.

A message from Mr. Vitale pops up on my screen via the internal messaging system, and I give it a disgruntled look.

Keep the schedule clear for the 26th of June and wear something comfortable that day. We're inspecting a building I'm interested in buying.

Just freaking great. I can't think of anything worse than spending an entire day alone with Mr. Vitale, and I'll fall behind with my other work.

Bringing up my emails, I search for the approval from HR for the vacation time I've requested. Adding a note to the email, telling him to keep in mind that I'll be out of the office for the whole week of the Fourth of July, I forward it to Mr. Vitale.

Within seconds, a reply pops up in my inbox.

Make sure all your work is done before you take the week off. In the future, your requests for time off will come directly to me, not HR.

"Yes, sir," I mumble. "At least he didn't cancel my vacation days."

Opening Mr. Vitale's electronic diary, I block out June twenty-sixth before continuing prepping for the meeting.

The work is so mundane that my thoughts turn to the date I had at *Paradiso*. It was so freaking dull but comforting at the same time.

Doyle is definitely not my cup of tea, but just talking to a man made me feel like I'm not a total hopeless case.

I've booked another date for tomorrow night, but this time, I'll be alone in the room with the man they assign to me.

It's a huge step I'm not sure I'm ready for. It's one thing having a drink with a man while we're surrounded by people, and a whole different scenario being alone in a room with a member of the opposite sex.

Maybe this whole thing is stupid, and I should cancel the appointment.

My fingers keep tapping on the keyboard while my thoughts revolve around the impending date.

I have to admit, I felt so much better after the conversation with Doyle. Not once did a feeling of panic and fear overwhelm me, and I almost felt normal.

That's all I want. I just want to feel normal and in control of my life again. I want to be able to go on dates like any other woman. I want to believe that not all men are out to hurt me.

Jesus, I just want my old life back.

"Miss Blakely!"

Startling at Mr. Vitale's sudden appearance next to my desk, I let out a shriek. My hand flies up to cover my mouth, and I gasp from being ripped out of my thoughts.

Is the man trying to give me a freaking heart attack?

His intense gaze is locked on my face, and it feels like he's trying to pry my deepest, darkest secrets from me with a single look.

Lowering my hand, I suck in a deep breath before saying, "Do you need something, sir?"

He stares at me for a moment longer, which makes me feel like squirming.

"It's lunchtime. Order the chicken sandwich you got last week."

"Yes, sir."

I watch as he stalks back into his office before I slump back in my chair.

Jesus. The man is way too intense.

Scooting closer to my desk, I dial the number for the deli and place an order for two sandwiches.

Just as I end the call, the phone rings, and I quickly answer, "Mr. Vitale's office, Samantha speaking."

"Hey, it's me," Jenny says. "You sound so professional. How are things up there?"

I let out a sigh and relax back in my chair. "Ugh. I miss the admin department."

"Yeah, I don't envy you at all."

I hear voices in the background and ask, "Are you out for lunch?"

"Yes. I'm at our favorite restaurant with a couple of the girls."

I make a whining sound. "I'm jealous. Bring me a chocolate milkshake, and I'll love you forever."

She lets out a chuckle. "Okay, but as soon as Mr. Vitale's office door opens, I'm gone. I don't want to be in the line of fire."

"Some friend you are," I tease her.

It was nice hanging out with Jenny on Saturday. Instead of going to the movies, we ordered Chinese takeout and stayed in. I got her up to speed on everything she missed while she was on vacation, and she told me how Aiden proposed to her.

When she asked me to be her maid of honor, I almost cried.

"I'm just finishing my meal then I'll be there with your milkshake."

"Thank you." I hear Mr. Vitale's door open and quickly say, "Talk to you later."

Ending the call, I turn my attention to my boss as he places a dry cleaning slip on my desk.

"Leave at four to collect my suits. Take them to my house and make sure they're hung neatly in the walk-in closet," he orders.

Oooh, I get to see where he lives.

Yeah, I'm nosy like that, and I'm not ashamed to admit it.

"Yes, sir."

He disappears back into the chamber of wrath, and I pick up the slip and tuck it into my handbag.

The rest of the day proceeds at an unbearable fast pace, and I don't even get time to drink half of the milkshake Jenny brought earlier.

As I leave the office at four, I feel victorious because not once did Mr. Vitale reprimand me for anything.

I'm totally taking it as a win that he's asked me to pick up his laundry. It means he's learning to trust me.

It takes me an hour to collect his suits, and when I take the stairs up to the front door, I realize I don't have a key to get into the house.

"Shit." My teeth tug at my bottom lip, and hoping he has a housekeeper, I knock.

When the door opens, I'm met by a burly looking man. "Yes?"

"I'm Mr. Vitale's assistant." I nod at the garment bags that are draped over my arm. "He asked me to collect his dry cleaning."

"Right." The man steps to the side, and when his phone rings, he gestures for me to enter the house before taking the call.

I walk into a massive open space that's all gleaming white tiles and luxurious.

Holy shit.

My mouth drops open as I glance at the impressive chandelier, the marble statues of women, and a lounge chair I wouldn't mind stealing.

I'm still staring at the foyer bathed in expensive décor when the man who opened the door says, "The main bedroom is on the third floor."

"Oh, right. Thank you."

When I walk toward a grand staircase, I notice the man doesn't follow me.

Yay! Maybe I can explore a little.

I take the stairs to the second floor and quickly peek up and down the hallway. The walls are covered with beautiful black and gold wallpaper.

Not wanting to push my luck, I head up to the third floor and as I approach an open door, I feel like I'm intruding on forbidden ground.

The moment I walk into the main bedroom, my mouth drops open again and I gape at Mr. Vitale's personal space.

The bedroom is easily three times the size of mine.

Wow. The man has good taste.

A king-size bed is positioned by floor-to-ceiling windows that overlook the city. Where the walls are black, the bed covers are a soft cream color. I move closer and trail my fingers over the silk, thinking this is where Mr. Vitale sleeps.

To the left of the bed is a lounge chair covered with black velvet and a small coffee table. A neatly folded newspaper lies on the table, and an image of Mr. Vitale reading the paper while sipping his morning coffee flashes through my mind.

Lucky bastard.

I glance into the bathroom, and my eyebrows fly up when I see stairs leading down to a sunken tub that can rival the best of jacuzzies.

I'd give one of my kidneys for a chance to soak in that baby.

There's a huge shower that can easily fit five people. The thing even has a bench and a fern in it.

The twin basins are made of black marble, and the round mirrors make me green with envy.

Stepping out of the bathroom, I head to the walk-in closet, and I let out a jealous huff when I see all the space the man has for his clothes.

"God, it's unfair that someone as grumpy as him gets to live in this beautiful house," I mutter as I unzip the garment bags. Hanging the suits and making sure nothing is out of place, I continue to rant, "Jesus, he has more shoes than I do."

Which is saying a lot, as I have an out-of-control shoe addiction.

When I'm done, and every suit is neatly in the closet, I glance at all the sweatpants and T-shirts but don't notice any jeans.

There's a display case in the middle of the walk-in closet, and I take a moment to look at Mr. Vitale's cufflinks, wristwatches, and ties.

Not wanting to be caught snooping, I let my eyes feast on all the beauty as I make my way back to the stairs.

I expected Mr. Vitale's house to be cold and soulless, but instead, I'm pleasantly surprised.

When I reach the first floor, there's no sign of the man who opened the door, and unable to suppress my curious nature, I walk toward a living room that's made up of my wildest fantasies.

The TV takes up an entire wall, and black velvet couches furnish the room. It doesn't look like they've been sat on.

There are ferns that remind me of the plants I saw in *Paradiso* and a glass table that holds a crystal decanter filled with an amber liquid, which I assume is some kind of expensive whiskey.

Movement draws my attention to the expansive windows and sliding doors, and I see a group of men out on the patio.

Instantly, my curiosity is doused, and fear creeps into my bones.

I turn around and rush out of the living room, only to bump into a chest that might as well have been made from steel. As I bounce backward, my hand flies up to rub my bruised nose, and my eyes lock on Mr. Vitale's narrowed gaze.

Shit.

"Sorry. I was just leaving."

It's only then I notice the two men on either side of Mr. Vitale, and forgetting that I was just caught snooping by my boss, my fear of men makes my body tremble.

At the best of times, I can handle dealing one-on-one with a man, but knowing there's a whole group outside on the patio and three more right in front of me, I panic.

Before Mr. Vitale can comment on why I'm still in his house, I dart around them and run to the front door.

As the solid piece of wood closes behind me, I think I hear Mr. Vitale call my name, but there's no way in hell I'm going back in there.

Chapter 7

Samantha

My breaths explode over my lips as I rush to the nearest subway, and on my way home, sweat beads on my forehead as I struggle not to have a panic attack.

My fingers grip my handbag tightly, and my shoulders are hunched as I do my best to avoid the other pedestrians on the sidewalk.

When I finally reach the safety of my apartment, I make sure all five locks are in place before sinking down on one of the couches.

I cover my face with trembling hands and try to focus on taking deeper breaths.

Feeling physically ill, my entire body is coated in a fine layer of sweat.

It's been a while since I had a panic attack, and it opens the floodgates, making the memories escape from where I keep them locked up in the darkest part of my soul.

Unable to move a muscle or make a sound, I can't even open my eyes. I think I'm lying on my bed.

I hear movement, then Todd's voice as he croons, "I'm never letting you go. We're meant to be together."

Why is he here? I was clear when I broke things off with him.

When he tried to control every aspect of my life and demanded that I have no contact with my family, I knew things would only get worse.

Why can't I move?

Why can't I speak?

I feel the bed dip as he climbs on, and when he crawls over me, a wave of repulsion floods me.

No! I broke up with him. He has no right to be here.

His hands move over my body, and when he reaches my left side, a sharp pain slices through my skin.

Stop! Oh God. Stop!

The pain increases as he cuts into me, and a tear escapes my closed eyes.

"If you weren't so stubborn, I wouldn't be forced to brand you," he whispers. "Don't worry. I'm going to carve your name over my ribs, as well."

I shake my head hard, and darting up off the couch, I rush to the kitchen, where I pour myself a glass of water. Swallowing the tepid liquid down, it takes all my strength to force the memories back to the deepest part of my soul, where I keep them locked up.

I'm in control of my body.

I can move.

I can scream for help.

I'm safe.

Slowly, the panic lessens until it's bearable, but then I'm struck with the thought that I must've looked a little crazy to Mr. Vitale.

Shit.

What do I say if he asks me about my odd behavior?

Dammit. I'll just admit I was admiring his home and didn't mean to invade his privacy. I'd rather have him berate me for snooping around than admit to him I panicked because I was surrounded by men.

Thank God I didn't have a full-blown panic attack in front of my boss.

Checking the time on my wristwatch, I let out a groan. It's already past six o'clock, and I barely have enough time to get ready for my appointment at *Paradiso*.

I should cancel. I'm not in the right frame of mind to be alone with a man in a bedroom.

No! I've worked so hard to get to where I am. I'm not giving up. Come hell or high water, I'm going to see this through. I'm going to regain the control that was stolen from me so I can freaking date again. There's no way I'm becoming a spinster with twenty cats.

Adamant to go through with my plans for tonight, I walk to my bathroom and take a quick shower.

When I've dried my body and lathered my skin with my favorite vanilla-scented lotions, I put on my light blue pants that I always feel pretty in and complete my outfit with a silver halter top and matching high heels.

Not bothering with too much makeup, I just swipe mascara onto my lashes and add a tint of pink to my lips.

Running out of time, I grab my handbag and rush out of my apartment.

During the subway ride to the heart of Manhattan, I remain determined to go through with my plans for tonight.

You'll be safe. There are security cameras everywhere in the club.

The thought makes me wonder how people have sex knowing there's an entire security team watching them.

Hey, maybe it's a turn-on for them.

The moment I leave the subway and walk toward *Paradiso*, my anxiety spikes.

I'm just going to spend an hour alone with a man in a bedroom. Nothing else will happen, and if the man tries something, the security guards will help me.

Nothing will go wrong.

Approaching the bouncer, I give him a nervous smile.

"Welcome, Miss Blakely," he says as he unhooks the red rope so I can enter the club. "Enjoy your evening."

"Thank you," I whisper, and as I walk down the hallway, my stomach tightens into a painful knot.

I can do this.

I'm met by one of the staff members, and once again, the ski mask with the skull printed over the face sends a chill down my spine.

Why can't they wear something less scary?

"Evening, Miss Blakely. Would you like to have a drink before I escort you to your room?" the same woman who welcomed me the other night asks.

"Definitely a drink first," I say before chuckling nervously.

"This way."

I follow her to the seating area, and when I sit down on a stool at one of the round tables, I force a smile to my face.

"A server will bring you a martini," she says before walking away.

Feeling more anxious by the minute, I glance at the other members. They're all relaxed and seem to be enjoying themselves.

It's just an hour with a man who won't touch me.

I take a deep breath and let it out slowly.

I'm a strong and confident woman.

The server brings my drink, and I quickly take hold of the glass and down half of it. As the alcohol hits my stomach, I feel queasy and leave the rest of the martini.

Getting up from the stool, I walk to the nearest staff member, whose petite frame indicates she's a woman, and say, "I'm ready to go to the room."

"Right this way, Miss Blakely," the woman says.

As I follow her toward a hallway, my muscles are tense, and my stomach spins with nerves.

There's no backing out. I can do this.

She opens a golden door, and I'm taken into a room that's decorated in the same black and gold as the rest of the club.

My eyes land on the bed, and avoiding it, I walk toward the armchair that's in the corner of the room.

Before I can even take a seat, a man comes in and the staff member says, "The only rule is no touching. Enjoy your time together."

Before I can catch my bearings, she leaves us alone, and the door shuts behind her.

Oh shit.

My eyes are locked on a man who can't be much older than me. He's not bad-looking, which only makes me feel more nervous.

He's taller and stronger than me.

Shit.

A smile spreads over his face as his eyes sweep over my body. "My name is Kevin. What's yours?"

"Ah." My tongue darts out to nervously wet my lips. "Samantha."

As my eyes dart to the door, he asks, "What do you want to do?"

My gaze snaps back to him. "We can sit."

I glance over my shoulder before I take a seat on the armchair.

Kevin plops down on the edge of the bed, and bracing his arms behind him, he stares at me as if I'm his next meal.

"I haven't seen you around here before," he says.

I glance at my wristwatch and see only five minutes have passed. Fifty-five to go.

"I'm new," I murmur while I position my handbag on my lap.

His eyes drop to where my hands are gripping my handbag, and he lets out a chuckle. "You look tense."

"Yeah," I mutter.

I wrap my arms around my waist and glance at the door again.

"Are you always this quiet?" he asks as he scoots up the bed so he can lean back against the pillows.

"Yes." Not wanting to be an absolute bitch, I force my gaze back to him and ask, "So…uhm…what do you like to do in your spare time?"

He shrugs as he crosses his ankles. "When I'm not at work, I'm here."

Okaaaay.

Silence falls between us, and after a couple of minutes, Kevin says, "Come lie down next to me. I promise I won't bite." Chuckling, he adds, "Unless you ask me to."

Yeah, that will never happen.

My arms tighten around my waist, and I shake my head. "No. I'm good here."

He lets out a sigh, then says, "Let's spice things up."

I'm just about to tell him that's not what I agreed to when he reaches for the zipper of his pants and pulls it down.

Unbearable fear and panic hit me instantly, and before he can even pull his dick out of his pants, my breaths speed up until they're sawing over my lips.

Chapter 8

Franco

Standing in front of the security monitor for Miss Blakely's room, I watch as she takes a seat in the armchair.

Mr. Forester's sitting on the bed, and even though I can't hear what they're saying, the conversation looks stilted.

My eyes latch onto Miss Blakely's face, and it's clear as daylight she's not comfortable at all.

When she wraps her arms around her waist in a protective move, I order, "Put on the sound. I want to hear what they're saying."

"Yes, sir," one of the men replies.

I step closer as he turns on the sound, and it's in time to hear Mr. Forester say, 'Are you always this quiet?'

The man makes himself comfortable on the bed as Miss Blakely answers, 'Yes.'

Christ, she looks like she's about to have a nervous breakdown. Where's the feisty woman I've gotten to know over the past three weeks?

'So…uhm…what do you like to do in your spare time?' she asks.

'When I'm not at work, I'm here.'

Minutes pass before Mr. Forester pats the covers and says, 'Come lie down next to me. I promise I won't bite.' Chuckling, he adds, 'Unless you ask me to.'

My eyes narrow on the man, and my body tenses when Miss Blakely adamantly shakes her head. 'No. I'm good here.'

Seeing how uncomfortable she is, causes a weird protective feeling to trickle into my chest.

From what I've seen tonight, I have a feeling something bad happened to Miss Blakely.

The thought has my eyes narrowing on the monitor.

It explains what happened earlier at my house. When Miss Blakely came barreling out of the living room and ran into me, it looked like she'd seen a ghost.

She has a problem being alone with men.

She didn't give me that impression at the office, though, which tells me how good she is at pretending.

Mr. Forester sighs, making it clear he's bored, then mutters, 'Let's spice things up.'

The moment he reaches for the zipper of his pants, Miss Blakely's features tighten with fear.

"Fuck," I snap as I swing around and make a run for the room they're in.

I slam the door open and order, "Get him out of here!"

My eyes lock on Miss Blakely, whose breaths are rushing over her parted lips, her eyes wide with terror.

Jesus fucking Christ. She's having a panic attack.

Crouching in front of her, I keep my tone as gentle as possible as I say, "You're safe, Miss Blakely."

Seeing how pale she is stirs something in my chest, and the urge to hold her almost overwhelms me.

Don't touch her. It's the only request she has.

Fuck.

"You're safe," I repeat. "I won't let anything happen to you."

The promise falls over my lips before I can even think about it.

I watch as she fights to regain control over her emotions, and it makes me respect her so much more.

Christ, she's strong.

Seeing the woman who's given me attitude at the office in such a vulnerable state makes another wave of protectiveness wash through me.

Samantha

My breaths keep bursting over my lips as my eyes lock with the staff member's worried brown ones.

There's something familiar about the man, and when I manage to calm down a little, it sinks in that Kevin is no longer in the room.

"Take your time," the masked man murmurs, his tone still soft. "Just know that you're safe."

I nod as I glance around the room before looking at the man crouching in front of me.

He made himself smaller so he wouldn't come across as a threat.

The thought has me calming down some more until I'm able to force a trembling smile to my face. "Thank you."

His dark brown gaze is locked on me as he asks, "Do you feel better?"

Weirdly, I do. There's just something about the man that makes me feel safe.

Nodding, I whisper, "Yes. Thank you."

He shakes his head. "No thanks needed. I apologize for what happened with Mr. Forester."

I nod again before taking a much-needed deep breath.

Rising to his feet, he moves to the bed, where he takes a seat on the edge. "You still have thirty minutes left. I'll sit with you if that's okay?"

I nod again, and then the realization sinks in that I didn't completely lose my shit. There was a hiccup, but I think I can do this as long as the man doesn't try anything.

Knowing he's a staff member of *Paradiso* helps set me at ease, and slowly, the chaotic emotions in my chest fade away until I'm just nervous.

Instead of undressing me with his eyes, like Kevin did, the man just stares at the wall.

He's bigger than Kevin, and when my gaze moves over his muscled frame, I wonder if he's the same man I saw the other night.

"Am I allowed to know your name?" I ask, my tone still tense from the little panic attack I had.

He shakes his head. "Unfortunately not."

Nodding, I ask, "Is it to protect your identity?"

"Yes." His eyes settle on me, and once again, I'm struck with the weird sensation that I've met him before.

His tone is still soft when he asks, "Do you feel better?"

"Yeah. I just didn't expect..." My hand nervously gestures between me and the bed, "...ah...that to happen."

"Again, I apologize."

I nod and glance down at my lap.

Silence fills the air, but this time, it isn't uncomfortable.

I close my eyes and focus on filling my lungs with deep breaths of air.

This is better.

Maybe it's because I know he's an employee of the club and not a member who's looking to get laid.

"You're doing very well," he praises me.

A smile tugs at my mouth. "Yeah?"

"Yeah. Only twenty minutes left."

Curious to hear his answer, I ask, "Don't you think I'm weird for requesting to sit in a room with a man for an hour and do nothing?"

"From what I witnessed tonight, I think you're brave."

His reply has my eyes snapping open and locking on him. "You think I'm brave?"

Still staring at the wall, he nods.

I don't know a single thing about this man, but his words mean a lot to me.

Feeling a hell of a lot more comfortable with the employee than I've felt with any man since I fled Houston, I continue to stare at him.

"Do you like working here?" I ask.

He shrugs, and his tone is still gentle when he answers, "It pays well."

"You won't get in trouble for sitting with me, right?"

He shakes his head. "Not at all."

My teeth tug at my bottom lip, and I wonder if I'm allowed to request to meet with him whenever I come to the club.

It won't hurt to ask.

"Next time I make an appointment, can I request that you join me?"

He stops looking at the wall, and when his eyes rest on me, I feel a little awkward.

"As long as you don't request anything sex-related."

"Dear God," the words burst from me, and my stomach lurches just from thinking about sex. "No, definitely nothing...ahh...like that. It's just to sit with me. A conversation here and there would be nice."

"I'm sure it can be arranged."

I'm filled with a sense of relief as I say, "I'd really appreciate it."

Before a heavy silence can fall between us, he asks, "Have you ever traveled?"

I nod. "Only to Canada to visit family. My grandmother used to live there."

"Did she move back to the States?"

I shake my head. "She passed away three years ago."

"I'm sorry to hear that." He's quiet for a moment, then says, "I like to travel as often as possible. I find other cultures interesting."

"Yeah?" I don't even notice that I'm completely relaxed. "Where have you been?"

"Thailand, the Netherlands, Germany, Spain." He seems to think about something before adding, "I've been all over South America."

"I'm jealous. It must've been quite an experience."

"It was."

"Do you have a favorite?" I ask.

"Thailand. I'd love to go back."

The corner of my mouth lifts. "I'll put Thailand on my list of places to see."

"What else is on your list?"

My smile widens as I chuckle. "Every country in the world."

"That's really ambitious of you," he teases me.

"A girl can dream."

This is what I wanted – just to sit and talk with a man.

When he glances at his wristwatch but doesn't say anything, I ask, "How much time is left?"

"There's no time limit. We can talk until you're ready to leave."

I check the time and see that my appointment ended five minutes ago. "Are you sure you won't get in trouble?"

"Dead sure. Don't worry about it."

My stomach growls loudly and it has me saying, "They should serve food here."

"We can order takeout."

My eyebrows lift with excitement. "Really? I would kill for a burger and fries."

He pulls a phone out of his pocket, and I watch as he calls someone and tells whoever is on the other end of the line, "Order a burger and fries and bring it to the room."

I'm once again struck with a feeling that I know him from somewhere.

When he ends the call, he moves off the bed to sit on the floor. He stretches his long legs in front of him, and it looks so comfortable, I decide to join him.

His eyes are locked on me as I get from the chair and sit down near the wall so I can lean back against it, leaving enough space between us to fit two people.

"So you're a burger and fries girl?" he asks, his tone unexpectedly playful.

"I'm actually a pizza girl, but I had it for dinner last night."

He lets out a chuckle, and the sound makes my smile widen.

"What do you like to eat?" I ask to keep the conversation flowing.

"Anything but..." he pauses for a moment, then clearing his throat, he says, "I'm not a fan of broccoli."

"I'm not too fond of it either."

"We have something in common."

I'm surprised when the door opens a few minutes later, and a staff member hands my takeout to my mystery man.

"Anything else, sir?" the other man asks.

"A bottle of water."

As soon as the staff member leaves, I ask, "Are you a manager here?"

My mystery man nods as he opens the paper bag to take out my food.

When he passes my burger and fries to me, I ask, "Is there any ketchup?"

He hands me two packets and our fingers brush. Instantly, my heartbeat quickens, and I quickly pull back. Trying to hide my reaction from him, I squirt the ketchup all over my fries.

Chapter 9

Franco

I'm not going to lie, I've never done anything remotely close to this.

Sitting on the floor with my PA is the last thing I expected to do tonight.

But it's weirdly satisfying.

Whenever I speak to Miss Blakely, I keep my tone soft and don't treat her like I would at the office, because I don't want her to run for the hills.

Passing a burger and fries to her, our fingers touch, but she quickly pulls back. Her features tighten, and while she's busy drowning her fries in ketchup, I watch as she sucks in a deep breath of air.

Haven't we touched before?

I search my memory, and realizing she's always kept a couple of inches between us makes me wonder what happened to her.

I can take a few guesses, but they all make me angry just thinking about them.

She might've annoyed me the first two weeks she worked with me, but since she got her act together, it's been, dare I say, pleasant.

Wanting to separate the time we spend together here at *Paradiso* from when we're at work, I ask, "Can I call you Samantha?"

Squashing her burger, she smiles at me. "Sure. I'd like that."

What is she doing?

When she sees me staring at her, she explains, "It's too big to fit into my mouth, so I have to flatten it."

Why do I find that cute?

The door opens, and Brian comes in with the bottle of water. He sets it down next to me before leaving the room again.

Grabbing the bottle, I place it between Samantha and me and continue to watch her eat her food.

Knowing we might spend a lot of time together in the future and not wanting to do something that will upset her, I say, "We should talk about the rules while you eat."

"What rules?"

"Yours. What do you expect from our meetings?"

She swallows the bite she just took, then answers, "I want to get comfortable spending time with you. If that goes well, then I'd like to try holding hands." Her shoulders slump and she sets the deformed burger down in the box. "I know it sounds weird."

My tone is still soft and gentle as I say, "Not at all. I assume something happened to you, and this is you trying to heal from it."

She nods as she reaches for the bottle of water, and only after she's taken a sip, she admits, "I tried going for therapy but it didn't work for me."

Anger begins to simmer in my chest as I get confirmation that someone hurt her so fucking badly she can't even be alone with a man.

It must've been difficult for her to come into my office.

She picks at the bun, breaking little pieces off, then gives me a smile that doesn't reach her eyes. "I figure if I can sleep next to a man, I might be able to date again. That's what I'm hoping to get out of these meetings."

"Just don't push yourself too hard."

She nods as she looks down at the food on her lap. "I won't." Lifting her head again, her eyes lock with mine. "Thank you for doing this."

"You're welcome."

She gestures at me, then asks, "What's with the scary ski masks? I understand it's to protect your identity, but couldn't the club have chosen something else?"

"You think they're scary?" A chuckle rumbles from my chest.

I don't want to know how she'll react if she were to find out I'm one of the heads of the Cosa Nostra. The woman will probably die of shock.

She scrunches her nose, which I find cute. "It's a skull. It doesn't inspire warm and fuzzy feelings."

"It fits the taboo nature of the club," I explain.

She picks up a fry and nibbles on it. When she's done, she wipes her fingers on a napkin and asks, "If we're going to spend time together, what do I call you?" A frown forms on her forehead. "Right now, I've got mystery man and masked man. Both sound silly. Any suggestions?"

Fuck. She has a point.

My mind races as I think for a moment, and coming up with nothing, I say, "You can call me whatever you want."

"Hmm." For the first time since I laid eyes on Samantha, a mischievous gleam sparkles in her eyes. "How about Bob?"

Before I can stop myself, I mutter, "Fuck no."

Samantha tilts her head, and her eyes narrow on me. "There's something familiar about you. It feels like we've met before."

Fuck. Fuck. Fuck.

Forcing a chuckle over my lips, I say, "I doubt that very much. I'd remember meeting someone as beautiful as you." An idea pops into my head. "How about Beast? You know, like Beauty and the Beast?"

Samantha lets out a loud bark of laughter, and I'm a little stunned as I watch her cry with laughter and tears stream down her face.

When she manages to catch her breath, she gasps, "That's so corny. Oh my God." She continues to laugh her ass off, and it brings a smile to my face.

I watch her wipe a tear from her cheek, and her voice is thick with laughter as she says, "I might as well call you Skull."

"Okay," I agree, which has more laughter bubbling over her lips.

"I'm just going to stick with my mystery man. It doesn't make me cringe."

Her mystery man. Why do I like that so much?

Samantha checks the time on her wristwatch, then her eyes widen, and she gets up. "I didn't realize it was so late!"

I check the time and see it's already past ten, meaning we've been in this room for over two and a half hours.

Climbing to my feet, I gather our empty box and wrapper and shove them into the paper bag.

"I'm so sorry," Samantha says as she hoists the strap of her handbag over her shoulder.

"Don't apologize. I enjoyed myself," I say to reassure her.

"Oh, good." A smile of relief spreads over her face as she walks to the door. Then she pauses and asks, "How do I book you for the next appointment?"

"I'll assign myself to all your appointments, so you don't have to worry about it."

"Great!" She looks a little awkward as she adds, "Thanks for tonight. I really appreciate it."

"Wait, I'll walk you to your car," I say before she can open the door.

"Oh, don't worry. I took the subway."

My right eyebrow lifts, and I shake my head. "I'm not letting you take the subway so late at night. I'll have one of the staff members drive you home."

"I don't want to inconvenience you."

"It's the least we can do after the mishap earlier."

Looking relieved, she asks, "Can a woman take me home?"

"Of course." Leaving the room with her, I say, "Take a seat up front, and I'll send someone to you."

Samantha turns to face me, and she looks hesitant. I'm about to assure her she'll be safe when she holds her hand out to me. "It was nice meeting you."

I glance down at her hand and ask, "Are you sure?"

She nods and widens the smile on her face. "I'm sure."

Reaching for her hand, my fingers wrap around her slender ones and I give her a gentle squeeze before pulling away.

"Have a good night, Samantha."

"You too, Mystery Man."

The corner of my mouth lifts as I watch her walk down the hallway, then I turn around and head to the security room so I can assign a driver to take her home.

Chapter 10

Samantha

Preparing a cup of coffee for Mr. Vitale, I can't stop thinking about last night.

It went so much better than I expected.

A smile plays around my mouth as I place the cup and two cookies on a tray.

Even though the evening started off rocky, it ended on a high note. I spent over two hours with a man, and not once did I feel panicky.

I'm on the right track, and I'm confident I'll be able to regain my trust in men with the help of my mystery man.

Obviously, I'll always be cautious when dating, and I'm not just going to allow anyone into my life.

But this is a good start, and where I would usually feel depressed after a panic attack, I feel optimistic.

Carrying the tray to Mr. Vitale's office, I set it down on the corner of his desk before heading back to my desk.

I'm bracing myself for Mr. Vitale's anger because I snooped around in his house, but I have an apology ready.

Just as I reach my chair, Mr. Vitale comes down the hallway. Today, he's dressed in a dark blue suit, and as always, the man looks way too handsome for his own good.

The usual nervousness I feel around my boss spins in my stomach as I say, "Morning, sir."

He doesn't even look at me as he mutters, "Morning."

I watch Mr. Vitale disappear into his office and follow him inside. "I just want to apologize for last night. You have a beautiful home."

"Close the door on your way out."

Asshole. It's not like I committed a crime.

I think.

Suppressing a huff, I shut the door behind me and take a seat at my desk. Within seconds, my inbox is bombarded with emails from my grumpy boss, and I get to work.

Fine, so I invaded his privacy a little. I said I'm sorry and I won't do it again.

Letting out the huff that's been impatiently waiting, I focus on my work so I can stay one step ahead of my boss.

The morning flies by at the speed of light, and before I know it, it's lunchtime.

Dialing Mr. Vitale's extension, I wait for him to grunt like he always does, then ask, "What would you like to eat, sir?"

"You can choose today," he replies.

Really?

"Pizza?"

"Sure."

He hangs up on me, but I couldn't care less because I'm getting my favorite takeout, and the company is paying for it.

I place an order for two pizzas, asking for all the toppings and extra cheese.

While waiting for our lunch to arrive, I dart between my desk and the boardroom, where I'm preparing everything for tomorrow's meeting.

When our food arrives, I grab a plate from the kitchenette and place four slices on it. Adding a bottle of water to the tray, I carry the meal to Mr. Vitale's office and knock before I open the door.

Placing the tray on his desk, I say, "I hope four slices are enough. Just let me know if you'd like more pizza."

"Thanks."

My mouth drops open, and I blink at the man as if he's lost his mind.

Did I just hear a thank you?

He gives me a dark glare when he notices I'm gaping at him. "You can leave, Miss Blakely."

Nodding, I hurry out of the office, and once I've shut the door behind me, I grin like an idiot.

And here I was thinking miracles don't happen anymore.

Franco

Having Samantha stare at me with a stunned expression just because I thanked her makes me feel like a dick.

Can you blame me, though? I went through years of shitty assistants, and having one that actually does her job is new to me.

Just don't get too friendly with her.

I don't want Samantha to put two and two together and realize I'm her mystery man.

Picking up a slice of pizza, a smile tugs at the corner of my mouth as my thoughts turn to last night.

I didn't lie when I told her I enjoyed spending time with her. Seeing Samantha away from the office showed me a different side to her.

For some unknown reason, I like the idea that she's a wildcat here and a wounded kitten at *Paradiso*.

Remembering how startled she was when I ran into her at my house, my mood sours a little.

Marcello is always at my place with a group of guards, and now that I'm sure Samantha has a problem being around men, I understand why she ran out of the house.

I'll never send her to collect my dry cleaning again.

I eat my lunch, and when Samantha comes in to collect the tray, I keep my eyes locked on the documents in front of me.

As she turns to leave, I mutter, "You can go home at five but be here at seven tomorrow."

"Yes, sir."

Once the door shuts behind her, I lean back in my chair and tap my fingers on the desk.

Why am I even doing this? Nothing good can come from spending time with Samantha.

Even though I have legitimate businesses, I'm still a criminal. I don't think being one of the heads of the Cosa Nostra will carry any weight with Samantha.

And even if it did, it doesn't matter because I don't plan on dating my PA.

I agreed to spend time with her because she's paid a steep price to be a member at *Paradiso*.

Yeah, that's the only reason I'm doing this.

Shaking my head, I get up from the chair and grab my jacket. Pulling it on, I stalk to the door, and leaving my office, I growl to Samantha, "I'll be out for the rest of the day."

"Oh. Should I cancel your four o'clock appointment?"

"Yes."

I head to the elevators, and only when I climb into the back seat of the G-Wagon do I feel less agitated.

"Where to boss?" Milo asks.

"The factory."

I'd rather check that the new printers I got a couple of months ago are printing high-quality counterfeit bills so I can get some time away from Samantha.

During the drive to the factory, Lorenzo is quiet as always while Milo hums to a country song playing on the radio.

I think spending less time at Vitale Health and more time at my other companies will be a wise move on my part. At least until Samantha doesn't need to meet with me at *Paradiso* anymore.

It will be safer that way.

For who? You or Samantha?

"You okay, boss?" Milo asks.

I'm pulled out of my thoughts and just nod in answer to his question.

"Did you fire the new PA?" he asks another question.

"No, Milo," I mutter. "I'm just thinking about work."

"Anything we can help with?"

I shake my head. "No."

Letting out a sigh, I glance out of the window.

Last night, when I got to be anonymous and just hang out with Samantha, it shined a huge spotlight on how busy I've been the past ten years.

I haven't had a serious relationship since I graduated from school, and I can't even remember when I last fucked a woman.

The Cosa Nostra and my companies take up all of my time. I'm not the most social person, but relaxing with Samantha was enjoyable.

Why am I obsessing over this? I'm not dating the woman. She gets to work through her issues, and I get to relax. It's a fucking win-win for both of us.

Annoyed with myself, I let out a huff, and it earns me a glance from Milo in the rearview mirror.

"I'm fine," I snap before he can open his mouth.

"Sure. You keep telling yourself that," he mumbles under his breath.

"Don't make me shoot you," I warn him.

"Please. I beg you. Shoot him and put me out of my misery," Lorenzo suddenly says. "I can't stand his constant humming to country songs."

Milo scowls at Lorenzo. "Hey, don't insult my taste in music."

Listening to the two men argue about country music, of all things, I let out a sigh and shake my head, but I'm thankful for Lorenzo changing the subject.

Chapter 11

Samantha

With Mr. Vitale hardly coming into the office, the past few days have been amazing.

Up until the moment I walked into *Paradiso*, I felt ready to conquer my fears and was excited to spend some time with my mystery man.

I've been looking forward to seeing him again, but I'm also nervous as hell because I'm moving to the next stage.

When I made the appointment, I requested that he sit on the armchair while I lay on the bed.

My heart lurches in my chest when I think about it. It won't be easy but I feel it would be a massive win if I can get through it.

But the fear of not being able to go through with it keeps me from leaving the table and going to the room.

He's waiting. Get up and go.

You won't know until you try.

Sipping on my second martini, I stare at the olive in the glass while I try to build up my courage.

I can do this.

He works for Paradiso, so I know he won't try anything.

I'm sure I'm safe with him.

I can do this.

Suddenly, someone sits down across me, and my head snaps up. My eyes meet my mystery man's dark brown ones briefly before I stare at the olive again.

Knowing I'm wasting his time, I say, "I'm sorry. I just need a couple of minutes."

"There's no rush, Samantha." His tone is so gentle it makes me feel slightly emotional. "We can just talk."

I shake my head, and taking a fortifying breath, I put the glass on the table and get up from the stool. "No. I want to try."

He stands up, and I'm suddenly overly conscious about how much bigger than me he is.

I wait for him to lead the way before I follow. My eyes are locked on his broad shoulders and muscled arms.

He could easily hurt me.

He could kill me.

A light layer of sweat beads on my forehead, and my breaths come faster.

When he opens the door and walks into the room, my feet come to a stop, refusing to take me a step further.

Shit.

My heart beats heavily in my chest, and it feels like the next step will throw me over the edge of a cliff without a parachute.

Don't panic.

"You're safe, Samantha," my mystery man says, his voice filled with a world of patience.

Nothing is going to happen.

When I force my feet to move, my arms wrap around my waist, and I hold myself tightly as I enter the room. My eyes lock on the bed, and hearing him shut the door, my lips part so I can take deeper breaths.

I watch as he takes a seat in the armchair, and leaning forward, he rests his forearms on his knees and links his fingers.

I step closer to the bed, and once I'm next to it, I stop to calm my racing heart.

"This is insane, right?" the question bursts from me, and unable to stop, I start to ramble, "All I have to do is lie down while you sit there. It should be easy." My breaths come faster and faster. "I should be able to do this."

"Samantha." When my eyes snap to him, he tilts his head. "Nothing about this is insane. You have all the time in the world and don't have to lie down right now."

The man's voice has some kind of magical power because I instantly feel calmer.

Nodding, I set my handbag down on the bed. "Thank you for being so understanding."

"There's no need to thank me. I'm not a therapist, but I'm glad I can help you in some way."

My gaze settles on him, and a smile wavers around my lips. "Are you always this nice?"

Instead of answering the question, he lets out a soft chuckle.

My eyes return to the bed, and I stare at the black covers.

Just get on it.

My hands curl into fists as I sit down on the side of the bed, and I have to close my eyes to focus on breathing through the wave of panic that threatens to overwhelm me.

"Can you talk, please?" My voice is filled with the tension I'm feeling.

"Earlier this week, I had to listen to two grown men argue about country music. It was the most tiring conversation I've ever listened to."

The corner of my mouth lifts. "Yeah? I take it you're not a fan of country music?"

"Not when I have to listen to it on a daily basis."

While he's speaking, I move further up the bed. My body tenses and my breaths speed up, but I keep going until I can lean back against the pillows.

My stomach churns, and the memories creep around the edges of my mind.

"What kind of music do you like?" he asks.

"Ah…" My tongue darts out to wet my dry lips, and my heart is beating so loudly it sounds like it's taken up residence in my ears.

My side is on fire, and my mind is reeling with horror as I feel his tongue swipe over my skin to lick up my blood.

"Samantha?"

My eyes fly open and snap to the corner of the room where my mystery man sits. I notice his fingers are tightly linked. It's the only sign that he's on edge.

"What kind of music do you like?" he repeats his question.

"Uhm. Anything. I'm not fussy."

I wrap my arms tightly around my waist and glance down to where the blue and white top I'm wearing covers Todd's name that he carved into me with a scalpel.

Licking my lips again, I ask, "Do you have any tattoos?"

"Yes."

My gaze darts to his. "Can you recommend a tattoo artist?"

"I'll give you the address before you leave."

My attention returns to the bed, and my muscles lock in place when I think about moving down into a lying position.

Come on! You can do this.

It takes a lot of strength to unwrap my arms from around my waist, and placing my hands on the covers, I slowly scoot down.

"After I spent time with you last week, I realized I don't get out much. I can't remember the last time I went on a date," he admits, much to my surprise.

"Really? Is it because you're too busy?" I ask as I slowly lower my head to the pillow.

When I'm in a horizontal position, I stare at the ceiling and listen for any movement from him.

"Yes. I've been swept up in my work and forgot there's more to life."

I hear him shift, and my eyes dart to the corner, only to see him leaning back in the armchair.

"I just wanted you to know I'm also getting something from these meetings."

I nod while my fingers dig into the covers. "I'm glad to hear that."

I try to close my eyes, but the moment they're shut, I'm bombarded with memories.

Even though I was in a relationship with Todd, and we've had sex before, feeling him push inside me this time makes a crack rip through the very foundation my entire life has been built on.

He lets out a groan. 'Do you feel how good we fit together, Sam?'

He thrusts into me again, and my mind screams for him to stop. Another tear escapes from the corner of my eye and disappears into my hair.

'I'll never let you leave me. If you try, I'll kill us both.'

I dart off the bed, and with my arms wrapped around me, I rub my hands up and down my biceps in an attempt to comfort myself.

"I'm here and won't allow anyone to hurt you," my mystery man says, his tone sounding harsher than usual.

The sound of his voice is so familiar I find myself stepping closer to him. When I'm next to the armchair, I sink down until my butt hits the floor and lean back against the wall.

Feeling disappointed with myself, I mumble, "It was worth a try."

"You'll get it right," he murmurs, sounding more confident in my abilities than I am right now. "There's no rush."

Still wanting to make a success of tonight, I glance up at him. "Can you come sit next to me?"

I watch as his powerful body rises from the chair, and when he moves closer and sits down beside me, I'm surprised when I don't feel a wave of panic.

Maybe it's because my eyes are open?

He's left a couple of inches between us, so I scoot closer until my arm brushes against his, which gets my heart racing.

I take a slow breath before I close my eyes.

With his voice no louder than a whisper, he says, "After my dad passed away from a stroke, my mother started getting panic attacks. It took years and a lot of medication before she managed to deal with her grief."

I keep my voice soft as I reply, "I'm sorry to hear that. It must've been hard for your family."

"It was, but with time, things got better."

He's right. It's been a year since I left Houston, and in a way, I've learned to live with the trauma.

What else can you do when giving up is not an option?

Chapter 12

Franco

Tonight is a fuck-ton more difficult than I expected it would be.

After spending time away from the office so I didn't have to interact with Samantha, I knew tonight might be uncomfortable.

But it's not uncomfortable. It's brutal.

All I want to do is hold her. The fucking urge is driving me insane.

I link my fingers again and rest my hands on my lap while I tell her about my parents.

When Dad had the stroke, I had no choice but to take over as the leader of the Vitale family.

Christ, I didn't know whether I was coming or going. People looked to me to run the business even though I had no fucking idea what I was doing.

"Were you close with your dad?" Samantha asks.

"Not really. I was seventeen and at a stage in my life where I didn't agree with anything my father said or did. Looking back now, I wish I had listened to him."

"Don't we all," she chuckles. "I argued with my mom about everything when I was a teenager."

Wanting to keep the conversation flowing, I ask, "What kind of tattoo do you want to get?"

I feel her arm brush against mine as she shifts a little. "I was thinking of bricks or blocks with some shading and a flower growing out of it."

When I glance at her, it's to find her looking at me.

She scrunches her nose and turns her gaze to her lap. "It means something good can grow in harsh conditions."

"I think it will suit you."

"Yeah?" Her gaze flits to mine again. "I also want to add the words 'stronger than ever' so it looks like graffiti on the bricks."

"The words definitely describe you." Knowing she might have a problem with the tattoo artist, I say, "The guy who did my tattoos is a friend. If you want, I can be there so you're not alone with him."

Her teeth tug at her bottom lip before she asks, "There isn't a woman who can do the tattoo?"

I shake my head. "I can ask around and see if I can find a different place for you?"

Letting out a sigh, she glances down again. "Will you be okay sitting with me?"

"Of course."

She nods, and while she nervously tugs at the seam of her shirt, she whispers, "Thank you. I really appreciate it."

Samantha turns her head, and I watch as she stares at my hands. Slowly, I unlink my fingers and lay my hand palm up on my thigh.

'Take my hand,' I silently encourage her.

She keeps staring, and as the seconds pass, a weird tension fills my chest. Christ, I've never felt such a desperation to touch a woman.

She shifts her hand to her thigh, and another few seconds tick by before she reaches for me and places her palm on mine.

The simple touch sends one hell of an electric bolt up my arm.

The air around us feels charged as I slowly weave my fingers with hers.

For a moment, I forget who I am.

I forget Samantha's my assistant.

While we both stare at our joined hands, I'm amazed by the emotions Samantha's touch stirs in my chest. Pride, protectiveness, empathy – but mostly the attraction I felt for her when she first started as my PA comes back in full force.

She's not the brainless woman I took her for during the first two weeks we worked together.

No. This woman is anything but stupid.

She's hardworking, intelligent, and so fucking brave it demands my admiration.

Clearing my throat, I ask, "How are you doing?"

Her thumb brushes over mine, then a stunningly happy smile lights up her face. "Surprisingly good." Her eyes fill with a mischievous expression. "It seems my mystery man has the magic touch."

Mystery man.

Right. She doesn't know who I am.

Taking a deep breath, I tighten my hold on her hand. Before silence can fall between us, I ask, "How long have you lived in New York?"

I know the answer, but her mystery man doesn't.

"A year. I used to live in Texas."

"Is that where your family is?"

She shakes her head. "No, they're in Seattle. I try to visit them as often as I can. I'll see them for the Fourth of July."

So that's where she's going for the couple of days' vacation she requested.

"Have you always lived in New York?" she asks.

"Yes."

"And your mom?"

I shake my head. "She passed away last year."

"I'm sorry," Samantha whispers.

"It's okay. She was eighty-one when she passed, and she had a full life."

Her eyebrows fly up, then she asks, "How old are you?"

"Thirty-five. I was a rainbow baby. Just as they gave up on having a child, I came along."

"Aww…they must've loved you so much." Hearing the warmth in her tone makes a smile tug at the corner of my mouth.

"They did." I let out a chuckle. "I was lucky."

"Do you have any other family in New York?"

Nodding, the Cosa Nostra flits through my mind. "Yeah, I have a large family."

I'm surprised when Samantha leans her head against my shoulder. She lets out a contented sigh, then whispers, "This feels good."

I turn my face to her and wish I could rip the balaclava off so I can smell her vanilla scent.

"You know what would be funny," she murmurs.

"What?"

"If we became friends."

"Why would that be funny?"

She tilts her head back to meet my eyes. "Men and women can't be friends."

"Why?"

She shrugs before settling her temple against my shoulder again. "Someone always ruins the friendship by falling in love, then the other party feels obligated to try, and everything just ends up going to hell."

"It sounds like you're talking from personal experience."

"Yeah," she whispers. "I am."

Samantha is quiet for a moment before she continues to talk. "I used to work at a hospital in Houston. I met a neurosurgeon there..."

She pauses for a moment, and her hand begins to tremble in mine. Realizing this is hard for her to talk about, I brush my thumb over her soft skin.

"We quickly became friends. He fell in love with me, and because I thought the world of him, I gave a relationship between us a chance."

I'm so caught up in what Samantha's saying, I can't stop myself from asking, "What happened?"

"I realized it wasn't going to work, and when I tried to put some distance between us..."

The air tenses around us, and she pulls her hand free from mine so she can wrap her arms around her waist.

"He became more and more controlling. Things got bad, and I left Houston to make a fresh start here."

Things got bad.

Anger fills my chest, and my jaw clenches as the muscles in my body tighten.

So the fucker who hurt her is a neurosurgeon in Houston. I'm sure I can find the hospital's name in Samantha's file at work. She must've had a work reference from her previous place of employment.

Knowing I need to say something, I focus on keeping my tone gentle as I say, "I'm sorry that happened."

She just shrugs and continues to stare at her lap.

117

Suddenly my phone starts vibrating in my pocket, and I pull the device out. Seeing Renzo's name flashing on the screen, I say, "I have to take this call. Give me a moment."

"Sure."

Getting up, I walk to the door and step out of the room before answering, "What's up?"

"There's a problem. One of the trucks was ambushed."

"Fuck," I hiss. I quickly pull the door shut behind me so Samantha won't hear me, then ask, "Which truck?"

"The one Steve was driving. Whoever stole my shipment sent us a message."

"What kind of message?"

"They fucking nailed Steve to the side of the trailer."

Christ.

"Tell me you're not by the truck."

"I'm not. I sent Carlo to take care of things."

"Tell him to be careful."

"Are you coming over so we can decide how to handle this?"

I glance at the shut door. "Yes. Just give me a few minutes to wrap things up at the club."

Ending the call, I head back into the room.

Samantha gets up and walks to the bed, where she grabs her handbag. "I didn't realize it was so late. I'm going to be dead at work tomorrow."

I check the time on my phone and see it's almost midnight. "I should've kept track of time. Sorry."

She takes a step closer to me, and gives me a grateful smile. "Thank you for tonight."

When she heads to the door, I ask, "How are you getting home?"

"The subway."

I shake my head. "I'll arrange for one of the women to take you home." Before I can stop myself, I add, "Or I can take you. I'm also leaving, so it won't be out of my way."

She stares at me for a moment, then nods. "Okay. That would be great."

"A woman or me?" I ask to make sure.

The corner of her mouth lifts. "You."

There's an intense sensation in my chest, and it feels like I beat one of her demons.

Shit, I'm pretty sure Samantha knows I drive a G-Wagon. I'll have to take Brian's car and tell Milo and Lorenzo to follow us at a safe distance.

"I'm just grabbing my car keys, then we can leave," I say as we step out into the hallway.

"Should I wait here?" she asks.

"Yes. I won't be long."

Hurrying toward the security room, my thoughts are torn between Samantha and the ambush on one of my trucks.

When I'm out of earshot of Samantha, I quickly call Milo.

"Yes, boss?"

"I'm using Brian's car to take Miss Blakely home. Follow behind us and make sure she doesn't see you."

"Got it."

"Be careful, Milo. One of the trucks was ambushed tonight."

"Fuck," my guard mutters. "I'll notify the rest of the men."

"After dropping off Samantha, we're heading to Renzo's place," I inform him before ending the call.

Chapter 13

Samantha

When I climb into the passenger seat of the BMW, I feel a little apprehensive.

I'm taking a huge risk by getting into a car with a man I barely know.

Barely...ha! I don't even know his freaking name.

When my mystery man settles behind the steering wheel, I watch as he adjusts the seat.

My eyebrow pops up. "Isn't this your car?"

"No, it's a friend's."

He starts the engine, and realizing he's going to drive through Manhattan with a balaklava on, I let out a snort. "You look like a bank robber. The cops are going to pull us over."

"Let's hope that doesn't happen," he mutters as he reverses the BMW out of the parking bay. "Where do you live?"

Knowing he can find my address on my membership form, I don't bother lying and tell him where to go.

We drive in silence for a minute or so before my nerves get the better of me, and I blurt out, "This isn't nerve-racking at all."

Turning left at a set of traffic lights, he says, "It's the same as being in a room with me. Try not to worry."

"It's not the same," I argue. "There are no security cameras. Right now, it's your word against mine."

"I'm not going to hurt you," he murmurs. "Besides, I enjoy your company and won't do anything to jeopardize our time together."

My eyes settle on him, and I watch as he steers the car.

Weirdly, I believe him when he says he won't hurt me.

Why?

Am I being gullible, or is my gut instinct right that he might be one of the good ones?

I thought Todd was one of the good ones. Look where that got me.

Forcing my thoughts away from Todd, I think about the past few hours I spent with my mystery man. Even though I couldn't lie on the bed for more than a few minutes, I feel I made some progress.

Holding his hand was nice.

It was more than nice. I felt safe with him and there was a fluttering in my stomach.

I even managed to tell him a little about my past, which was a first for me.

When the BMW comes to a stop, I'm yanked out of my thoughts and realize I stared at my mystery man all the way home.

Look who's being the creepy one.

"Thanks for the ride," I say while pushing the door open.

As I climb out, my mystery man also gets out of the car. He looks up and down the street before glancing at my apartment building.

I watch as he walks around the front of the BMW, then he says, "I enjoyed tonight."

"Me too." I take a step toward the entrance. "Drive safely."

He nods and keeps watching me as I walk into the building.

When I lock my front door behind me, a smile tugs at my lips.

I might not know who my mystery man is, but he's helping me a lot.

Walking to my bathroom, I wash my face and brush my teeth.

I feel safe in that room because security will rush to help if something happens.

Then again, I just spent ten minutes alone in a car with a man who's a virtual stranger to me.

Which means I feel safe with him.

Right?

I spit out the toothpaste and rinse my mouth before I head into my bedroom. Pulling the covers back, I look down at the bed and wonder whether I've made any progress at all.

Maybe the sense of security I get at the club is keeping me from freaking out.

Shit.

The thought crosses my mind to ask my mystery man to meet me at my apartment for the next meeting, but I banish the idea before it has a chance to take root.

Letting out a huff, I climb under the covers and punch my pillow.

I need to sleep now. I'll worry about this tomorrow.

Franco

When I walk into Renzo's penthouse, it's to see Domiano, Angelo, and Dario already seated in the living room.

Everyone has a grim expression on their face, and the air is tense with anger.

That's how the Cosa Nostra works. If you attack one of the five heads, you have to deal with all of us.

I head straight to the liquor cabinet to pour myself a tumbler of whiskey.

"What took you so long?" Renzo asks.

"I had to drop my PA off at home." Taking a sip of the whiskey, I turn around and see everyone's watching me.

"Jesus, did you make her work until midnight?" Dario asks, not looking impressed with me. "No wonder your assistants never last longer than three months."

"No, I didn't make her work until midnight," I mutter.

Everyone's eyebrows fly into their hairlines, and I let out a sigh. "No, I'm not fucking my PA. Can we stop talking about her and focus on the problem?"

When I take a seat, Renzo passes his phone to me. "Look at the photos."

I scroll through them, and seeing that Steve's eyes are gouged out, and his body is positioned the same as Christ's was when he was crucified, I'm filled with rage.

It's a brutal way to die. I'll make the fuckers pay for what they did to Steve.

"I think it's safe to say whoever ambushed the truck is trying to send us a message," Renzo says.

"Do you think it's because of the route the truck was on or because they were after the weapons?" Angelo asks.

I let out a sigh. "Seeing as they emptied the truck, they were probably after the submachine guns."

"Fuckers," Renzo growls. "That was an important shipment."

"I'll check with my contact in Paraguay. I might be able to arrange a shipment of Heckler & Kochs," Damiano says.

Renzo gives him a grateful smile. "That will help a lot, brother."

"So what are we going to do about this?" Dario asks.

I shake my head. "We have to find out who's behind the attack."

"It could be one of the cartels," Angelo mentions.

I shake my head. "They'd send Steve's body to us in pieces. This doesn't feel like their work."

"I'll see what I can find out," Dario offers. The man is a wizard when it comes to hacking into systems and finding shit.

"There's not much we can do right now," Damiano says as he rises to his feet. "Put everyone on high alert just in case this is the start of something."

Angelo gets up as well. "I better get back to my wife."

I give the men a chin lift before they leave, then turn my attention to Renzo and Dario.

When Dario just keeps staring at me, I glare at him. "Don't even fucking ask."

His tone is filled with laughter when he goes against my wish and asks, "So, are you fucking your PA?"

"Fuck off," I mutter before downing the rest of the whiskey in the tumbler.

"I'd like to hear the answer as well," Renzo joins in.

"No, I'm not."

"You don't attend any functions unless we force you to," Dario says. "And you weren't working late with her."

"Christ, you're like a dog with a fucking bone," I growl. "I'm just spending time with her. It's nothing romantic."

Both men give me a skeptical look.

"You're just spending time with her." Dario shakes his head at me. "Suuuuure."

"I'm just helping her deal with some shit," I admit, so they'll shut up about the matter.

"You're helping your PA? Willingly?" Renzo asks, his voice thick with laughter. "Hell has officially frozen over."

I set the tumbler down and climb to my feet. "I'm going home."

"Aww, just as we're getting to the interesting part," Dario taunts me.

When I walk to the private elevator, they burst out laughing like a couple of fucking teenagers.

I step inside, and as the doors start to close, I give them the middle finger.

Fuckers.

My phone starts to vibrate, and I quickly pull it out of my pocket. Whenever I get a call at one in the morning, I know it's not good news.

Seeing Brian's name flashing on the screen, I answer, "I've already returned your car."

"That's not why I'm calling."

The elevator doors open, and I walk to where Milo and Lorenzo are waiting by the G-Wagon.

"What's up?"

"It's Miss Blakely. She wants to know whether you can call her."

No, I can't. I spend half the day talking to her over the phone. She might recognize my voice.

"I'll deal with it," I mutter before hanging up. Looking at Milo, I say, "Let's go home."

I have a couple of burner phones at the house. I'll send her text messages, that way, my identity will remain anonymous.

Chapter 14

Samantha

Sitting in my living room, instead of sleeping, I stare at my phone.

This really could've waited until tomorrow, and he'll return your call tomorrow. Go. To. Sleep!

When a message comes through, I grab the device and quickly open it.

You asked me to call. Is everything okay?

"Shit," I mutter.

I type my reply and press send.

I'm sorry for bothering you like this. We can talk tomorrow. I don't want to keep you up.

While I program the number under MMM, another text comes through.

MMM: You're not keeping me up. What's wrong?

Samantha: I just wanted to ask you something.

MMM: What?

I hesitate for a moment before I type out the question.

Samantha: Do you do house calls?

MMM: Why?

Samantha: I'm worried the club is giving me a false sense of security, and while I think I'm getting better, I'm actually making no progress at all. I want to test the theory.

Feeling like I'm asking too much, I quickly add another text.

Samantha: Don't feel obligated in any way. I'll understand if you say no.

MMM: When do you want me to come over?

Samantha: When are you free?

MMM: Now.

My eyes go wide as saucers, and my heartbeat sets off at a crazy pace.

This is why I reached out to him. Chickening out will make me look childish. Before I can change my mind, I send my reply.

Samantha: Okay.

When I put my phone down on the coffee table, the thought crosses my mind that I'm going to be dead tired at work.

I wonder if Mr. Vitale will have an aneurysm if I call in sick?

Probably.

I get up from the couch, and when I walk into my bedroom, I see my reflection in the mirror.

"Shit!"

Darting to my closet, I yank out a pair of leggings and a T-shirt and quickly change out of my pajamas. I pull my brush through my hair, and looking semi-decent, I head back to the living room.

Unable to sit, I stalk up and down, my eyes darting to the front door every few seconds.

Suddenly, my phone vibrates with an incoming message, and I almost tackle the coffee table to get to the device.

MMM: I'm coming up the fire escape, so I don't give any of your neighbors a heart attack.

My eyes dart to the window, and feeling nervous as hell, I go to open it. A moment later, a black figure appears, and as he climbs into my living room, I begin to think I have some kind of death wish.

My mystery man straightens to his full length, then our eyes lock.

Yep, I've just let a stranger into my apartment. I'm officially insane.

He doesn't try to move closer, but instead asks, "How are you holding up?"

Hearing the gentle tone of his voice helps ease some of the nerves spinning in my stomach.

"I'm not sure," I answer honestly.

He takes a step closer, and it has my heart rate spiking. When he's within reaching distance, he holds his hand out to me.

I swallow hard on my anxiety, but as I place my hand in his, I feel the same sense of comfort with him I felt at the club.

I have made progress!

The confirmation has a smile spreading over my face. "It's not a false sense of security." My eyes meet his. "I'm making progress."

His eyes crease at the corners as if he's smiling back at me and I suddenly hate the stupid ski mask.

"If I promise to ignore you in public and keep your identity a secret, will you take the ski mask off?"

Letting go of my hand, he shakes his head. "It's the only rule I have."

I sigh but don't push him further. "Okay." Crossing my arms over my chest, I ask, "Is it against the rules to meet here?"

Again, he shakes his head. "Is that what you want?"

I'm not sure.

Moving around him, I walk to one of the couches and take a seat. "I'm in two minds about it."

He sits down on the other couch, then murmurs, "I'm okay with whatever you decide."

Glancing a the kitchen, I ask, "Would you like something to drink?"

He points at the ski mask. "Thanks for the offer, though."

My gaze settles on the coffee table between us, and I consider which option would work best for me. Here or the club.

I won't have to take the subway every other night.

"I think I'd like to meet here," I say.

"You have my number. Just text me when you want me to come over."

"Will your boss be okay with it?"

He lets out a soft chuckle. "I own *Paradiso*."

Holy shit.

He is the boss.

I gape at him for a moment. "You're the owner?"

He nods and chuckles at my surprised reaction.

"Okay...wow..." A frown forms on my forehead. "In that case, I have a complaint."

"What?"

"Seriously, you could've chosen better masks."

Laughter bursts from him. "You *really* hate the balaclavas."

"A lot." Not wanting to insult him any further, I change the subject. "I'm sure you're busy and don't have time to spare. Why did you agree to meet with me?"

"I wanted to make sure nothing went wrong again." He rests his forearms on his thighs and links his fingers. "It's clear you're dealing with something traumatic, and I want to help."

"That's really kind of you."

He glances around my apartment, then asks, "What are your plans going forward? It will help if I know what to expect from future meetings."

Hoping he'll go along with everything, I reply, "After I manage to lie on the bed with you in the room for at least ten minutes, I'd like to try it with you lying beside me."

Without even thinking about it, he agrees. "Okay. What then?"

"I'd like to try hugging you."

He nods.

"That's all I have for now."

There's a moment's silence, then he asks, "You opened up a little to me earlier. Do you want to try telling me more about what happened?"

Instantly, my muscles tighten, and my anxiety spikes a little. "I don't know about that. I don't want to burden you with the details."

"It won't be a burden, Samantha. Maybe if you talk about it, it will help."

"I haven't told anyone." I shake my head. "I don't think I can."

"As long as you know I'm here whenever you feel like talking."

I give him a thankful smile. "I appreciate it very much."

He checks the time on his wristwatch, then says, "It's almost three-thirty. You better get some sleep."

I let out a groan before chuckling. "My boss is going to kill me."

"Hopefully, he doesn't." My mystery man gets up and walks to the window.

"Thank you for coming over," I say as I rise to my feet.

"You're welcome."

When he disappears down the fire escape, I move closer and shut the window.

Feeling like tonight went really well and hopeful about our future meetings, I walk to my bedroom and flop down on my bed.

"Ugh, why do I have to work? Why couldn't my family be stinking rich so I can sleep in?"

Chapter 15

Samantha

God, I feel like death warmed over.

Mr. Vitale has been relentless this morning. You'd swear he's the one who didn't get any sleep.

Asshole.

Just as the thought crosses my mind, an incoming call comes through from his office.

Answering it, I try to sound upbeat as I say, "Yes, sir?"

"My office. Now!"

God, I hate him.

"I'm coming." He doesn't hear my reply, because he's already hung up.

I let out a whining sound as I get up from my chair and have to resist the urge to stomp my feet like a two-year-old.

Opening the door to the chamber of wrath, I go inside.

"Cancel all my appointments for the next two days," he barks. "And fix all the mistakes on this contract."

Papers fly across his desk, and I dart forward to catch them. Before I can stop myself, I snap, "Do you have to be such an asshole?"

When he raises an eyebrow at me, my words register in my tired brain.

I did not just say that to him!

I start blinking at him, and then an apology falls over my lips, "Oh my God. I'm so sorry, Mr. Vitale."

His intense eyes stare a hole into my freaking soul before he says, "You look sick. Maybe you should take the rest of the day off."

Surprised, I squawk, "What?"

"Go home, Miss Blakely. I can manage without you for one day."

A frown forms on my forehead. "I'm not sick. I can work."

"Go home before I change my mind and make you work until midnight!" he barks.

I spin around and make a beeline for the door, but before I can escape the chamber of wrath, he snaps, "And you better be back to your full potential tomorrow!"

"Yes, sir." I almost freaking curtsy. "Thank you, sir."

Why the hell am I thanking the king of bastards?

Still, at least he didn't fire me for calling him an asshole.

I switch off my computer and grab my bag from the drawer.

Never again am I staying up that late.

Leaving the building, I head to the subway station, and once I'm seated on a train, it becomes the fight of my life to stay awake.

The moment I walk into my apartment, I let out a groan and drop down on the couch. I kick off my high heels, and curling up into a fetal position, it only takes a minute or two before I'm fast asleep.

———————————

Waking up, I'm confused and don't even know what day it is.

It takes me a moment to remember what happened earlier, and now that I've had some rest, dread pours into my veins.

God, after all the hard work I've put in over the past few weeks to impress Mr. Vitale, I just had to screw things up.

I pull my handbag closer and dig my phone out of it. When I check the time and see I only slept for two hours, I dart up and rush to the bathroom to fix my makeup and hair.

Maybe I can still salvage things. I'll work late tonight to make up for the shit show this morning.

When I look good as new, I hurry out of my apartment and take the subway back to work.

Nerves tighten my stomach, and I brace for the wrath of God as I walk into the building.

During the ride up to the top floor, I nibble anxiously on my bottom lip and when the elevator doors open, my legs feel a little weak.

No matter what happens, I'm going to work my butt off.

When my desk comes into view, I see Gloria from the sales department sitting in my chair.

Surprise flutters over her face. "Mr. Vitale said you're sick."

"I'm not." I give her a grateful smile. "Thanks for covering for me, but I'll take over."

"Thank God," she sighs. Getting up, she shakes her head. "I don't know how you do it."

I watch as she walks away then take a seat at my desk. After I tuck my handbag in the bottom drawer, I check all the emails and notice Gloria couldn't keep up with Mr. Vitale.

The poor woman.

I put the wireless headset on and fix the contract I botched up this morning. After I email it to Mr. Vitale, I get to work on all the emails.

I don't know how much time has passed when I suddenly hear, "What are you doing here?"

I startle so bad, that I dart up from my chair and shriek, "Jesus! My freaking heart!"

Seeing Mr. Vitale glare at me, I ramble, "I thought you were out for the rest of the day? I felt better, so I came back to work. I'm sorry."

Why the hell am I apologizing for coming to work?

He drops a signed contract on my desk. "Courier it to the lawyers."

"Yes, sir."

His eyes burn on my face for a moment too long, then he says, "I'm leaving."

"Yes, sir."

When he walks away, I slump down on my chair and let out a sigh.

If the stress of working for the man doesn't kill me, the heart attack he tries to give me every other day will.

Just as I'm about to get back to work, my cell phone vibrates with an incoming message. Picking up the device, I unlock the screen, and seeing a text from my mystery man, a smile spreads over my face.

MMM: I'm just checking in to make sure you're alive, and your boss didn't kill you.

Samantha: He came close to wringing my neck a couple of times, but I survived.

MMM: I'm glad to hear that.

Samantha: Did you manage to get some sleep?

MMM: Not a single wink.

Shit.

I feel rotten when I read his reply.

Samantha: I'm so sorry. Can you at least squeeze a nap in today?

MMM: Don't worry about me. I'll talk to you later.

I place my cell phone on the desk and turn my attention back to my work. Putting the contract in an envelope, I schedule a pick-up time with the courier Vitale Health always uses.

I take call after call while typing up reports and letters, and when I come up for air, it's to see it's past six already.

Getting up from my chair, I stretch my body before I grab all the documents from the printer. I grab my stapler off my desk and head to the empty boardroom so I can use the large table.

Stapling all the reports and contracts, I set them down in neat piles before double-checking all the letters for any errors I might've missed when I typed them.

Happy with my work, I gather everything and carry it to Mr. Vitale's office.

Just as I take hold of the doorknob, it twists beneath my hand. I'm yanked forward as someone opens the door, and I slam into a hard wall of muscle.

Hands grab hold of my arms, and as the documents fall to the ground, my eyes lock on Mr. Vitale's face.

It only takes a second before it registers that his hands are gripping my biceps.

He's touching me.

Before I can start panicking, he lets go of me and takes a couple of steps backward.

Feeling rattled, I suck in a deep breath of air before I look at the documents scattered on the floor.

"Why are you still here?" he asks in his usually grumpy tone.

My voice is tight from the shock as I answer, "I wanted to get all the work done."

I crouch down and gather all the papers.

I didn't have a panic attack.

In the past, something like this would've set me off.

It means my meetings with my mystery man are really working.

Intense relief fills my chest, and it makes me overemotional.

I stand up again, and rushing past Mr. Vitale, I place the stack of documents on his desk.

When I turn around he mutters, "Go home, Miss Blakely."

Geeze, the man really doesn't want me at the office today.

"Have a good evening, sir."

I head back to my desk, and as I switch off my computer, I hear male voices rumbling from the elevator's direction. Just then, two men come down the hallway, and the sight of them makes a shiver race over my body.

Dear God, they look just as intimidating as Mr. Vitale.

They're both tall, and the expensive suits they're wearing are clearly tailor-made for their bodies.

One of the men notices me, and a smile spreads over his attractive face. "Well, well, well, if it isn't the infamous PA."

What does that mean?

"Shut up, Dario," Mr. Vitale snaps from where he's standing in the doorway to his office. His eyes flick to me. "Why are you still here?"

"I was just about to leave," I say.

I grab my handbag and wait for the men to pass my desk, but Dario stops in front of me.

With a playful grin, he holds his hand out to me. "Dario La Rosa. Just let me know when you're tired of his bullshit. I'm looking for a good assistant."

Oh shit.

My eyes drop to his outstretched hand, and unable to be rude to Mr. Vitale's business acquaintance, I place my hand in his.

As if a switch is flipped inside me, a fine layer of sweat beads over my skin, and fear floods my veins.

My breaths burst over my lips, and they're so loud it's all I can hear.

Every muscle in my body locks up, and my feet refuse to move.

'You call this a meal?' Todd roars as he shoves my face into the plate of spaghetti and meatballs. 'Then you fucking eat it!'

I can't breathe, and placing my hands on the table, I try to push against Todd's brutal grip around the back of my neck.

Suddenly, I'm yanked away from the plate. Before I can catch my bearings, he slams me against the wall, and the blow to my head makes my vision go black.

"You're safe....No one's going to hurt you...Jesus fucking Christ... Samantha, you're safe..."

I manage to suck in a breath of much-needed air, but then the panic attack has me bursting out in tears, and it becomes harder to breathe.

Hands frame my face, and Mr. Vitale's face appears before mine. "Look at me, Samantha!"

His harsh tone rips me out of the terror I'm stuck in.

"Take a deep breath," he orders, and like a good little PA, I obey.

"That's good," he praises me, which is all it takes to make me come to my senses.

Pulling his hands away from my face, he takes a seat on the chair next to me and it's only then I realize we're in his office.

There's no sign of the other men.

Forget about that and focus on calming your emotions.

It feels like an elephant is sitting on my chest, but as the seconds pass, the pressure eases until my breathing returns to normal.

With my head bowed, I wipe the tears from my face.

When I feel semi-normal again, the realization sinks in that I just had one hell of a panic attack in front of my boss.

Today is not my day.

Feeling smaller than an ant, I whisper, "I'm sorry."

"It's fine," his voice rumbles. He sounds agitated with me.

My heart sinks, and gathering the meager strength I have left, I lift my head and meet Mr. Vitale's dark eyes.

Instead of firing me, he says, "Take a moment, and once you feel better, go home. I'm leaving with the other men, so you'll be alone."

I nod, and as he gets up from the chair, I blurt out, "I'm really sorry for today."

"It's okay, Miss Blakely. We're all entitled to a bad day once in a while." He pauses, and his eyes drift over my face. "Get some rest tonight."

I nod and watch as he leaves the office.

"How is she?" I hear Dario ask.

"Better. Let's go," Mr. Vitale grumbles.

Hey, at least I'm not the only person he growls at.

Letting out a sigh, I cover my face with my hands, and then disappointment washes over me.

I'm not making any progress.

But why am I okay with my mystery man?

It takes a moment before I realize I also didn't freak out when Mr. Vitale was touching me. Instead, he managed to calm me down.

Okay, so maybe it will take a little longer before I'm okay with touching random, strange men.

Chapter 16

Franco

After having dinner with Renzo and Dario, I stop at *Paradiso* to check on things.

Once I've changed into my uniform, I take a moment to send Samantha a message.

MMM: How are you?

While I wait for her reply, my thoughts go back to the panic attack she had. It was fucking bad, and it's clear our meetings haven't helped as much as I thought.

My phone vibrates in my hand, and I quickly read the message.

Samantha: Honestly?

MMM: Yes.

Samantha: Not so good.

MMM: Do you want me to come over?

Needing to be there for her, I whisper, "Please say yes."

Samantha: Please. I'd really appreciate it.

"Thank fuck."

MMM: I'm on my way. Open the window.

I'm up and out of my office at the speed of light, and as I rush through the back entrance to the club, Milo and Lorenzo kill their cigarettes and give me a worried look.

"What's wrong?" Milo asks.

"Nothing. I'm going to Samantha's place," I say as I open the back door of the G-Wagon.

My men pile into the vehicle, and when we're on our way, my thoughts return to the clusterfuck of a day I've had.

This morning I was extra harsh with Samantha so she doesn't figure out who I am. I also wanted her to go home and rest, but that fucking backfired on me.

She wasn't supposed to be at the office when Renzo and Dario arrived, and when Dario held out his hand to her, I didn't intervene because I wanted to see whether our meetings were helping her.

Watching Samantha struggle to breathe while her green eyes were drowning in terror is up there with the worst shit I've ever seen. And I've seen some fucked up shit in my life.

Milo stops the G-Wagon near the side of the building, and as I open the door, I say, "I might be a while."

"The balaclava," Lorenzo reminds me.

"Fuck," I mutter as I quickly pull it over my head, and when I get out of the vehicle, I run toward the fire escape.

One day someone is going to see me and call the police on my ass.

When I reach Samantha's open window, I climb through and find her pacing in the living room.

Her head swings to me, her eyes wide and her features drawn tight.

Christ, I need to hold her.

"Can I hug you?" I ask as I slowly move closer to her.

Her face crumbles, and her head bobs up and down.

I close the distance between us, and the moment my arms wrap around her, a sob escapes her lips.

I pull her tightly to my chest, and even though the fucking balaclava is in the way, I press a kiss to the top of her head.

I can't describe what I feel as I finally get to hold her in my arms, but it's so fucking powerful it leaves me breathless.

She places her hand against my chest, and her fingers fist the fabric of my shirt.

"I'm not getting better," she whimpers.

"You are. You're letting me hold you."

She pulls away from me. "I tried to shake a man's hand today and ended up having a panic attack in front of my boss." She lifts her hand and tucks her hair behind her ear. "God, he's going to fire me."

"He won't."

"You don't know him like I do," she argues. "The man has no soul, never mind a heart. He has a new PA every couple of months. I made so many mistakes today he's probably plotting my death."

Christ, it sounds like she hates me.

"I seriously doubt that."

She starts to pace again and cover her mouth with her hand when a sob bursts from her.

Fuck this.

I stalk toward her and pull her back into my arms. "Don't worry about work right now. Let's focus on you."

She nods and pulls away from me again. I hate letting go of her, but I don't want to make things worse.

When she takes a seat on the couch, I sit on the coffee table so I'm close to her.

Leaning forward, I hold my hand out to her with my palm facing up.

Her eyebrows are drawn together, and she looks so fucking sad it takes a swing at my heart.

She doesn't hesitate and places her hand in mine. When my fingers wrap around hers, I say, "You just need time. Rome wasn't built in a day."

She takes a deep breath and lets it out slowly. "I hope you're right."

When my thumb brushes over her skin, her eyes settle on our hands.

"What can I do to make you feel better?" I ask.

"You're already doing it." A smile wavers around her lips as she looks at me. "At least we've ticked hugging off the list."

We continue to hold hands and she's quiet for a while before she whispers, "I hate him."

Her words deliver a blow to my heart.

"Your boss?"

She shakes her head. "My ex."

I almost ask her what's the fucker's name so I can have him killed but stop myself in time.

She stares at our hands again. "I keep thinking I should've done a million things differently. I shouldn't have become friends with him. I should've broken things off the first time he got aggressive. I should've gotten a restraining order against him instead of just breaking up and assuming he'd stay away. I should've gone to the police when…"

Fear and disgust ripple over her face, and unable to keep quiet, I ask, "Did he hit you?"

A look of shame tightens her features as she nods.

Getting up from the table, I take a seat next to Samantha and link my fingers with hers. She leans her head against my shoulder and closes her eyes.

"It wasn't your fault," I whisper.

"I keep telling myself that." She squeezes closer against my side. "Maybe I'll believe it one day."

Letting go of her hand, I lift my arm around her shoulders, and she places her hand against my abdomen.

We're quiet for a good ten minutes before she says, "Don't forget about the tattoo. I'd like to get it as soon as possible."

Fuck, it completely slipped my mind.

"I'll make an appointment first thing tomorrow morning."

Silence falls between us again, and when her body relaxes next to me, I glance down only to see she's fallen asleep.

You're definitely making progress, baby.

Careful not to wake her, I rest my chin on top of her head and close my eyes.

It feels so fucking good to sit beside her with my arm around her shoulders.

With my free hand, I reach for the balaclava and lift it enough so I can press my lips to her hair, and I take a deep breath of her vanilla scent.

Chapter 17

Samantha

God, I can't wait for next week. I need a vacation, even if it's only a week.

As I leave the subway and walk toward work, my phone starts to ring, and seeing it's Mom, I smile as I answer, "Hey, Mom."

"Hi, sweetie. I can't wait to pick you up at the airport on Saturday. I was thinking we could start your vacation with a spa day. What do you think?"

My smile widens at the thought of getting a full body massage. "Yes! I'd love that."

"Great. I'll make an appointment for us," Mom says.

"Thanks, Mom." At the end of the block, I turn right and move closer to the buildings to avoid the other pedestrians before I admit, "I can't wait to see you and Dad."

"We miss you too, sweetie. Unfortunately Matt won't be here. He's so busy with the new account he landed."

"Aww, that's a pity," I mutter. I haven't seen my brother since Christmas and make a mental note to give him a call.

When I reach the office, I say, "I have to go, Mom."

"Okay. Have a good day, sweetie."

"You too."

Ending the call, I walk into the building, and after greeting the girls at reception, I take the elevator up to the top floor.

Since I had the panic attack last week, Mr. Vitale hasn't brought it up. He also hasn't mentioned anything about my poor performance that day.

Luckily, nothing has gone wrong since, but I'm worried about today. We have to inspect the building he wants to purchase, which means I'll be alone with him.

Ugh. Why can't he do the inspection without me?

I'm wearing a gray pantsuit and ballet flats, seeing as my boss told me to wear something comfortable for the day.

When I reach my desk, I place my handbag in the bottom drawer and switch on my computer.

Just as I take a seat, Mr. Vitale comes stalking down the hallway.

Shit.

The phone is still on voicemail, so reception couldn't warn me.

"Morning, Mr. Vitale. I'll bring you a coffee now," I say before I dart in the direction of the kitchen.

"Don't bother with coffee," he mutters, then he raises an eyebrow at me. "Are you ready?"

"Yes." I quickly grab the tablet I'll need to take notes and my handbag.

When I reach for the computer, Mr. Vitale says, "Leave it on. Gloria will sit here for the day."

I nod and have to jog to catch up as he stalks back to the elevator.

When we climb inside, I put a safe space between us and switch on the tablet so I can get the notepad ready.

"We'll be escorted by two guards, but they'll take a different vehicle," Mr. Vitale mentions.

Of course, the man will have bodyguards. He's a billionaire, after all. I'm just thankful they won't be riding with us.

The elevator doors slide open, and as we walk to the exit, Mr. Vitale says, "Gloria will spend tomorrow and Friday with you so you can show her how I like things done before you go on vacation."

"Okay."

When we step out onto the sidewalk, two scary-looking men move closer to us, but before I can panic that we're about to be mugged in broad daylight, Mr. Vitale says, "This is Milo and Lorenzo, my guards."

I manage a quivering smile. "Nice to meet you."

They nod at me and wait for us to get into a G-Wagon before heading to the SUV behind us.

When Mr. Vitale starts the engine, I'm surprised I don't feel panicked about being alone in a car with him.

It's probably because I work for the man and we spend a lot of time together.

Relieved that I'm semi-comfortable with my boss, I bring up the details of the building and go over them for the third time.

I've already compiled a list of other buildings to compare with the market value of the one Mr. Vitale wants to purchase. I want to make sure it's not overpriced.

When ready for the inspection, I notice there's a weird silence between us. Stealing a glance at Mr. Vitale, I take in his attractive face.

It's a pity the man is so grumpy. I think he'd make ovaries explode in the office if he smiled occasionally.

We pull up to the building that's situated near a shipyard, and I ask, "What will the building be used for?"

"A financial company."

Leaving my handbag in the vehicle, I climb out. I notice a woman standing near her car and glance at the guards as they park the SUV behind the G-Wagon.

At least I'm not the only woman here.

When Mr. Vitale catches me staring at the guards, he says, "Don't worry about them."

That's easier said than done.

I follow my boss toward the woman, and when we reach her, she gives us a wide smile. "Thank you for meeting with me today, Mr. Vitale."

My grumpy boss just nods.

I shake the woman's hand and say, "I'm Samantha, Mr. Vitale's assistant."

"Jessica. Nice to meet you."

With the introductions out of the way, we head inside.

"This six-story building has two –"

"I'd prefer to inspect the property without you," Mr. Vitale interrupts her rudely.

"Oh. Okay. I'll wait here. Let me know if you have any questions."

Poor woman.

Suddenly, one of the guards comes running into the building, shouting, "Down, boss!"

Windows shatter, and as Mr. Vitale tackles me off my feet, I watch as a bullet hits Jessica in the side of her neck.

A horrifying scream is ripped from me, and when I slam into the tiled floor, my eyes are locked on Jessica.

She gasps for air as blood spurts from the gunshot wound.

I've felt fear before, but the emotion seizing my mind is nothing compared to that.

Seeing Jessica exhale her last breath and her eyes lose all life is the most horrific thing I've ever witnessed.

"Run, boss. We'll keep them off as long as we can," I hear one of the guards shout.

My breaths explode over my lips, and a cry is ripped from me as Mr. Vitale yanks me to my feet.

More bullets slam into the walls and tiles, and I hear the guards firing their guns.

Mr. Vitale pushes me toward the stairs, shouting, "Go, Samantha!"

The intense shock makes it feel like every inch of my skin is being pricked by thorns.

I'm yanked toward the emergency stairs and stumble a couple of times because Mr. Vitale is moving much faster than I'm able.

As we enter the stairwell, I hear a bullet slam into the wall a couple of inches behind me and let out a terrified shriek.

Mr. Vitale grabs my hand in a brutal hold, and I'm yanked up the flights of stairs.

My lungs are on fire from the breaths sawing over my lips, and there's a sharp pain in my side from the sudden exercise.

I think we're on the fourth floor when Mr. Vitale abandons the stairs, and we rush into a lobby. When he finally comes to a stop in an empty hallway, I gasp like a fish out of water while trying to catch my breath.

My mind refuses to process what's happening, and I feel as if I'm stuck in some kind of alternate universe where nothing makes sense.

I watch as Mr. Vitale checks something on his wristwatch and wonder why the hell he needs to know what time it is.

"I've pressed the panic button. Backup will be here soon," he says.

I can only stare at my boss as he shrugs his jacket off, and then the man pulls a gun from behind his back.

What. The. Hell?

His eyes lock on my face, and the severe expression tightening his features demands my attention.

"We're under attack. You need to do everything I say."

"W-w-why," I stammer through the terror. "W-what?"

Picking up his jacket, he tosses it into a small office, then I'm grabbed by the hand and pulled down the hallway.

"I'll explain everything later. Right now, we just have to stay alive until backup arrives."

Stay alive. Jesus.

I'm yanked into an empty office and pushed against the wall.

"Stay behind me, and don't make a sound," Mr. Vitale orders.

Our dire circumstances register with one hell of a force, and my body begins to tremble like a leaf in a shitstorm.

"Oh my God," I gasp.

Why the hell are people attacking us?

Do they want to kidnap Mr. Vitale for ransom?

My eyes lock on the gun in his hand, and seeing my grumpy boss hold a weapon looks weird.

"Find him!" someone shouts out in the hallway.

"Shit," I whimper, and a grim sense of dread fills my chest.

Suddenly, Mr. Vitale darts forward, and in absolute horror, I watch as he kicks a man who's wearing a combat uniform in the gut. The man staggers back, and Mr. Vitale shoots him right between the eyes.

The gunshot is so loud it makes me shriek with fright.

Mr. Vitale grabs the dead man's weapon and checks how many bullets it has.

With him having the bigger weapon, he shoves his gun into my hands, then says, "If something happens to me, find a place to hide. If anyone comes near you, shoot them."

"I-I've never f-fired a g-gun," I stammer, the gun heavy in my hand.

"Just point and pull the trigger," he mutters as he tucks the hilt of the bigger weapon between his elbow and chest, and looking pretty badass, he steps out of the office.

Shocked out of my mind, I stand frozen.

I hear more gunshots, then Mr. Vitale shouts, "Come, Samantha! Stay behind me."

Somehow, I manage to move, and as soon as I leave the office, I shift closer to Mr. Vitale until I'm almost glued to his back.

When he takes a step, I match it, and every time he shoots someone, a wave of shock hits me.

This is insane.

As we move past the lobby, the elevator doors open. Two men step out, and Mr. Vitale manages to shoot one of them while shoving me so hard I fall onto my butt and slide a couple of inches backward.

In a stunned stupor, I watch as my boss becomes a freaking ninja. Lunging his powerful body into the air, he avoids a bullet and delivers a kick to the side of the man's head. As the man stumbles to the side, Mr. Vitale lands effortlessly on his feet.

Holy shit. That was badass.

He ends the man's life by burying two bullets in his chest, then swings around and rushes to where I'm still sitting flat on my butt.

Chapter 18

Franco

It's been ten minutes since I pressed the panic button on my wristwatch.

Renzo and the others have received my exact location and will be here soon.

I grab hold of Samantha's bicep and haul her to her feet before pulling her toward the stairs.

I'm fucking worried about Milo and Lorenzo. With men getting past them so quickly, it means we're being attacked by half an army.

As we cautiously take the stairs up to the sixth floor, my phone starts to vibrate. I quickly dig the device out of my pocket, and seeing Milo's name flashing on the screen, I answer, "Where are you?"

"Third floor. You?"

"In the stairwell. We're heading to the sixth floor."

"I'm coming."

I end the call and put the phone back in my pocket, then glance at Samantha's pale face.

"How are you holding up?" I ask.

She shakes her head. "I'm not."

"It will be over soon."

When we reach the door to the sixth floor, I gesture with my finger in front of my lips for her to keep quiet.

Holding the submachine gun I took from one of the fuckers ready, I nudge the door open an inch and check the lobby. Not seeing anyone, I move forward.

On high alert, my eyes keep darting everywhere as I lead Samantha to another empty office.

My voice is low as I say, "Help is on the way."

Her head bobs up and down, her eyes wide and filled with terror.

Silence falls around us, and I stand ready near the door. I hear the elevator ping, and the doors slide open.

My muscles tighten, and my finger brushes against the trigger.

The moment I hear footsteps nearing the office we're hiding in, I move forward. I'm met by three men and manage to shoot one in the chest and another in his thigh. Grabbing the one with the chest wound, I use him as a shield while I finish off the other two.

Just then, Milo comes running down the hallway.

I exchange the submachine gun for one of the others lying on the floor and check the clip before I look at Milo and ask, "Where's Lorenzo?"

He shakes his head, a flash of heartache tightening his features.

No.

As the loss of Lorenzo grips my heart, I shake my head.

"He took a bullet for me," Milo mutters.

Christ.

I clench my jaw as relentless heartache pours into my chest. He was one of my best men and I considered him a close friend.

We hear the elevator doors open, and Milo pushes me back into the office where Samantha is hiding.

Suddenly, gunfire erupts from outside the building, and it makes the corner of my mouth lift. "They're here."

"Thank fuck," Milo breathes.

I lock eyes with him. "Ready?"

When he nods, we dart out of the office and open fire on the fuckers.

The moment it's safe, I shout, "Come, Samantha."

Within seconds, she's right behind me, and we rush to the stairwell so we can head down to where the other four heads of the Cosa Nostra are eliminating the enemy.

As we move from the fifth floor to the fourth, men come running up the stairs, and Milo and I open fire on them.

We step over the dead bodies and keep killing the fuckers as we make our way toward the ground floor.

Suddenly, Samantha lets out a shriek. I swing around, and seeing one of the fuckers has his hand around her ankle, I bury a bullet in his head to make sure he fucking dies.

Grabbing hold of her hand, I pull her closer and position her between Milo and me before we continue to move.

Slowly, the sound of gunfire fades away, and by the time we reach the ground floor, we're met with a sea of bodies in the main lobby.

Samantha

Horrified out of my ever-loving mind, I gag at the sight of blood and death in the lobby.

Overcome with the most sickening feeling I've ever had, I cover my mouth with my hand as if it will stop me from vomiting.

I take in the bodies, the blood, the weapons, and the other men who all look scary as hell.

I recognize two of them from when they came to the office last week.

"Jesus Christ," the scariest of the group mutters before he crouches down and searches the pockets of a dead man.

Mr. Vitale takes the gun from my trembling hand and tucks it behind his back into the waistband of his pants.

Guns. Blood. Death.

I shake my head, unable to process the immense shock and terror I experienced today.

I'm surrounded by men.

"Fuck. It's the Slovak mafia," one of the men growls. "I recognize the tattoos."

Mafia?

"Who the fuck did you piss off, Franco?" Another asks.

What is going on?

Mr. Vitale drops the submachine gun on the floor and moves closer to the other men. "Fuck if I know."

The trembling in my body grows, and unable to just stand here, I begin to walk. I have to step over bodies and pools of blood, and it makes my breaths come faster and faster.

"Samantha!" Mr. Vitale calls me.

One of the men moves toward me, and Mr. Vitale shouts, "Don't touch her."

Slipping on the blood, I land on my butt, and my hands slap against the tiles. I feel the sticky liquid beneath my palms.

Lifting them, I see red, and I lose my mind.

Unable to think clearly and drowning in horror, I begin to scramble to get up.

Blood.

There's so much blood.

I'm barely able to register that Mr. Vitale picks me up and carries me out of the building, where there are more bodies.

So much death.

I can't.

"You're safe. It's going to be okay," I hear Mr. Vitale say.

No, I'm not. I'll never be okay again, not after everything I witnessed today.

I'm placed on the hood of a car, and Mr. Vitale's hands frame my face. He forces me to look at him.

"Take deep breaths. You're safe."

My body listens to him while my mind tries to flee from all the violence.

I don't know how I do it, but I manage to calm down enough to take a deep breath.

Mr. Vitale actually looks worried about me as he says, "I'm so fucking sorry you had to see that."

Realizing he's touching my face, I pull away and whisper, "Don't touch me."

He immediately takes a couple of steps away from me, then he glances toward the entrance of the building, and his face turns to stone.

I follow the line of his sight and watch as a man is carried toward us.

When they lay the man down near us, Mr. Vitale moves closer and crouches next to him. He places his hand on the man's chest, and it's only then I recognize the expression on his face. Grief.

The man was important to him.

Mr. Vitale rises to his full height and asks, "Renzo, can you handle this for me?"

"Of course," Renzo replies. "Dario, give me a hand."

As I look at all the men, power and rage come off them in waves, and it taints the air I breathe.

Who are they?

I don't realize I asked the question out loud until Mr. Vitale answers, "They're friends."

"Let's get out of here," one of his friends orders.

Mr. Vitale's eyes lock on me, then he says, "Let's go."

I slip off the car's hood and follow him to the G-Wagon, where the remaining guard is waiting for us.

"Bring the SUV, Milo," Mr. Vitale instructs before he opens the passenger door.

The tablet. I have no idea what happened to it.

Feeling numb, I climb into the vehicle and pull on the safety belt.

When Mr. Vitale starts the engine, I look out of the window and think to ask, "What about the police?"

"Don't worry about them," he mutters.

As we drive away from the building, I lower my head and try to make sense of what happened today.

My voice sounds drained of life as I ask, "Did they try to kidnap you?"

"No."

I don't understand how I'm able to have a conversation right now.

"Then why did it happen?"

"They wanted to kill me," Mr. Vitale answers, making it sound like this is an everyday occurrence for him.

Before I can ask another question, he pulls his phone out of his pocket and answers, "Vitale speaking."

Slowly, I turn my head to glance at my boss. He looks a hell of a lot calmer than I feel.

The man is really made of stone.

"Lorenzo didn't make it. Renzo and Dario took his body." He listens to whatever the other person says, then replies, "It was the Slovak mafia...yeah, get everyone ready for war...I'm five minutes away."

He ends the call, and all I can do is blink at him.

Why would the mafia want to kill Mr. Vitale? Did he do something to piss them off?

When he drives through a pair of large black gates, my eyes widen at the sight of all the men.

"No," I whisper.

Mr. Vitale hits the brakes, then picks up his phone again and makes a call. "Have everyone go to the guesthouse until I have Miss Blakely inside."

Within seconds, all the men head to the side of the property and soon I can't see them anymore.

Mr. Vitale drives to where other cars are parked, and when he gets out, I don't move a muscle.

He opens the passenger side door and orders, "Come, Miss Blakely."

It's only then I realize he called me Samantha while we were being attacked. Now I'm Miss Blakely again.

Despite feeling reluctant, I climb out of the G-Wagon and follow Mr. Vitale into the house, which I recognize from when I dropped off his dry cleaning.

He walks to a liquor stand and pours a glass of whiskey. Bringing the tumbler to me, he says, "Drink it all."

Yeah, I don't think alcohol is going to make me feel better.

Still, I take the drink and swallow the burning liquid.

His eyes lock with mine, and then he says, "You can't tell anyone at the office."

"I'm pretty sure it's going to be all over the news," I mutter.

"It won't."

I set the tumbler down on the stand and notice the dried blood on my hands.

My mind recoils, refusing to process the death and violence I saw.

Mr. Vitale takes hold of my wrist, and I'm pulled to a restroom, where he shoves my hands into the sink. Turning on a faucet, cool water runs over my skin, and I watch as the blood swirls down the drain.

My mind begins to race, and I'm bombarded with gruesome images.

Jessica being shot in the neck. The blood squirting from her. Her lifeless eyes.

The gunshots.

Being hunted.

The terror.

The hopelessness when I realized I might die.

Mr. Vitale killing all those men.

The bodies.

The blood.

My shoulders shudder, and a silent cry is torn from my chest.

Mr. Vitale places a hand on my shoulder, and before I know what I'm doing, I move closer and bury my face against his chest.

Maybe the trauma I suffered today is bigger than my fear of men.

Maybe I just need to be comforted so badly that I don't care whether he's touching me.

Right now, it doesn't matter.

His arms wrap around me, and I feel his mouth press to my hair before he says, "I'm so fucking sorry. You were never meant to see that part of my life."

"W-why d-d-did it h-happen," I sob, needing to understand why we were attacked and so many people had to die.

His tone is filled with power when he says, "I'm one of the five heads of the Cosa Nostra." He pauses, then adds, "The Sicilian mafia."

What?

It takes a moment for his words to sink in.

Mr. Vitale is a mobster?

Is that even the right word?

Who the hell cares?! The man is…is…

Oh. My. God.

Chapter 19

Samantha

With a fresh wave of fear flooding my veins, I yank away from Mr. Vitale.

Our eyes lock, and suddenly, I see his ruthless nature written all over his face.

One of the five heads.

The other men.

Oh God. I was surrounded by the leaders of the Sicilian mafia.

It feels like I'm having an out-of-body experience, and what has been a pretty mundane reality until today, warps into something unrecognizable.

Spinning around, I rush out of the restroom and into the foyer. Spotting the front door, I make a beeline for it.

Suddenly, Mr. Vitale darts in front of me, and obstructing my escape, he says, "You can't leave until we've talked about everything."

"The hell I can't," I shriek, my voice shrill from all the shocks I've had. I move away from him, and feeling bewildered, I say, "I work for a mafia boss. Great." My hands fly to my hair and grip fistfuls. "Oh God. I won't survive going to prison."

"You're not going to prison," he snaps.

Hearing his annoyed tone, I spin around and level him with a glare. "I'm working for a criminal!"

He holds up a hand. "Calm down."

The words make me unreasonably angry. "Don't tell me to calm down!"

He lowers his hand and just stares at me, and for some reason, it makes me want to strangle him.

When I glance at the front door, he says, "You can leave after we've talked."

My eyes snap back to him, and crossing my arms over my chest, I practically spit the words at him as I say, "Then talk."

"Vitale Health is a legitimate company. You haven't taken part in any criminal activities."

I have.

The memories of Mr. Vitale killing those men flash through my mind, and my anger takes a back seat to my fear.

This man is dangerous.

Tears threaten to overwhelm me as I say, "I saw you kill people and then left the scene of a crime. The police will think I'm an accomplice."

"They won't."

He takes a step closer, but I quickly move away from him.

He sucks in a deep breath as if he's trying to stay calm, then says, "I have the police commissioner in my pocket, which means I'm above the law, Miss Blakely.

Dear God. He can probably make me disappear, and my family will never know what happened to me.

More fear pours into my chest, and all I can do is shake my head.

He must see I'm terrified of him because he says, "I'll never hurt you."

He did protect me today.

Still, he's a head of the Sicilian mafia.

Holy shit.

I keep getting slapped upside the head by everything that's happened.

"Vitale Health is a legitimate company," he says again.

Jesus, how do you hand your resignation to a mob boss?

For a moment, I'm at a loss for words and can only stare at the man.

I remember how easily he fought those men. How he killed them without blinking an eye.

He's done this before, and he'll do it again.

My voice is hoarse as I say, "I can't work for you anymore." I lift my hand to my clammy forehead and wipe over it. "I'll leave New York."

I'll run like I did a year ago and make a fresh start somewhere else.

Mr. Vitale shakes his head and takes a step closer to me, which has me moving backward. "You're not resigning, and you're not going anywhere."

I'm unsure whether the man is threatening me, but to err on the safe side, I decide not to argue with him, because I'd like to live to see another day.

I don't know much about the mafia. Only that they're ruthless, and people end up in bodybags when they try to cross them.

My mind starts to race again, and I'm bombarded with a million questions I want to ask him. The first one to escape my lips is, "The other men... they're the other heads of the Cosa Nostra, right?"

Mr. Vitale nods. "Yes."

"And the men I saw when we arrived here?"

"My army."

Right. Of course, he'll have an army.

Nodding, I wrap my arms tighter around myself. "I'd really like to go home now."

His intense eyes search my face, then he asks, "Will I see you at work tomorrow?"

My features tighten as I struggle not to burst into tears. "C-can I take tomorrow and Friday off, please? Just to process everything."

"Will you be back after your vacation?"

Swallowing hard on my fear for this man, I can only nod.

He tilts his head, his gaze sharpening on me. "I'd hate to lose you, Miss Blakely. You're the best PA I've ever had."

My eyebrows furrow, and breaking eye contact, I lower my gaze to the tiled floor. "Can I go?"

"I'll have someone take you home."

I quickly shake my head. "No, thank you."

He moves, and I watch as he grabs a coat from the closet near the door. Seeing the confused look on my face, he explains, "You have blood on your pants. This will cover it."

I glance down and see the red stains all over my gray pants.

I take the coat from Mr. Vitale and shrug it on. The fabric swallows my body, and I'll probably die of heat on my way home.

"Thank you, sir," I whisper, and when I have to walk past Mr. Vitale, my muscles tense up, and a tremble rushes through me.

"See you after your vacation, Miss Blakely."

"Yes, sir."

God. Everything he says sounds like a threat.

The moment I pull the front door shut behind me, I let out a breath of relief. I dart down the steps of the mansion and run toward the subway station.

Franco

As the front door shuts, I walk to the living room and pour whiskey into the tumbler Samantha used earlier. I pick it up and down it all in one go.

Fuck.

Now that I don't have to keep my emotions in check anymore, I throw the tumbler across the room, and it shatters against a wall.

Christ. I lost Lorenzo.

And Samantha knows I'm a capo.

There's a good chance she won't come back to work, and God only knows how today has affected her.

Within seconds, men pour into the living room.

Milo looks tense as he says, "I heard glass shatter."

"I threw it against the wall," I mutter, upset with myself for stressing Milo even more.

Lorenzo was his best friend, and the last thing he needs is making his already shitty day worse.

"Take some time off, Milo. I'll be fine."

He shakes his head, and when he walks closer to me, the other men leave to give us some privacy.

"I'm not leaving your side until every last one of those Slovakian fuckers are dead."

Lifting my hand, I grip his shoulder. As I stare at him, I can see he's struggling to keep his grief at bay.

I tug him closer and give him a brotherly hug. "We'll kill them all."

He nods as he pulls back and sucks in a deep breath. He crosses his arms over his chest and looks down at the floor as he murmurs, "It was a quick death. At least he didn't suffer."

Marcello enters the living room and holds the burner phone out to me. "You got a text from Samantha."

During the day, I leave the device with him so Samantha doesn't accidentally see it. I take it from him and read the message.

Samantha: I need to see you.

Samantha: Please.

I quickly type out a reply.

MMM: I'll be there in twenty minutes. Open the window.

"I'm heading over to Samantha's place," I inform Milo and Marcello. "Send two men to check what happens at the building we were attacked at. I want to know who comes and goes when those fuckers collect their dead."

"I'll get Santo to assign a couple of guys."

"Make sure they're not seen. I don't want to lose anyone else today."

Marcello nods, then says, "I'm coming with you. You need the extra protection. Santo can take over from me and run things here."

"That sounds good." When I walk to the archway that leads to the foyer, Milo mentions, "You need to change your clothes."

Fuck. I need to get my shit together before I give myself away tonight.

I don't think Samantha is ready to find out I'm her mystery man.

I head to my bedroom and quickly strip out of the suit. I put on my *Paradiso* uniform and grab the balaclava before leaving the house with Milo and Marcello.

During the ride to her apartment, I make a call to Renzo.

When he answers I ask, "What did you do with Lorenzo?"

"His body is at the morgue."

"Thank you."

"Anytime, brother." His attention is pulled away by someone else, then he says, "Damiano wants to know when you're coming over. We need to have a meeting."

"I just want to make sure Samantha is okay."

"I understand. It must've been one hell of a shock for her."

"Yeah," I murmur. "Thanks for the help today, Renzo."

"You'd do the same for me."

I end the call and suck in a deep breath of air.

As soon as I'm sure Samantha's doing better, I'll deal with the Slovakians.

When Milo stops the SUV at the side of the apartment building, I quickly pull on the balaclava.

Marcello gets out of the vehicle with me and escorts me to the fire escape.

"I don't know how long I'll be," I tell him.

"Take your time. I'll get Milo something to eat from across the road."

Nodding, I climb up the steps, and when I enter Samantha's apartment through the window, I find her sobbing on the couch.

She's changed out of the pantsuit into a pair of leggings and a T-shirt, and her hair hangs in damp curls around her shoulders.

"Hey," I whisper so I don't scare the shit out of her.

Her head snaps up, and seeing me, she darts from the couch and plows into my chest.

I wrap my arms around her shuddering body, and lowering my head, I keep my tone soft as I say, "I'm here, baby. I've got you."

She cries harder, and it has me lifting her into my arms. I walk to the couch and sitting down, I position her on my lap before holding her tightly again.

"That's it, baby. Let it all out."

I close my eyes, and while she breaks down in my arms, I find comfort in being so close to her.

Right now, I'm not a capo.

I'm not her boss.

I'm just an ordinary man who gets to hold the woman he's fallen in love with.

Chapter 20

Samantha

After I cried my heart out, I made myself a cup of coffee, which I'm sipping on while I sit next to my mystery man on the couch.

He has his arm wrapped around my shoulder, and it makes me feel safe.

"I had a bad day at the office," I whisper over the rim of my cup.

That's the understatement of the century.

"Want to talk about it?" he asks, his tone gentle and caring.

Not wanting to put him in any danger by telling him about Mr. Vitale being a mafia boss, I shake my head. "I can't."

I can't tell anyone about what happened.

It's something I'll have to stay quiet about until the day I die.

Feeling exhausted and emotionally drained, I let out a miserable sigh and mutter, "I need to do something that will take my mind off what happened today."

My mystery man pulls his arm away from my shoulders and says, "I'll be back in a few seconds."

He gets up and walks into the restroom.

I rise to my feet and take the cup to the kitchen. Placing my hands on the side of the sink, I stare at nothing in particular as the past day's events hang over my head like a dark cloud.

Jesus, I can't believe what happened today.

Mr. Vitale is one of the heads of the Cosa Nostra.

After I got home, I took a quick shower before Googling the Sicilian mafia. Everything I read about the mafia group increased my fear tenfold.

Mr. Vitale made it clear he won't let me resign, and I get a feeling if I try to run, he'll come after me. Not because I'm an excellent PA, but to silence me.

Shit.

What do I do?

When the restroom door opens, I turn around and look at my mystery man, who's quickly becoming one of the most important people in my life.

I could've called Jenny or caught an early flight to Seattle, but instead, I messaged him.

"We can leave in fifteen minutes," he informs me.

"Leave? Where are we going?"

"To get the tattoo you want."

For a moment, I'm overwhelmed because I've wanted to get the tattoo done for a while now. Every time I see Todd's name carved into my skin, it's a reminder of what he did to me.

Closing the distance between me and my mystery man, I wrap my arms around his waist and press my cheek to his chest.

It feels amazing to touch a man after not being able for so long. I didn't realize how much I missed it until now.

And it's all because of him – my mystery man.

"Thank you," I whisper.

When he engulfs me in a hug, a sense of safety calms the storm of emotions in my heart. "You're welcome, baby."

He's called me that more than once, and it has me tilting my head back so I can look up at him. My voice is shaky as I ask, "What's happening between us?"

"Whatever you want," he murmurs.

"What if I want a relationship?"

He lifts his hand to my face and brushes his fingers along the curve of my jaw. "Is that what you want?"

My heartbeat speeds up and pulling my arms from around his waist, I reach a hand up to the ski mask. He allows me to trail my finger over the skull, and I wish I could see his face.

"Yes. I'd like to try with you," I admit.

"Whatever you want, baby."

Our eyes lock, and his soft brown irises make a kaleidoscope of butterflies flutter in my stomach.

Slowly, he lowers his head but stops an inch from my face.

"Is this okay?" he whispers.

"Yes."

He closes the last of the distance and presses his mouth to mine. I can feel the heat of his breath through the mask before he lifts his head.

Again, we stare at each other, but when I try to take hold of the fabric so I can lift the ski mask, he grabs me by my wrist and shakes his head.

"Not yet."

"When?" I whisper.

"Soon. I just need a little more time."

Franco

I called Marcello and told him to have a car waiting outside with the keys in the ignition so I can take Samantha to the tattoo place. They'll follow us in the G-Wagon.

I should be meeting with Renzo and the others, but I can't make myself leave Samantha. Not until I'm sure she'll be okay.

As I look at the woman who's making me feel things I've never felt before, I pray to all that's holy she falls in love with me.

If I can make her love me, then she might accept it when she learns I'm her mystery man. I don't know what I'll do if she rejects me.

I'll probably kidnap her so she can't leave me.

I feel my phone vibrate and know it's a signal from Marcello that everything is ready.

"Let's go, baby," I say as I take her hand.

When I pull her toward the window, she tugs against my hold. "I'm leaving through the front door. I'll meet you outside."

Right.

Not even thinking about what I'm doing, I wrap my other hand around the back of her neck and press a kiss to her mouth. Even though the balaclava is in the way, I can still feel her lips.

Christ, I want this woman so bad I'll do anything to make her mine.

Love me back, Samantha.

I let go of her and climb out the window so she can close it behind me.

Heading down the fire escape, I jump to the ground and rush to where the Mercedes is parked. I glance up the street and see the G-Wagon, then climb behind the steering wheel.

I don't wait long before Samantha opens the passenger door and gets into the car.

Starting the engine, I guide the vehicle into traffic, and as we drive to Dante's tattoo place, I ask, "Are you feeling better?"

Samatha shrugs and glances out the window. "It comes and goes." She turns her gaze to me. "I don't think it's fully sunk in yet."

Yeah, I don't think so, either. She's way too fucking calm. Either that or this woman is the strongest person I know.

When I park the car behind the building where the tattoo parlor is, we get out of the Mercedes. I take Samantha's hand and lead her to the back entrance.

"Will you be okay with Dante touching you?" I ask.

"Dante? Is he the tattoo artist?"

"Yes."

"Only time will tell," she murmurs before we go inside.

Dante's busy getting everything ready, and when he sees us, a grin spreads over his face.

I informed him about Samantha and that he needs to be gentle with her. I also told him he can't call me by my name around her, and I'll be wearing a balaclava.

"Did you close the store?" I ask.

"Yes. No one will bother us." He gets up from his stool and comes to shake my hand. "It's been a while. How are you?"

"Good." I gesture to my woman. "This is Samantha."

He gives her a friendly smile. "Nice to meet you." Pointing to the tattoo chair, he says, "Take a seat."

Letting go of Samantha's hand, I watch as she positions herself on the chair before I move closer so I can stand next to her.

"Great," Dante murmurs. "I was told you want a tattoo of shaded bricks with a flower growing out of them."

Samantha nods. "And I want the words 'stronger than ever' over the bricks as if it's graffiti."

Dante nods, then asks, "Where do you want the tattoo?"

Her features tighten, and she looks more nervous than usual as she gestures at her side.

When I realize it will be a couple of inches beneath her breast, there's a burst of jealousy in my chest because Dante will be working close to what I consider mine.

Mine?

Christ, I'm falling too fucking fast for this woman.

"Okay." He gives her a questioning look as he takes a seat on a stool. "Can you lift your shirt so I can clean the area?"

She hesitates, and I figure it's because she's nervous about Dante touching her, so I place my hand on her shoulder. "I'm right here."

She nods and swallows hard before gripping the hem of her shirt, slowly pulling it up.

I notice haphazard scars on her skin as the fabric moves up, and a frown forms on my forehead.

Then I get to see more of the scars, and it spells out a name.

Todd.

The rage hits me so hard that I take a step back as if I've taken an actual punch to the gut. My lips part with shock, and my vision tunnels on the name carved into her skin.

The fucker branded her.

I'm going to check Samantha's personnel file to see which hospital she used to work at in Houston. Then I'm going to find out which fucking neurosurgeon's name is Todd.

And then I'll kill the fucker.

Dante masks his reaction a hell of a lot better than I do. I'm just thankful I'm wearing the balaclava because the last thing Samantha needs to see right now is the anger on my face.

She tucks the fabric neatly beneath her breasts, then turns her head so she's looking at me.

I grab the extra stool, and taking a seat near her head, I take her hand and press a kiss to her knuckles before I lock eyes with her.

"How are you holding up?" I ask.

She sucks in a deep breath, and instead of answering my question, she whispers, "Don't let go of my hand."

"I won't," I assure her before I nod at Dante to begin.

The moment he wipes the area clean, she jerks and her fingers tighten around mine.

I see panic flare in her eyes, and bracing my other arm at the top of her head, I move so close to her that I can feel her breath warming the balaclava.

"You're doing great, baby."

She nods, and I notice she's holding her breath.

"Breathe," I murmur close to her mouth.

Dante pulls away from her, and she sucks in a deep breath.

"I'm just going to prep the area," Dante warns her.

This time Samantha doesn't jerk when he touches her, and it makes me so fucking proud of her.

At this moment, I don't think about the hell that broke loose today and the war I'll have to fight in the coming weeks.

There's only Samantha and how brave she is.

Chapter 21

Samantha

Standing in front of my full-length mirror, I hold my shirt up so I can see the tattoo.

Dante did a fantastic job. I can't even make out any of the scars.

Todd's name is buried beneath the words 'stronger than ever,' and I never have to see the scars again.

Feeling very emotional, a tear trickles down my cheek.

Just as I'm managing to deal with the trauma Todd inflicted on me, I have to face what happened yesterday.

With a tired sigh, I lower my shirt and walk to where my luggage is waiting in the living room.

Needing to get out of New York, I changed my flight from Saturday to today.

As I pick up my handbag, my phone starts to ring, and I dig it out. When I see Mr. Vitale's name flashing on the screen, my body is doused in ice.

He's no longer Mr. Vitale, my grumpy boss, but Franco Vitale, one of the ruthless heads of the Cosa Nostra.

He's a killer.

Instantly fear bleeds through me, and my hand trembles as I swipe across the screen to answer the call.

"Y-yes, sir?"

"Morning, Miss Blakely. How are you today?" his voice rumbles over the line.

God, he sounds aggressive.

"F-fine," I stammer.

"I see you've changed your flight, and you're heading to Seattle today."

An intense cloak of dread wraps around me.

He's watching my every move.

Not only is the man above the law, but he's able to get my information from an airline. It registers just how powerful he is and that I don't stand a chance against him.

"I...I...I –"

"Get a lot of rest because when you're back at the office, you'll have to fix everything Gloria fucks up while you're gone."

That's his way of telling me I better return to work.

His tone sounds downright dangerous as he adds, "Enjoy your time with your family."

Is he threatening to kill my family?

Thorns of fear prick at my skin, and the words just fall over my lips, "Don't hurt my family. Please. I'll be back on the eighth."

He lets out an annoyed-sounding sigh. "It wasn't a threat, Miss Blakely. I won't touch your family. You need the break, and I hope you enjoy your vacation."

Oh.

When I keep quiet, he adds, "I don't kill innocent people, and I'll never hurt you."

Too brave for my own good, I ask, "What will happen if I resign as your assistant?"

"I won't accept your resignation, Miss Blakely. Have a safe flight. I'll see you on the eighth of July."

The call ends, and lowering my trembling hand, I watch as the screen goes black.

Shoving the phone into my handbag, I grab my luggage and rush out of my apartment. As if all the demons from hell are chasing me, I hurry to the subway.

I need to get away from New York and the Cosa Nostra. In Seattle, I'll be able to think clearly and make sense of the mess I find myself in.

When I walk through the doors at the airport, Mom catches my attention by jumping up and down.

During the six-and-a-half-hour flight, I focused on calming myself down, but as I walk to my mother, my emotions are all over the place, and I can't stop the tears from falling.

When I reach her, we hug, and I cling to my mother.

She notices I'm crying and coos, "Aww, sweetie. What's wrong?"

"I just missed you."

It's only half a lie. I did miss her.

She pulls back, and smiling at me, she wipes my tears away with the pads of her thumbs. "You need to visit more often."

I nod, and as we walk to the exit, I say, "If I had more vacation time, I would."

When we reach Mom's Prius, I feel a little better.

I'm going to put on the best performance of my life so I don't worry my parents. They can't find out about Mr. Vitale being a mob boss or that we were attacked yesterday.

Once we're both seated in the car and Mom's driving away from the airport, she asks, "Are you tired from the flight?"

I shake my head. "No. I napped a little."

"Oh, good. Do you want to go shopping? I want to get some things for the Fourth of July."

"Sure."

She grins at me before turning her attention back to the road. "The whole neighborhood decided to BBQ in the park."

I inject some excitement into my voice. "That sounds nice."

"Oh, did I tell you Ms. Jameson and Mr. Parker got married?"

"Wow. Seriously?" I gasp.

The elderly couple have been on and off for as long as I can remember, so I'm surprised to hear they finally got married.

"Yes. They eloped in Vegas." Mom scrunches her nose. "But they're still living in separate houses. Every night, Ms Jameson shouts at Mr. Parker to come over for dinner."

I let out a chuckle. "You mean Mrs. Parker, or is she keeping her last name?"

"God only knows. Those two have the weirdest relationship I've ever seen." Mom turns left at a traffic light, then says, "Matt is doing well at work, and Wendy is about to pop. Once they have the baby, I'll probably go to Portland to help out."

"Do they know what they're having?"

Mom shakes her head. "They want to keep it a surprise, but her butt is so big I think it's a boy."

"I hope you didn't tell her you think her butt is big," I say, my eyes wide on my mother.

"Of course not."

Mom steers the car up the driveway, and as I open the door, Dad steps out onto the porch and waves at me.

Being home helps ease the tension from my body, and as I hurry toward my dad and give him a hug, I push all the thoughts about Mr. Vitale and the Cosa Nostra to the back of my mind.

"Welcome home, Sammie," Dad murmurs before he pushes me back so he can look at me. "How is the New York life treating you? You look too skinny. Are you eating enough?"

I give Dad a comforting smile. "I've just been busy at work. I plan on picking up a lot of weight over the next week."

"Good. I've roasted some almonds for you to snack on."

The smell of roasted almonds is synonymous with Dad. It's something he's done all my life.

We walk into the house, and the familiarity of my family home settles around my shoulders like a warm blanket.

This is just what I needed to catch my bearings.

"We're just dropping off the luggage, then we're going shopping," Mom informs Dad of our plans.

"Ribeye steak is on sale at Joe's. Grab three, then I'll grill them for dinner," Dad says as he follows us to my bedroom.

"Oh, I was going to make the pot roast Sammie loves so much."

"Fine, I can grill them tomorrow," Dad relents.

A smile plays around my lips, and walking into my childhood bedroom, I glance at the posters of Nirvana and the Red Hot Chili Peppers still up on the walls. My parents have kept the room exactly as I left it.

The single bed is covered in a pink bedspread, and the desk where I did my homework has a vase with daisies standing in the center.

"Let's leave Sammie to freshen up," Mom says as she pushes Dad out of the room, then she smiles at me, "We'll be on the porch, sweetie."

"Okay. I won't take long."

When the door shuts behind them, I slump down on the edge of my bed and fall backward on the covers.

God, I could sleep for a week.

My phone buzzes, and I let out a groan as I dig in my handbag for the device. When I look at the screen, a smile spreads over my face, and I open the message.

MMM: Your flight should've landed already. Are you in Seattle?

Samantha: I just got to my parents' house and was going to send you a text.

MMM: How's the tattoo?

Samantha: It just feels like I have sunburn. Nothing I can't handle.

MMM: I'm glad to hear that. I'll let you go so you can spend time with your family.

Samantha: Thank you for checking in on me.

MMM: Of course. Wanted to make sure my girlfriend reached Seattle in one piece.

His girlfriend.

Samantha: I'm probably the only woman on the planet who doesn't know her boyfriend's name.

MMM: Soon. I promise. Talk to you later.

I drop the phone on the bed and stare up at the ceiling.

I'm insane. Who dates a man whose face she hasn't seen?

Me. That's who.

Chapter 22

Franco

I've stayed away from Vitale Health and *Paradiso* because I don't want the Slovak mafia attacking me at my companies where innocent people can get hurt.

Working from home, I'm surrounded by an army that's ready for war.

Dario has converted my living room into his personal office space. Whenever I have to pass through the living room to get to the sliding doors, I almost break my neck, tripping over all the fucking computer cables.

Renzo has practically moved in, and I can't do a fucking thing without the man breathing over my shoulder.

I'm on a call with Paulie. I sent him to Houston to get information on Todd's whereabouts.

"About a year ago, he was in a pretty bad car accident," Paulie informs me. "Apparently, he was released from the hospital two months ago, and no one has seen him since. Word around town is he's gone to his cabin to recover."

"Find out where the cabin is and check it out," I order.

"On it, boss."

As I end a call with Paulie, I glare at Renzo. "Stop babysitting me."

"I will once the Slovakians have been taken care of," he mutters, his eyes locked on the screen of his laptop.

"Christ," I grumble as I walk out of my office.

Heading through the living room, I glance at Dario. "Find anything new?"

He shakes his head. "Nope. Just the usual bullshit."

Exiting the house through the sliding doors, I walk to where Marcello is giving orders to the men to search the city for the Slovakians.

"Tell your informants they'll make good money if they give us a solid lead," he says to the men.

As they walk away to carry out the job, Marcello turns to face me. "Milo called. The funeral is on Monday. He's on his way back."

I nod, feeling a stab of grief. "As soon as he's here, prepare to leave. I want to go to the truckyard."

"Yeah, I'm worried about the shipment that's going out today. I've told all the drivers to carry weapons and changed their routes."

Over the past few years, Marcello has taken on the position of the underboss of the Vitale family. It's an unspoken agreement between us.

The gates open, and my eyes flick to the SUV as it comes up the driveway. I watch as Milo climbs out of the vehicle before walking to us.

"Everything's ready for tomorrow," he says, his face grim from the grief of losing his best friend.

Lorenzo was always the quiet one between the two, but since his death his silence hangs heavy around us.

Placing my hand on Milo's shoulder, I give him a squeeze. "Thank you."

"We're heading to the truckyard," Marcelo informs him.

The burner phone vibrates in my pocket, and I pull it out. Opening the message from Samantha, the corner of my mouth lifts.

Samantha: My mom just whacked my dad with a spatula. Just so you know, I take after her.

MMM: You're telling me I should hide all the spatulas?

Samantha: Just giving you time to back out.

MMM: Never.

Samantha: I have a question.

MMM: What?

Samantha: So there are security cameras in all the rooms at *Paradiso*. Does that mean you watch people having sex?

MMM: I go out of my way to avoid it and have employees who take care of that part of the business.

Samantha: Shoot. Here I was, hoping you have some juicy stories to tell me.

As the smile on my face widens, I glance at Marcello as he walks to the guest house where I keep my stash of weapons in an underground armory.

There's also an entrance into the armory from my office in the main house, which doubles as an escape route.

The phone vibrates in my hand again, drawing my attention back to my conversation with my girlfriend.

I'm taking advantage of calling her that before she finds out who I am and dumps my ass.

Samantha: Just kidding. I have to go and save my dad from my mom.

MMM: Talk to you later, baby.

When I tuck the device back into my pocket, Marcello comes walking toward me with an armored vest. He hands it to me, saying, "Just in case there's another attack."

I take the vest from him and shrug it on. While I adjust it around my chest, I head to the sliding doors. "Give me five minutes then we'll leave."

"We'll be at the G-Wagon," he replies before walking to where Milo is having a smoke break.

I go into the house and find Renzo breathing over Dario's shoulder for once.

"I'm heading out," I inform them.

Renzo's head snaps up. "Where to?"

"The truckyard. I have a shipment of cash going to Castro and Diaz. It can't wait. I need the medical equipment."

"I'll tag along," he says.

Not bothering to argue, I nod and head back outside.

"Marcello, grab an armored vest for Renzo," I say when I reach the men.

Milo finishes the cigarette, and pulling his gun from behind his back, where he keeps it tucked into the waistband of his pants, he checks the clip.

Renzo shrugs his jacket off and unhooks the chest holster that holds his two Colts. When Marcello returns with the vest, he puts it on and tucks his weapons into the slots.

When everyone's ready, we pile into the G-Wagon, and with Milo behind the steering wheel, we head to the truckyard.

The drive is tense, and we all keep our eyes peeled for anything suspicious.

"Are you changing the routes?" Renzo asks.

"Yeah. Marcello already took care of it," I answer while turning my attention to my friend.

"Good." His eyes meet mine. "I've arranged a small army to guard you and your men at the funeral. Just let us know when it is."

"Thanks, brother."

Milo's voice is somber as he says, "It's Monday at eleven a.m."

Renzo nods before glancing out the window again. Before silence can settle around us, he asks, "So, what's going on between you and your PA."

"We're dating…kind of," I mutter. When Renzo's eyes flick to me, I add, "I wear my uniform from Paradiso, so she doesn't know who I am."

"What the fuck?" A frown forms on his forehead. "It feels like you're leaving out a huge fucking chunk of the story."

214

I let out a sigh and mutter, "She came to the club because she's trying to deal with something that happened to her. One of the men she was paired up with fucked up, and I took over. It's been a month, and we've grown close since."

"So she thinks her boss and her partner at *Paradiso* are two different men?" He chuckles while shaking his head. "Brother, that's some fucked up shit."

I let out a sigh. "Trust me, I know."

"How the hell are you going to explain this to her? I'm pretty sure the woman hates you." He glances at Marcello and Milo. "Right, guys?"

"Yep," Milo mumbles.

"I'm hoping she'll fall in love with me and forgive me for deceiving her."

Renzo lets out a bark of laughter and almost wets himself next to me. When he catches his breath, he says, "Good luck with that."

Milo stops the G-Wagon near the warehouse, and as I climb out, my eyes scan over the fleet of trucks.

Everything seems to be in order, and heading into the warehouse, it's to find my men hard at work. They're filling mattresses with counterfeit banknotes before wrapping the mattresses so they look brand new.

I walk over to the piles of counterfeit notes and check a couple while Marcello talks to the drivers, making sure they know which routes to take.

"The new printers are better than the old ones," Renzo comments.

"Yeah," I agree. "It's almost impossible to tell the difference between these notes and the real thing."

When the men start to load the shipment into the trucks, I head outside, and crossing my arms over my chest, I watch as they fill the trailers with mattresses.

Renzo takes up position next to me and asks, "What are you going to do if Samantha freaks out when she learns you're both men?"

"I'll kidnap her and keep her until she forgives me," I mutter.

I feel Renzo's eyes on me. "I can't tell if you're joking."

I meet his gaze. "I'm serious."

His eyebrows lift. "I can't see how that will help your case. If anything, it will terrify the shit out of her."

I know he's right, but what else can I do, besides letting her go?

I take a deep breath and exhale slowly. "That's why I'm hoping she'll fall in love with me."

We're quiet for a while, just watching the men work, then Renzo says, "Hold up. Do you wear the balaclava when you see her?"

I nod, and when he bursts out laughing, I level him with a scowl.

His voice is thick with laughter as he says, "So you're her masked man?"

Before I can nod, he bends over at the waist, and his laughter echoes over the yard.

"Fucker," I mumble while a smile tugs at the corner of my mouth.

He tries to straighten up and grabs hold of my shoulder. With watering eyes, he says, "Okay, so seriously, what does she call you?"

Knowing he'll get a kick out of it, I mutter, "Mystery man."

When Renzo drops to the ground, he can barely say, "I'm calling you that from now on."

"Try, and I'll shoot you."

"It's worth a bullet."

Shaking my head at my friend, I walk away to check with Marcello whether everything is on track.

Chapter 23

Samantha

Watching Ms. Jameson (who's made it abundantly clear she's keeping her last name) load a very disgruntled Mr. Parker's plate with potato salad, a snort escapes me.

He keeps trying to stop her, saying he doesn't want so much.

"You will eat every vegetable on your plate before you're allowed to have meat," she orders sternly.

"You're going to kill me with all these vegetables," he argues.

"At least you'll die healthy," she mutters.

"How does one die healthy?" Mr. Parker asks his wife. "Seriously, Matilda, do you hear yourself when you speak?"

She points the spoon at him, and the potato salad falls off, dropping to the grass between them.

"Why are you sitting all alone?" Mom says as she takes a seat beside me. "Go mingle with the neighbors and have some fun."

I point at the elderly couple. "Shhh. I'm watching the show."

"Are they at it again?" Mom asks.

"Ms. Jameson says Mr. Parker has to eat all the vegetables before he can have meat, and he's not standing for it," I catch her up with what's happening.

"Lord only knows why they got married," Mom chuckles. "They bicker all the time."

"Hmm, sounds like another couple I know," I tease her.

"Your father and I don't bicker."

"No, you just whack him with the spatula."

She grins at me. "The Bible says spare the rod and spoil the child. I figure it's the same with husbands. It's my way of showing your father I love him."

Letting out a burst of laughter, I look at Ms. Jameson and Mr. Parker again. They've finally moved away from the table and are sitting at a bench. Ms. Jameson keeps pointing at what Mr. Parker should eat next.

"Let's grab some food," I say to Mom.

We head to the table, and I help myself to corn on the cob, a hot dog with pickle and parsley relish, corn-stuffed zucchini, and some pickled green beans.

"Are you going to eat all of that?" Mom asks with wide eyes.

"I'm going to try. I promised Dad I'd pick up some weight while I'm here."

"Just leave some space for the rhubarb pie I made."

"Oh, trust me, I will."

When we take our seats again, I pick up the hot dog and take a huge bite while my eyes scan over all the families eating and having fun.

My eyes lock on a man on the other side of the park, but he disappears behind a tree before I can get a good look.

A chill ripples down my spine, and my heart lurches in my chest.

Just as I'm about to start panicking, thinking I saw Todd, the man appears again, and using a cane, he limps toward a car.

Letting out a breath of relief, I watch as he climbs in his car and drives away.

Jesus, that almost gave me a heart attack.

I wish I could stay longer, but I have to fly home in a couple of hours.

Sitting at the kitchen table, I sip on a cup of coffee while my mind races to find a way out of this mess.

Mr. Vitale made it clear he won't allow me to resign, so I have no choice but to go back to work.

Besides, even if I tried to run, I'm sure he'd track me down in a heartbeat.

"Hey, Sammie," Dad says as he comes into the kitchen. He pours himself a cup of coffee and takes a seat at the table. After he drinks a couple of sips, his eyes drift over my face, then he says, "So, are you going to tell your old man what's bothering you."

"Nothing." I smile at Dad to set him at ease. "I'm fine.

"I know you better than yesterday." He lifts an eyebrow at me. "What is it? Do you need money?"

I shake my head. "No." Lowering my eyes to my cup, I circle the rim with my finger. "Work has just been busy, and my boss is impossible to please."

"Why don't you look for another job?"

Thinking quick, I say, "It won't look good on my resume if I leave the company so soon."

"Yeah, but it doesn't help if you're unhappy. No job is worth your peace of mind."

"I know." I reach across the table and give Dad's forearm a squeeze. "I'll be okay. Don't worry about me."

"It's my job to worry about you."

Mom walks into the kitchen and takes one look at us then asks, "What are you talking about?"

"We're conspiring to take over the world," I answer.

"God help us all." She lets out a chuckle, then asks, "What time do you want to leave for the airport?"

Never.

Getting up from the chair, I take my cup to the sink. "I just have to pack the last of my things, then we can go."

"By last of your things, you mean you haven't packed at all," she teases me.

I chuckle as I walk out of the kitchen to take a quick shower before throwing everything in the suitcase.

Sitting on the side of the bed, I unlock my phone and send my mystery man a text.

Samantha: I'll be back in New York at five. Do you want to come over tonight?

I set the device down beside me and put on my ballet flats.

Within minutes, a reply comes through.

MMM: What time do you want me there?

Samantha: Anytime after five.

MMM: It's a date.

Tucking my phone into my handbag, I drag my luggage to the front door before I join my parents in the kitchen again.

Dad's eating a bowl of oatmeal with a disgruntled expression, and it has me teasing my mom. "See, you also force Dad to eat healthy stuff like Ms. Jameson forces Mr. Parker."

Mom slants her eyes at me. "It's for his own good."

With Mom standing behind Dad, she's not able to see as he mouths, *'It's disgusting.'*

Mom takes the bag from the trashcan and says, "Make sure your father eats every last bite while I take this out."

"Okay."

The moment she disappears out the backdoor, I reach for the bowl and shovel the oatmeal into my mouth. I manage to make a huge dent in it before I have to pass the bowl back to him.

"This is why you're my favorite daughter."

I roll my eyes at him and swallow before I mutter, "I'm your only daughter, Dad."

"Right."

Mom comes back inside and takes one look at the almost empty bowl, then says, "What did you do with the rest of the oatmeal?"

"I told Dad I'd visit for Thanksgiving and Christmas if he ate his breakfast."

Smiles erupt on my parents' faces.

"That's wonderful news," Mom exclaims, then she taps Dad on the shoulder. "See, it's good when you eat your oatmeal."

Dad gives me a wink, then tells Mom, "I'd eat anything you put down in front of me to have Sammie here for Thanksgiving and Christmas."

Mom washes her hands, then asks, "Are you ready to go, sweetie? We don't want to be late for your flight."

"Yes." I make a whining sound as I get up and pout. "It sucks being an adult. I wish I could stay longer."

"Us too, sweetie."

I kiss Dad on the cheek. "Thanks for an amazing week, Dad."

"Anytime. Let us know when you land safely in New York."

Nodding, I follow Mom to the front door and haul my luggage to the Prius.

The drive to the airport is quiet, and by the time Mom drops me off, my heart is heavy with dread.

I give her a quick hug. "I'm going to miss you."

"Me too, sweetie." She pulls back, and her eyes drift over my face. "I love you."

"Love you too, Mom."

Taking hold of my luggage, I pull it behind me as I walk into the airport. I check in and go through security while my thoughts revolve around everything that's happened.

Tomorrow, I have to go back to work and what? Pretend like nothing happened?

I was wary of Mr. Vitale before I knew he was a mob boss, but now I'm downright terrified of the man.

Chapter 24

Franco

When I climb through Samantha's window, there's no sign of her.

I move toward the bedroom, and looking inside, I see her standing on her toes so she can put her luggage on the top shelf.

Christ, it's good to see her.

I walk closer, and coming up behind her, I take hold of her hip.

"Oh Jesus," she gasps before stumbling backward and colliding with my chest.

"Welcome home," I say, my tone soft. I lean down until my mouth is by her ear. "I missed you."

She turns around, and giving me a playful look of warning, she says, "Don't sneak up on me. You'll give me a heart attack."

"Sorry, baby."

She wraps her arms around my waist and says, "I missed you too."

"I missed you more." I lift my hands and brush my palms over her bare shoulders and arms. "You look beautiful in this dress."

"I'm glad you like it." She grins up at me. "I got it in Seattle."

My eyes search her face before I ask, "Did you have a nice time?"

"The best." She turns around and closes the closet doors, then says, "I ate way too much food. The vacation did me a world of good."

"I'm glad to hear that."

She comes to stand in front of me again. "How was your week?"

Fucking exhausting.

I shrug. "I kept busy with work." I bring my hand to her face and brush a finger along her jaw. "What do you want to do tonight?"

She pulls away from me and says, "I don't know if it's worth going through the list because it's not helping. Even though I don't get panic attacks with you, I still crap myself around other men."

227

"All men?" I ask because she doesn't lose her shit when I touch her as myself and not her mystery man.

She thinks for a moment, then mutters, "For some reason, I'm kind of okay with my boss. At least I was before…"

Samantha doesn't have to finish the sentence. I know she's talking about before the attack and finding out I'm one of the heads of the Cosa Nostra.

Wanting to help her deal with her demons, I say, "I think we should continue working through your list. You never know what might help."

She nods then gestures at the bed. "I can always try lying down with you."

I look at the light green covers with a leaf pattern printed on them. "How do you want to do this?"

"I'll lie down first and close my eyes, then you can lie beside me. Don't say anything. I just want to listen to you moving."

"Okay."

She kicks off her shoes, and I watch as she climbs onto the bed. She fixes her dress before she lies down, and taking a deep breath, she closes her eyes.

I give her a minute before moving closer and placing my knee on the bed.

My eyes stay locked on her face, looking for any sign that she's panicking as I move into a lying position.

Samantha takes a deep breath and lets it out slowly. She keeps her eyes shut for a bit longer, then opens them and turns her head to look at me.

"I think this is a waste of time. I'm comfortable with you, so I don't think anything you do will make me panic."

Turning onto my side, I prop my head on my hand and say, "Maybe it will help if you talk about what happened."

She thinks about it for a moment, then admits, "It's difficult. Every time I try, it's as if I get transported back to it."

"You were okay while Dante tattooed you because I was there. Give it a try."

She turns onto her side and locks eyes with me. "Okay, but don't get your hopes up."

With my other hand, I take hold of hers and brush my thumb over her skin. Her gaze lowers to our joined hands, and she remains quiet.

My eyes drink in the sight of her beautiful face, and I'm so fucking happy she's back. It's been a long ten days without her.

I missed my wildcat at the office and my vulnerable kitten at night.

Her tongue darts out to wet her lips again, then she says, "The domestic abuse isn't what destroyed me. It's what happened after I broke up with him."

I know the fucker carved his name into her, so I'm bracing for the worst.

She's quiet for a long while before she says, "I used to wake up in the mornings feeling like I had a hangover, even though I didn't drink any alcohol. It happened for a couple of weeks."

A frown forms on my forehead as I listen to her.

"I felt weird…as if I couldn't connect with my body."

Her eyebrows draw together, and her voice trembles as she says, "Turns out he was drugging me."

Jesus Christ.

"I only found out because, for some reason, I came to after he drugged me." She pauses, and I watch as she struggles to get the words out. "I couldn't move or open my eyes. I couldn't speak."

Indescribable anger rushes through me until my heart races in my chest.

Fuck, I can't even imagine how she must've felt being a prisoner in her own body.

"I was so scared," she whispers, her voice hoarse. Her eyes dart to mine, and I see the horror and trauma she's been forced to live with, trembling in her green irises.

It's a blow to my heart, but what she tells me next grinds my soul to dust.

Samantha

As Todd climbs onto the bed, I'm unable to move a muscle or make a sound.

It feels like I'm a prisoner in my own body, and it makes me feel claustrophobic as panic and fear bleed through me.

There's a sticky substance between my legs, and it has my stomach churning because I know what it means.

Todd had sex with me while I was unconscious.

He raped me.

My heartbeat speeds up as my mind races, putting all the puzzle pieces together.

For how long has he been drugging me? Since that first morning I woke up feeling like a bus ran me over?

I thought I was losing my mind.

I feel him crawl over my body again, and it makes every fiber of my being fill with disgust.

How many times has he raped me?

His hands roam over my breasts and down my side, then suddenly, I feel a sharp pain as something cuts into my skin.

Oh God. Stop!

"If you weren't so stubborn, I wouldn't be forced to brand you," he whispers. "Don't worry. I'm going to carve your name over my ribs, as well."

No!

The pain increases with every cut, and my heartbeat speeds up until it's nothing but a terrifying flutter in my chest.

When he's done and my side is on fire, I feel his tongue swipe over my skin to lick up my blood.

"Mmm...you taste so good."

Jesus. He's deranged.

While my mind reels from the nightmare I'm in, intense fear coats my skin because I don't know what he's going to do next.

Todd settles over my body, and I feel his erection between my legs, which makes my stomach roll violently while my soul cringes back from the disgust and degradation I'm forced to endure.

When he shoves himself inside me, it feels as if my soul is trying to detach itself from my body.

He lets out a groan. 'Do you feel how good we fit together, Sam?'

I'm overcome with anger, hatred, and a broken feeling that keeps growing until it's a gaping hole that sucks my mind into a world of darkness.

My body feels every thrust.

My lungs breathe.

My heart beats.

My mind is consumed by the depravity that's being inflicted on me.

He thrusts into me again, and my mind screams for him to stop. Another tear escapes from the corner of my eye and disappears into my hair.

'I'll never let you leave me. If you try, I'll kill us both.'

Todd's movements become choppy, and he starts to grunt like a pig before he comes inside me. His full weight bears down on me, and his breaths hit my ear.

"You're such a good girl. Don't move," he taunts me.

The bed dips and I hear him walk to the restroom. When he comes back, he touches the cuts on my side, making them burn like fire.

"My turn."

I hear him hiss and assume he's carving my name on his skin.

"See how much I love you, Sam? I've branded myself for you."

Leave! Please. Just leave me alone.

I feel the bed move again, and as he climbs on top of me, my mind screams. He begins to kiss me, his tongue and spit coating my lips, and I feel insanity take me as he rapes me again.

Chapter 25

Franco

My body trembles with rage, and I'm clenching my jaw so fucking hard I'm a second away from cracking a tooth.

The fucker.

What he did to her is unspeakable, yet she finally managed to talk about it.

The fucking fucker. Paulie better find Todd Grant so I can rip his ballsack off and shove it down his throat.

"He finally left. I don't know how long I laid there before the drug he gave me wore off. I got up and cleaned myself, then packed what I could into my car and left Houston."

Her voice is void of emotion, and it cuts fucking deep into my soul.

"I know I should've gone to the police, but I was so traumatized, all I could think to do was run."

It feels as if my soul is hemorrhaging from hearing the hell she had to endure.

"I don't know how he drugged me. I don't know what he did to me while I was unconscious. All I know is I lost a part of myself, and I don't think I'll ever get it back."

I want to pull her into my arms, but I'm scared it will stop her from talking. She's finally opening up, and I don't want to do anything that will jeopardize it.

She lets out a sigh that sounds like it came straight from her soul. "Wow. It feels cathartic to finally say it out loud. It's true what they say…" Her eyes lift to mine. "the burden becomes lighter if you share it with someone."

My voice is hoarse as I murmur, "I'd take it all if I could, so you didn't have to carry any of it."

She inches closer to me, and I finally get to wrap my arms around her. Holding her tightly, I press a kiss to her hair and hate the fucking balaclava for being in the way.

"I'm so fucking sorry that happened to you," I whisper, so my voice doesn't sound harsh because she might recognize me then.

I fold my body around hers in an attempt to get as close as possible to her.

"You're so fucking strong, Samantha. You amaze me."

"I don't want what he did to me to define the rest of my life," she admits.

"It won't. You've already made so much progress."

236

She tilts her head back so she can meet my eyes. "Any progress I've made is thanks to you."

"No, baby. You did it all on your own."

We stare at each other while a violent storm rages inside me. I can't fathom how this woman survived such a nightmare, yet here she is.

Now I understand why she fears men. Her trust has been obliterated.

Needing to know, I ask, "Do you trust me?"

She doesn't hesitate and nods.

"Close your eyes, baby."

She shuts them, and I wait a few seconds, then say, "Don't open them until I tell you to. Okay?"

"Okay."

As I pull the balaclava up, my heart beats faster.

If she opens her eyes now, I'm fucked.

Closing the distance between us, I press my mouth softly against hers.

She gasps against my lips, then her hand darts up to my face, and I feel her palm against my jaw.

At first I kiss her gently, but then Samantha's tongue brushes over the seam of my mouth. Our tongues touch, and as I enter her mouth, a soft moan escapes her.

The urgency in me grows, and needing more, I deepen the kiss.

I feel the connection I have with her in the deepest parts of my soul.

I love this woman.

Pushing her onto her back, my teeth tug at her bottom lip before I devour her as if she's the last meal I'll ever have.

I taste every inch of her mouth and knead her lips until they feel hot against mine.

I pour everything I feel for her into the kiss because I don't know whether I'll get another chance again.

Samantha

The way my mystery man kisses me makes me feel loved and treasured.

He sweeps me away from the memories of Todd and takes me to a world where I'm whole.

I've been violated and destroyed, but I'm intact, and it's because of this man.

It feels like every choice I made, everything that happened to me, led me to this moment.

It led me to him.

Slowly, he ends the kiss and presses my face against his neck. I feel as he adjusts his mask into place before he holds me tightly.

His voice is filled with emotion as he says, "You're such an amazing woman, Samantha. I've fallen in love with you, which is a feat in itself because I've never felt this way about anyone."

Placing my hand against his ribs, I ask, "Then why won't you show me your face?"

He's quiet for a while before he explains, "I'm scared you'll reject me."

"I won't."

He pulls back, and our eyes meet. "What if I'm not who you expect?"

"I'm not expecting anything. I don't care if you have two noses and purple hair. I want to see what the man I'm falling for looks like. I want to know your name. I want to get to know everything about you."

I can see he's thinking about it, then he says, "Can I have a couple more days?"

Seeing the worry in his eyes, I nod. "Okay."

As my apartment grows dark, we lie on my bed and stare at each other.

"Are you really falling in love with me?" he asks softly.

I scrunch my nose. "Insane, right? Only I would fall for a man whose face I've never seen." I lift my hand and trail my fingers over the ski mask. "Every part of me is drawn to you. The connection I feel to you is unbelievably strong."

His hand covers mine, and he presses my palm to his chest. "Feel that?"

"Your heartbeat?"

He nods, his eyes staring so deep into mine I'm sure he's looking at the darkest parts of me. "Every beat is for you. I need you to remember that when I take off the balaclava."

"Stop worrying." I give him a reassuring smile. "I don't care what you look like, or what your name is. I just want to put a face to the man I'm falling for and call you something else besides my mystery man."

His fingers wrap around mine as he whispers, "No matter what happens, I want you to know I love you." He wraps his arms around me and hugs me to his chest. "I have to go."

"Okay."

When he pulls away from me, we climb off the bed and I follow him to the living room.

My mystery man stops a couple of feet from the window, and wrapping his hand around the back of my neck, he tugs me closer.

"On Wednesday night, I'll come get you. I'm going to blindfold you and take you to my place, where I'll take off the balaclava. Are you okay with that?"

I'll be able to learn more about him if I see where he lives.

"I don't understand why I'll be blindfolded, but okay."

"I don't want anything to give away my identity until we're in my house," he explains.

"What would give away your identity?" My eyes widen. "Are you famous?"

"Something like that," he chuckles. He closes the distance and presses a quick kiss to my lips. "See you Wednesday night."

"I look forward to it."

I watch as he climbs through the window and disappears down the fire escape.

Excitement bubbles in my chest, but then I think about work tomorrow, and the smile drops from my face.

Chapter 26

Samantha

It feels like my stomach is spinning from the anxiety coursing through me.

When I step out of the elevator, my hands begin to tremble, and I keep swallowing hard on the lump of fear stuck in my throat.

I've worked for this man for over a year. I've been his PA for six weeks.

I'm just going to pretend he's not a mob boss and do my work.

Reaching my desk, I stare at the mess. There are sticky notes everywhere, a dirty coffee mug, and candy wrappers.

I read the note stuck against my computer's screen.

Sorry. There was just too much work. Gloria.

Pulling it off, I let out a sigh as I toss it in the trashcan. I place my handbag in the bottom drawer and switch on my computer before I put on the wireless earpiece and take the phone off voicemail.

Taking a seat at my desk, I check all the sticky notes and organize the work into piles.

By the looks of things, Gloria did nothing but eat candy at my desk.

When the phone rings, I quickly answer, "Mr. Vitale's office, Samantha speaking."

"The eagle has landed," Charlotte, from reception whispers. "I repeat. The eagle has landed."

The corner of my mouth lifts. "Thanks. I owe you."

"Anytime."

Ending the call, I get up and head to the kitchen. When I prepare Mr. Vitale's coffee, my hands won't stop trembling.

With every passing second, my heart beats faster, and my anxiety spikes.

Vitale Health is a legitimate company. I'm just the PA to the CEO. There's no such thing as the mafia.

Damn, no matter how I try to convince myself, it's not working.

I work for one of the heads of the Cosa Nostra. There's no way to sugarcoat it.

When I reach for the box of cookies, I notice it's almost finished and make a mental note to get more during lunch.

I arrange the coffee and two cookies on the tray and carry it to Mr. Vitale's office. As always, I set it down on his desk, but when I turn around, it's to see him stalking toward the office.

Crap. It's too late to run to my desk.

He's wearing a black suit and looks like he's on a mission to kill someone. His eyes lock on me, and I feel the intensity in them burn right through me.

God help me.

"Morning, Miss Blakely," he says, his tone clipped. "I trust you had a good vacation?"

"Morning, Mr. Vitale," I reply, my voice sounding like I sucked on a helium balloon.

He walks to his desk and takes off his jacket. When he drapes it over the back of the chair, my eyes lock on the gun tucked into the waistband of his pants.

Jesus.

Did he always carry a gun?

"Do you need something?" he asks as he takes a seat at his desk.

"Ahhh…" I swallow hard. "Will you reconsider accepting my resignation?"

"No." His eyes narrow, and it makes fear slither down my spine. "Let's make a couple of things clear. One, you will not resign. Two, you will not mention who I am to anyone. Three, stop looking at me like you're about to shit yourself. I said I won't hurt you, and I'm a man of my word."

I nod like a crazy person.

Too brave for my own good, I ask, "You say you won't hurt me, so what will happen if I just leave?"

The look in his dark brown eyes tells me not to even try.

"I'll find you and drag you back, kicking and screaming, if I have to. I'd hate to do that, so don't force my hand."

Right. Kicking and screaming.

He nods in the direction of the door. "Get to work, Miss Blakely. You have a lot to catch up on."

I spin around and hightail it to my desk. When I plop down on my chair, the air wooshes from my lungs.

My phone rings and seeing Mr. Vitale's extension, I let out a groan before I answer, "Yes, Sir."

"Shut the door behind you."

"Yes, sir."

"Also, I'm only here for an hour, so if you need anything signed urgently, get it ready."

"Yes, sir."

The call ends, and I get up to shut the door before returning to my desk.

I throw myself into my work, hoping it will distract me from the mob boss in the office next door.

My fingers fly over the keyboard, and I try to get as much ready as possible for Mr. Vitale to sign, because the sooner he leaves, the better.

An hour later, when he comes out of his office, I place a pen on top of the pile of documents and say, "Please sign everywhere I've marked with an X."

He picks up the pen, and leaning over my desk, he scribbles his signature on the first document.

I quickly remove it from the pile, and as he keeps signing beside every X, I keep taking the papers so he doesn't lose momentum.

Within minutes, he's done, but instead of setting the pen down on the desk, he holds it out to me.

I hesitate at first but push through and take it from him.

"Don't schedule any appointments for this week," he orders. "I'll only be in the office for an hour tomorrow morning, so have everything ready when I come in."

"Yes, sir." I swallow hard on the constant lump in my throat. "Have a nice day, sir."

His eyes lock with mine. "You too, Miss Blakely."

When he walks away, I deflate in my chair and wipe the sweat from my forehead.

Thank God he won't be here the whole day.

I take a moment to gather my bearings before I straighten in my chair and get back to work.

While I deal with one job after the other, my thoughts turn to yesterday, and slowly, a smile spreads over my face.

Just two days, and I'll finally see my mystery man's face.

After he left, it sunk in that I finally shared my trauma with someone and he didn't run for the hills.

Instead, he kissed me and told me he loved me.

And boy, what a kiss.

It was toe-curling and mind-blowingly good, and I felt it in my soul.

Just two days.

I can't wait.

I swear, the man can look like Quasimodo from *The Hunchback of Notre Dame,* and it won't change how I feel about him.

Chapter 27

Samantha

I'm so exhausted someone could knock me over with a feather.

After one hell of a busy day, I'm taking a quick shower, and once I'm done, I quickly dry myself and lather my skin with lotion.

I've chosen to wear another new dress for my mystery man, hoping he'll like it as much as the one I wore on Sunday.

While I get dressed, my thoughts turn to work. The only good thing is Mr. Vitale hasn't been in the office much.

The sad part is, I think I'm starting to accept he's a mafia boss, and I'm not sure how I feel about it.

I mean, on one side, the job pays really well and I'm just a PA doing regular PA work. On the other side, he's one of the heads of the Cosa Nostra.

Ugh, why do I bother fretting about it? It's not like I can do anything to change my situation.

After I put on a pair of ballet flats, I quickly brush my hair and swipe some mascara on my lashes.

When I walk into the living room, I see a black scarf lying on the coffee table.

The blindfold.

I glance around the apartment but don't see my mystery man.

Walking closer, I pick up the scarf and wrap it around my head.

Jesus, I can't see a thing. Not even a shadow.

Not even a minute passes when I hear movement. I feel someone behind me, then he murmurs, "You look breathtaking, baby."

A smile spreads over my face. "I wore the dress for you."

"I'm honored."

His hands frame my jaw, and when he presses a kiss to my lips, I realize he's not wearing the ski mask.

My excitement grows tenfold, and I start to feel downright giddy.

My mystery man (not for much longer) wraps an arm around my lower back and leads me out of my apartment.

I keep wanting to put my arms up in front of me so I can stop myself from bumping into a wall or something.

He lets out a chuckle. "Trust me."

"If you let me walk into something, I'm going to whack you with a spatula," I say, my tone playful.

He chuckles again, and by the time he helps me into the car, I can't contain my excitement.

With my eyes blindfolded, I'm overly conscious of every move he makes. I smell his spicy aftershave, which has hints of wood and coffee.

During the drive to his house, he puts on some music and doesn't try to make conversation.

I'm too excited to try and think of something to talk about, so I keep quiet, hoping the next turn we take will bring us to our destination.

But it doesn't, and he keeps driving.

When I grow impatient, I mutter, "Geez, do you live on the other side of the city?"

"No," he chuckles just as the car starts to slow down. "We're here."

"Finally," I whisper, suppressing the urge to clap my hands like a toddler on Christmas morning.

He brings the vehicle to a stop and says, "Wait for me to open the door."

"Okay."

I hear him move, and a few seconds later, the passenger door opens. He takes hold of my hand and helps me to climb out, before wrapping his arm around my lower back so he can lead me into the house.

"Careful, there are steps," he murmurs.

I must look like an idiot as I try to gauge how high the steps are, but luckily, I don't fall.

When the air changes and our steps sound different on the floor, I assume we're inside his house.

"There are stairs, so I'm just going to carry you," he mutters right before I'm airborne.

My mystery man holds me bridal style, and as laughter bursts from me, I wrap my arms around his neck.

"Careful. A girl can get used to being carried around," I tease him.

"I don't mind," he chuckles.

It feels like we go up three flights of stairs before I'm placed down on my feet again.

Having been patient for so long, I ask, "Can I remove the blindfold?"

"Not yet." His hands frame my face. "I just want to do one more thing."

"What?"

I feel his breath on my lips, then his mouth covers mine. He doesn't deepen the kiss but instead keeps still as if he's savoring the moment.

It almost feels like a goodbye, which confuses me.

He pulls away, and taking hold of my shoulders, he turns me around so I'm standing with my back to him. As I feel him untying the knot, I find myself holding my breath.

This is it.

The fabric falls away from my eyes, then he says, "I love you, Samantha. Don't ever forget that."

My heartbeat speeds up, and I open my eyes.

The first thing I see is a black lounge chair and a coffee table.

Why does it look familiar?

I glance to my left and see a king-size bed that's positioned by floor-to-ceiling windows that overlook the city.

I feel my face go numb before I realize why the room looks familiar.

No.

"Turn around," he says.

I'm filled with a world of confusion because the man behind me still sounds caring and kind.

No.

When I remain frozen, and my body starts to tremble, I hear him move, and I quickly pinch my eyes shut.

"Samantha."

"No."

"Open your eyes."

"No."

Memories of my time with my mystery man flash through my mind.

Holding his hand.

Hugging him.

Crying in his arms.

Kissing him.

Telling him my darkest secret.

I feel his hand touch mine, and yanking away, my eyes fly open.

My vision focuses on Mr. Vitale. He's wearing his Paradiso uniform and not the usual impeccable suit.

My gaze darts to his face, and in stunned disbelief, I stare at every handsome inch of him.

I shake my head wildly. "I…I…"

Suddenly, anger rips through my chest, and before I can stop myself, my hand flies through the air, but he moves faster than me and grabs hold of my wrist, stopping me from slapping him.

"How dare you," I hiss as my face crumbles under the chaotic emotions warring in my chest.

He steps closer, and his tone is soft when he says, "I love you."

"No!" I scream as I try to pull my wrist free from his hold. "You played me for a fool. Why? What did I do to you to deserve this?"

A sob bursts from my chest, only making me more angry because I don't want to cry in front of him.

I begin to struggle against him, and he lets go of my wrist, but before I can move away from him, his arms lock around me.

He imprisons me against his chest, and feeling his strength, I know it's no use fighting. But I can't stop myself from trying.

"Let go!" I demand.

"I know it's a shock, but I'm still the same man you fell in love with."

God.

I shake my head wildly and push with my hands against his chest. "No, you're not. The man I fell in love with is kind, and patient, and caring, and gentle," I ramble. "You're the complete opposite."

When he tightens his hold on me, I cry, "Let me go. Please."

He keeps an arm wrapped around me, and placing his hand behind my head, he presses my face against his chest.

I smell his aftershave, and it makes a fresh wave of tears burst from me.

"You're safe with me, baby."

He sounds like my mystery man, but he looks like Mr. Vitale, who's made my life a living hell at the office.

The fight leaves me when I realize the man I fell in love with doesn't exist. It was all some kind of sick game.

I told him everything. He comforted me.

He told me he loved me.

"It was all a lie," I cry as my heart breaks. "How could you do that to me?"

"None of it was a lie," he argues, his tone urgent. "I meant every word I said to you."

As I cry my eyes out, the pieces fall into place.

That's why I don't have a panic attack when Mr. Vitale touches me. It's because somehow my body recognized him while my mind refused to see the signs.

"God, how could I be so stupid?"

It's because I needed someone so badly.

"You're not stupid," he says before pressing a kiss to the top of my head.

If I keep my eyes closed, I can pretend Mr. Vitale isn't here.

Unable to deceive my heart with false hope, I open my eyes and face the cold, hard truth.

"Let me go," I say for what feels like the hundredth time.

"I will if you promise to give me a chance to explain."

"I promise," I mutter.

The moment he pulls his arms away from me, I shove at his rock-hard chest and put a safe distance between us.

My eyes burn on Mr. Vitale with rage, and I want to slap myself upside the head for being so blind.

He gestures to the lounge chair. "Have a seat."

My tone is tight as I say, "I prefer to stand."

My gaze lowers to his mouth, and the realization hits again. It feels like a ten-pound hammer knocks me right off my feet.

Oh. My. God. I kissed Mr. Vitale.

I told him I was falling in love with him.

I shared everything with him.

Chapter 28

Samantha

As the shock keeps rippling through me, I cover my mouth with my hand.

My eyes are glued to Mr. Vitale's face, and it takes a moment before I can process his expression. His features are torn with worry.

It's weird seeing him like this. Even when we were attacked, he kept his cool.

He's always come across as broody, rude, and overly arrogant.

This isn't my mystery man who's only shown me patience and affection.

I shake my head again, unable to believe I've been so stupid.

In my defense, why would a billion-dollar CEO also run a taboo sex club? During the day, he's always abrupt while barking orders at me, and at night, he's gentle.

It didn't even cross my mind the two men might be one and the same person, because they were worlds apart.

Sure, at times, it felt like there was something familiar about him, but it never stuck.

"This was not a game to me," Mr. Vitale says with a pleading look. "When I had to step in because your partner fucked up, I took over because you're my assistant. I couldn't let some idiot upset you. I wanted to help you, Samantha."

I cross my arms over my chest and lower my eyes to the floor.

His voice sounds a little hoarse as he continues, "That first night we spent together made me see how strong you are. I was amazed and wanted more time with you."

At my expense.

"You started making progress, and I didn't want to ruin that." He pauses for a moment, and I hear him take a deep breath. "I fell so fucking hard and fast for you. I couldn't risk losing you, so I continued being an asshole at work so you wouldn't catch on."

Silence falls between us, and I know he's waiting for me to say something, but I can't bring myself to speak.

"Close your eyes," he whispers.

I shake my head hard.

258

"Please," he begs, sounding like my mystery man.

My eyebrows draw together, and I struggle not to cry as I shut my eyes.

I hear him move closer, and my body tenses.

He's a couple of inches away from me when he whispers, "You're safe with me."

My throat constricts, and I shake my head.

When his fingers brush over the curve of my jaw, I flinch.

"I'm so fucking sorry." His tone is gentle and caring, and it screws with my mind.

I'm torn between my love for my mystery man and my hatred for my boss.

The two emotions war in my chest, shredding my heart to pieces.

His palm cups my cheek, and I gasp at the storm it causes inside me.

"I love you."

I hear the truth in his words, but I can't equate them with something Mr. Vitale would say.

My heart keeps breaking, and unable to stop a sob from escaping, it bursts over my lips as I cry, "Why couldn't you be Quasimodo? Why did you have to be the man who's given me so much hell at work? Why do you have to be a

259

mafia boss?" My breaths quiver over my lips, and my chest shudders. "I want my mystery man back."

His arms wrap around me, and he gently pulls me into a hug. "I'm still your mystery man."

I shake my head against his chest.

His touch is soft as he takes hold of my chin. He nudges my face up, and when I feel his breath fan over my lips, he says, "I'm still here, baby."

His mouth brushes against mine, and a sob sputters from me.

With my eyes closed, he's the man I've fallen in love with.

"I don't want to lose you," I whimper against his lips.

"You won't." The words sound like a promise.

He kisses me tenderly, and I feel the strong connection between us.

Lifting his head an inch, he whispers, "Look at me, baby."

"No," I sob. "You'll disappear."

"I'm right here. You can feel me."

Another sob ripples over my lips as I slowly open my eyes.

The moment my gaze focuses on Mr. Vitale, everything feels wrong.

The corner of his mouth lifts slightly, then he says, "I'm the mystery man you fell for."

My eyes search his dark brown irises, and I don't see the annoyance I've gotten used to in the office. Instead, his gaze is filled with affection.

I lower my eyes to his shirt as I try to process my boss and my mystery man being the same person.

My boss – my arrogant, rude, head-of-a-crime-family, dangerous asshole boss – is my mystery man.

Pulling away from him, I cross my arms over my chest again, then admit, "I don't know how to process this, Mr. Vitale."

"Franco," he murmurs. "My name is Franco, Samantha."

This is insane.

I fear him, yet I can't stop this insane attraction I have for him. I can't just magically flip a switch and erase my feelings for him.

The hate and love keep warring in my chest, and right now, I have no idea which emotion will prevail.

Lifting a hand, I wipe my palm over my forehead before saying, "I need time to wrap my mind around everything."

"I understand."

My anger surfaces again, and my eyes snap to his stupidly handsome face as I exclaim, "Do you? Really?"

"I know this is a shock for you, but we can work through it."

I let out an incredulous burst of laughter while shaking my head. "Yeah, I'm not so sure about that."

His features tighten, and I watch him change from my mystery man to my boss. His tone is determined as he says, "I won't lose you."

Throwing my arms open, I yell, "You never had me!"

He moves fast, and before I can even think about backing away, his fingers wrap around my throat. With his face an inch away from mine, he says, "You're mine, Samantha. I will do everything in my power to keep you from leaving me."

He doesn't hurt me, and seeing the flare of panic in his eyes, I realize he means every word.

His palm moves up to my jaw, and his expression softens as he whispers, "I've never felt this way about anyone. Give me a chance to prove I'm the man you fell in love with." He tilts his head and gives me a pleading look. "Please."

"I have to think about everything," I say. My tongue darts out to wet my lips before I continue, "I can't just magically change how I feel."

He stares at me for a moment, and I see this is difficult for him as well.

"Do you have any questions you want to ask me?"

I shake my head. "I'm not ready to talk."

"You can call me anytime," he says. "Or just message me."

An incredulous chuckle ripples over my lips. "Yeah? On which phone?"

"It doesn't matter."

Right.

"I'm going home."

I turn around, and walking out of the bedroom, I head to the staircase.

I hear him behind me, then he says, "I'll take you home."

"No." I rush down the stairs, just wanting to get out of this mansion.

"Samantha." His tone is harsher. "This is not up for discussion. I'm taking you home."

The moment I dart into the foyer, Mr. Vitale grabs me by my forearm, and I'm dragged through the living room and out onto the veranda.

"You're insufferable!" I snap at him.

"And you're stubborn." He opens the passenger door. "We make a great pair."

"Like hell, we do," I mumble before climbing into the G-Wagon.

I pull the safety belt over my chest and clip it in place before I cross my arms over my chest.

When Mr. Vitale slides in behind the steering wheel, I turn my face away from him and stare at the mansion.

The drive to my apartment is filled with tension, and when he parks the G-Wagon in front of my building, he says, "I'll see you at work tomorrow."

I shove the door open. "Only because I don't have a choice in the matter."

Getting out, I slam the door shut, and without a backward glance, I walk into the building.

When I lock my front door behind me, my body begins to tremble. I rush to my bedroom and strip out of the stupid dress I wore for him.

Immense anger and heartache rip through me, and sitting on the floor with my back against the bed, I pull my knees up and wrap my arms around them. I bury my face in the crook of my arm and cry my eyes out.

Just as I thought I found a good man, he turns out to be my boss. And a freaking mob boss.

Why does it keep happening to me?

Chapter 29

Franco

I didn't close an eye last night.

I kept replaying everything in my mind, wondering if there was a better way to handle the situation.

As the elevator doors slide open, my heart pounds in my chest.

I don't know what I'll do if Samantha's not here.

I walk down the hallway, and as her desk comes into view, I let out a sigh of relief.

Thank fuck.

"Morning, Samantha," I say, my tone soft.

She doesn't stop typing and keeps her eyes locked on the screen. "Morning, Mr. Vitale."

Her features are tight, and from the dark circles beneath her eyes, it's clear she didn't get any rest last night either.

"Can you come to my office?"

She doesn't stop working. "Is that a question or order, sir?"

"It's a question."

"Then the answer is no."

I have to suppress the urge to drag her to my office and instead ask, "How are you holding up?"

"I'm fine, Mr. Vitale."

The printer starts working, and Samantha gets up from her chair. Instead of giving me a wide berth, she pushes me out of the way and begins sorting the papers into piles.

I can feel the anger come off her in waves and brace myself for one hell of a day as I walk to my office.

Shrugging my jacket off, I drape it over the back of my chair. I take a seat at my desk, and reaching for the cup of coffee Samantha placed on my desk, I take a sip.

When I turn my computer on and open my emails, I notice from the timestamp on the first email that Samantha's been at work since six thirty.

I let out a sigh as I pull both the cellphones out of my pocket, setting them on the desk.

There's a knock at the door, and before I can answer, Samantha comes in.

She places a stack of documents on my desk. "I need you to sign everything before you leave the office."

"I'm here for the whole day," I inform her, keeping my tone gentle.

Her eyes lock on the two phones for a moment, then she swings around and walks out of the office.

A moment later, she returns with her cellphone in her hand, and I watch as she types a message.

The burner phone lights up, and taking hold of the device, I unlock the screen.

Samantha: My boss is an asshole.

I knew she would be upset, but it hurts watching her struggle to comprehend that I'm her mystery man.

MMM: Yeah? Do you want me to beat him up?

Her eyes flick to me, then she types again.

Samantha: If only that were possible. Turns out you're an asshole as well. How stupid of me to think you're one of the good ones.

MMM: I never claimed to be good.

She shoots me a glare before typing out a message.

Samantha: You made me believe you were good!!! You made me believe I was safe with you. I freaking told you everything. Do you have any idea how shitty that feels? I gave you my trust, and you used it to play me for a fool. What kind of person does that?

MMM: The kind that doesn't want to lose you. The last thing I wanted was to hurt you. You can still trust me.

Samantha: GO. TO. HELL.

She spins around again and hightails it out of my office. She yanks the door shut, the sound reverberating through the room.

MMM: How am I supposed to do that when I've found an angel?

She doesn't reply and I type another message.

MMM: You can be angry at me for the rest of our lives as long as you give me a chance to show you I can make you happy.

Samantha: How do you plan on making me happy when our entire relationship is built on lies?

MMM: I only omitted I'm your boss, so you would get comfortable with me. Everything else has been the truth.

My regular phone vibrates, and a frown forms on my forehead when I see she's texting me on that number.

Samantha: I have questions. How could you be so nice to me at night, but during the day, you treated me like shit? How can you claim to love me, but you threatened me when I wanted to resign?

Franco: 1. You were making progress, and I didn't want to do anything to ruin it, so I kept faking to be an asshole at the office. 2. I've never threatened you.

Samantha: If your job as a mob boss doesn't work out, you should go into showbiz. You're one hell of an actor.

Samantha: BTW...You're a freaking mafia boss!!!!

The burner phone vibrates, and I switch devices again.

Samantha: I don't know what to do. I miss my boyfriend.

MMM: I'm right here, baby.

Samantha: No, you're not. The man I fell for never existed.

I suck in a deep breath, and feeling frustrated as fuck, I get up from my chair and stalk out of the office.

Samantha's head snaps up, and her eyes widen on me.

I grab hold of her chair and spin it so she's facing me. Grabbing hold of the armrests, I lean over her until we're face-to-face.

My voice is a low rumble. "I exist."

Her green irises darken with anger. "Yeah, sure. The asshole version of you is standing right in front of me.

I lean another inch closer. "So is the man who told you he fucking loves you."

"Telling and showing are two different things, Mr. Vitale. You told me many things while you showed me how shitty you treat the people you claim to love."

270

Jesus fucking Christ.

I frame Samantha's face, and keeping her in place, I slam my lips against hers. She gasps, and it gives me entrance to her mouth.

My tongue sweeps over hers, and my soul groans from how good she tastes.

Samantha grabs hold of my forearms, and instead of trying to shove me away, her mouth wars with mine for control.

The kiss is angry and wild. It creates a violent storm in my chest and fills me with a need to consume this woman.

I move an arm to her back, and yanking her to her feet, I squash her against my body as I continue to ravage her mouth.

Samantha brings her hands to my biceps, and she clings to me.

Our lips knead, our teeth tug, and our tongues memorize the taste of each other.

Not caring a flying fuck whether anyone can walk in on us, I lift her and sit her down on the edge of her desk. My mouth frees hers so I can pepper desperate kisses over her jaw and down her neck.

I hear her breaths explode from her before she lets out a soft moan that's filled with desire.

When I push her knees apart, her hand slaps against my chest, and she tries to shove me backward.

"Wait," she gasps.

Reluctantly, I pull away, and when our eyes meet, I realize I was going to fuck her on her desk.

I put more space between us, and we keep staring at each other as we catch our breath.

"I might be an asshole, but you can't deny the connection we have," I say, my voice hoarse from all the emotions. "I felt it in your kiss, and I see it in your eyes."

Her cheeks are pink, and her lips swollen. She looks like a fucking goddess as she glares at me, and her voice is tense with anger. "I don't care about the connection."

I step closer to her again. "You do, or you wouldn't have returned my kiss."

"We come from different worlds," she argues.

"That doesn't change a fucking thing, Samantha," I snap.

She darts off the desk, and jabbing her finger at my chest, she hisses, "It changes everything. Your world is dangerous and filled with crime. You'll get me killed."

"I won't." I grab hold of her hand and yank her against me. "I'll protect you with my last breath. I've proven I can keep you safe."

Her eyebrows draw together as some of her anger fizzles away. "You're one of the heads of the Cosa Nostra."

"Which means no one will touch a hair on your head." I place my hands on either side of her neck and lean down until there's only an inch between us. "I'll burn New York City to the ground for you. Every ounce of power I possess will belong to you. There's nowhere safer on this planet than by my side."

Her eyes begin to shine with unshed tears. "You deceived me."

My voice is soft as I promise, "I'll spend the rest of my life making it up to you."

Chapter 30

Samantha

Pulling away from Mr. Vitale, I switch off my computer.

When I grab my handbag from the bottom drawer, he asks, "Where are you going?"

"Home," I mutter.

"It's only ten-thirty."

I let out a sigh as I look at him. "I'm going home so I can think about everything you said. Unless you want me to stay at work. In which case, you'll wait longer to find out whether I'm sending you to hell or giving you a chance."

He moves out of the way. "You can go home."

"Thank you," I mumble as I walk past him.

Honestly, I need to process the freaking hot kiss he laid on me. I can't focus on work while my lips still tingle.

Leaving the building, I head to the subway, and when I reach my apartment, I can still feel Mr. Vitale's lips on mine.

Then, a realization hits me. I didn't have a panic attack when Mr. Vitale kissed me.

That's a win, right?

My phone begins to ring, and I almost ignore it but change my mind because it might be my parents.

Looking at the screen, I see Jenny's name.

"Hey," I answer.

"Where are you? I called your desk to see if you wanted to join me for lunch and almost had a heart attack when Mr. Vitale answered."

I walk to one of the couches and plop down on it. "I'm at home. Mr. Vitale gave me the rest of the day off."

"Why? Are you sick?" she asks.

"No, I just have something I'm dealing with."

"Oh? Do you want to talk about it?"

I'm quiet for a moment, then say, "I fell in love with a man, and it turned out he wasn't who I thought he was."

"What? Hold up," she gasps. "You fell in love and didn't tell me?"

"I was busy at work and then went on vacation. And you're busy with the wedding planning. We haven't had time," I say in my defense.

"Mrs. Jones is in a meeting, so I have time now. Spill it."

"Ugh. It's all too confusing to explain."

"Come on. Try. You can't leave me hanging like this," she argues.

"I met the man a month ago. He was perfect, and I fell in love, but last night, I discovered he was not who I thought he was. He wants to work through it, but I'm not sure that's a good idea." I let out a sigh. "So now I'm stuck in limbo."

"What do you mean he's not the person you thought he was? Did he suddenly grow a vagina? Ooh, is he a spy?"

"No," I mutter. "I can't explain it."

"Okay, but you said he was perfect?" Suddenly, she gasps. "Shit, did he hit you?"

"No!" I sit upright and shake my head. "He would never hurt me."

Hearing myself say the words, it sinks in.

He might've betrayed me, but he'd never physically hurt me.

"Oh, thank God. I was worried there for a second," Jenny says. "What made him perfect?"

"He was gentle and caring. I could tell him anything, and he made me feel safe," I tell her.

He made me feel safe.

Even when we were attacked, he was focused on keeping me alive.

My eyes widen, and I murmur, "Jenny, I have to go. I'll call you later."

"Okay."

I end the call and stare at the window Mr. Vitale always climbed through when he came over.

'Don't touch her.'

His words echo through me, and then I remember how he managed to calm me down when I had a panic attack at the office.

After the attack, he came to my apartment to comfort me instead of dealing with the mess. He lost a friend that day, but he put me first.

Holy shit.

Lowering my face to my hands, I suck in a deep breath of air.

When he kissed me today, he was one hundred percent himself, and I couldn't push him away. The moment his lips touched mine, I couldn't hate him.

He's right. There's no denying the connection between us.

Thoughts of Mr. Vitale consume me, and I can't help but love the man, even though I try not to.

He's a mafia boss. How do I look past the cold, hard truth that he's a killer?

God only knows what other shady things he's involved with.

Even if I forgive him for deceiving me, I can't date one of the heads of the Cosa Nostra. That's insane!

Right?

Franco

I left the office right after Samantha to meet with Renzo and Dario at Renzo's penthouse. The last thing I'm in the mood for is work, but the shit needs to get done.

"How did it go with the shipment?" Renzo asks when he hands me a tumbler of whiskey. "I didn't hear anything about an ambush, so I assume it reached Castro and Diaz."

"Yes. Changing the routes worked," I mutter.

Dario places his laptop on the coffee table, and turns it so I can see the screen.

There's a photo of a group of men, and one of them is circled in red.

"What am I looking at?" I ask.

"Ivan Varga," Dario answers. "He's the head of the Slovak mafia."

"Great, now I know who to kill." My eyes flick to Dario. "Whereabouts?"

"He was last spotted in Hell's Kitchen."

"So he's not there anymore?" Renzo asks.

"No, he keeps moving," Dario mutters before pointing at another man in the photo. "This is Miro Vargo, Ivan's brother. He's in Miami. If we grab him, it might bring Ivan out of hiding."

My eyebrow lifts. "Let's do that."

"I have a shipment of arms coming in," Renzo says. "After I've taken care of it, I'm good to go."

I glance at Dario as he mutters, "I'm pretty much open."

"I'll check with Angelo and Damiano," I say.

Renzo drops down on one of the couches, then mutters, "Damiano's in Sicily."

A frown forms on my forehead. "When did he leave?"

Renzo lets out a chuckle. "Brother, you were at the poker game last week. How do you not remember Damiano left right after?"

"Fuck," I mutter. "I'm a little preoccupied."

"I bet you are. Between your PA and the fucking Slovak mafia, your plate is full.

Dario's eyebrows lift. "PA? Has she finally left your ass?" There's a flash of shock on his face. "If you fired her, give me her number so I can offer her a job."

I level my friend with a dark glare. "No, she hasn't left me. Stay away from her. She's mine."

Dario sees the grin widening on Renzo's face, then asks, "Your PA or your woman?"

"Both."

A burst of laughter escapes Dario, and he slaps his thigh. "Finally! I was really starting to think you bat for the home team."

"The fuck?" I mutter.

He wags his eyebrows at me. "I've seen you checking out my ass."

"The fuck?" I repeat as I imagine strangling his neck.

"Hey, no judgment," Dario chuckles.

I shake my head at him. "Do you have a sudden death wish?"

"I like flirting with danger," he taunts me.

I shake my head again, and rising to my feet, I down the last of my whiskey before saying, "I'm leaving before the La Rosa family has to find a new head."

As I walk to the private elevator, I hold up my middle finger to Dario, who gives me a bark of laughter.

When the doors begin to shut, I hear Renzo say, "One of these days, he's going to shoot you."

"Not if he shoots you first," Dario chuckles.

I let out a sigh as the elevator takes me to the underground parking, and stepping out, I see Milo having a cigarette while Marcello keeps glancing around the area.

We're all fucking tense since the attack.

As I reach them, I say, "Dario found out Ivan Vargo is in New York. He was last seen in Hell's Kitchen. Get the men to search the area from top to bottom."

"On it," Marcello replies.

We all pile into the G-Wagon, and as we leaving the underground parking, I pull both my phones from my pocket.

There are no messages from Samantha, which has my worry growing. I know she has to process everything, but what if she can't forgive me?

What if she tells me to go to hell?

My jaw clenches, and I shake my head because it's not an option.

I don't care what I have to do to keep her. There's no way I'm letting her go.

Chapter 31

Samantha

Walking into my apartment, I glance at the window and let out a sigh when I see another bouquet of flowers.

My freaking place looks like a flower store!

Yanking my phone out of my handbag, I press dial on Mr. Vitale's number.

Not even a second passes when he answers, "What's wrong?"

"I can't move around in my apartment," I complain. "Stop with the flowers, Mr. Vitale."

I glance around at all the colorful arrangements and shake my head.

It looks like a unicorn puked everywhere.

"I'll stop on one condition," he murmurs.

"I'm not ready to talk about us," I warn him.

It's been over two weeks, and I still can't bring myself to make a decision. One moment, I'm willing to give things a try between us, and the next, I shut it down because Mr. Vitale is, and always will be, a mafia boss.

"I want you to call me Franco," he murmurs.

"Oh." I narrow my eyes. "Is that it? Will you stop leaving flowers at my window?"

"Yes."

"Fine," I sigh as I drop my handbag on the couch and walk to the window to retrieve the latest peace offering.

"So you didn't throw any of the flowers I left for you in the trash?" he asks.

"Of course not. They didn't do anything wrong."

He chuckles, and the sound has my heart beating faster.

I've barely seen him because he's staying away from the companies until he's dealt with whoever attacked us.

That's another reason why I'm hesitant to give things a chance between us.

"How did things go at the office today?" he asks.

"Good." I tuck the device between my ear and shoulder and lift the arrangement into my apartment. Shutting the window, I say, "I'm not talking with you about work. That's what office hours are for."

"Fair enough." His tone is laced with amusement. "What would you like to talk about?"

"Nothing. I just called to tell you to stop with the flowers. I'm hanging up."

Before I can end the call, he admits, "I miss you."

I press my lips together so I don't say the words back to him and make a non-committal sound.

"Can I come up?"

A frown appears on my forehead. "You're here?"

"Yes. I dropped the flowers off a couple of minutes ago."

I shake my head. "I don't think that's a good idea."

"Please."

I glance at the window, and seeing Franco standing there, I startle.

"You're sneaky," I whisper into the phone.

"All is fair in love and war."

I move closer to the window and lock eyes with him through the glass.

We stare at each other for close to a minute while I try to sort through my feelings about him being here.

Giving in, I end the call and unlock the window.

Franco pushes it open, and I watch as he climbs inside. When he straightens to his full height, he tucks his phone into his pocket.

This is the first time he's come through the window wearing a suit and not his uniform from *Paradiso,* and it makes everything more real.

It merges my mystery man with my boss, and my confused mind gets a little more clarity.

My heart, on the other hand, starts to beat faster and faster until it's a mere fluttering in my chest.

When I started working at Vitale Health, I had a crush on Mr. Vitale.

Just like every other woman in the building.

Of course, it died a quick death when I became his PA, but now it's back. Add to that my love for my mystery man, and I feel a little overwhelmed.

I move to one of the couches and sit down. Staring at the coffee table, I try to shove my feelings down because I need to be sensible about the situation.

Franco takes a seat next to me, and he places his hand palm up on his thigh.

My eyebrows draw together as I lay my hand in his.

His fingers weave with mine, then he says, "Christ, I missed you."

I missed you too.

Lifting my hand to his mouth, he presses a kiss to my skin.

My heart wars with my mind, and I feel a little lost.

"Want to talk about it?" he asks.

Closing my eyes, I lean against his shoulder. I smell his aftershave and feel how solid he is beside me.

"Even if I can look past you deceiving me, it won't matter, because you're one of the heads of the Cosa Nostra." I suck in a deep breath and let it out slowly before I continue, "At the end of the day, you're a criminal."

He takes a deep breath and tightens his hold on my hand before he mentions, "Honestly, the Cosa Nostra does a hell of a lot for the city. We provide jobs to thousands. We keep the gangs in check. We keep drugs off the streets. It's one of the reasons the police look the other way. We do half their job for them."

I didn't know that.

"We don't shit where we eat, Samantha."

I stare at his hand as I ask the most crucial question, "How many people have you killed?"

He's quiet for a moment before he answers, "I don't keep count." He lets out a sigh, then adds, "But I can promise you, I've never killed an innocent person."

I pull my hand free from his, and leaning forward, I rest my elbows on my knees and rub my hands over my face.

My voice is filled with confusion as I say, "I know you want an answer from me, but I can't give you one. Not right now."

"I understand, but while you think about things, can I at least see you?" He places his hand on my back, and the touch feels comforting. "Since I'm working from home, so the company doesn't become a target, I barely get to spend time with you."

True.

Maybe that's part of the problem. I'm still stuck in the past where Franco and my mystery man are two different people. I'm not getting to know him any better.

Nodding, I turn my body to face Franco and lean my shoulder against the back of the couch.

The corner of his mouth lifts, and seeing him smile makes butterflies erupt in my stomach.

"You should smile more," I mention.

"I'll make a conscious effort for you."

Sitting in my apartment and having a normal conversation with him makes him feel less like my boss.

Franco's eyes drift over my face, and I see his affection for me shining from them.

He looks at me as if I'm precious to him.

"What are you thinking about?" he asks.

My tongue darts out, and I wet my lips. "How different you are away from the office."

He lifts his hand to my face and trails his fingers along the curve of my jaw. "Remember when I said our appointments were helping me as well?" After I nod, he continues, "You made me realize how cold and empty my life is. You've added warmth and light to my life, and I don't want to lose it."

His words warm my heart, and when his hand wraps around the back of my neck, I don't stop him as he pulls me closer.

His other hand takes hold of mine, pressing my palm to his chest. I feel his heart beating, and it makes me remember what he said before he allowed me to see his face.

'Every beat is for you.'

He lowers his head, and as his mouth brushes against mine, the intense connection we have threatens to overwhelm me completely.

Before he can deepen the kiss, I pull back and whisper, "We need to take things slow until I've come to a decision."

Franco nods and stares at me as if he's trying to memorize my face. After a few seconds, he presses a kiss to my forehead, then pulls away from me and climbs to his feet.

I stand up as well, and as he walks to the window, I say, "You know you can use the front door, right?"

He lets out a chuckle. "I'll use the window for old times' sake."

I watch as he climbs onto the fire escape, and when he disappears from my sight, I take a deep breath.

That went better than I expected.

Maybe there's still hope for us.

Chapter 32

Franco

I know I've said I'll force Samantha if I have to, but it's the last thing I want to do. Especially after what that fucker did to her.

At least she hasn't told me to leave her alone.

Where I think quick on my feet, Samantha is an overthinker. I'll just have to be patient with her.

"I'm hungry," Renzo complains as we walk toward the back of Angelo's club, Fallen Angels, for a quick meeting.

"Grab something to eat while we're here," I mention while I ignore the half-naked women entertaining the customers.

Big Ricky, Angelo's personal guard, gives us a chin lift and steps aside so we can get to the office.

Renzo stops to shake Big Ricky's hand, then asks, "Can you get one of the servers to bring me a plate of hot spicy wings?"

"Sure," Big Ricky replies. "Anything else?"

"Curly fries smothered in bacon and cheese," Renzo adds.

Big Ricky glances at me, and it has me saying, "Nothing for me."

We continue down the hallway, and walking into Angelo's office, it's to see Damiano and Dario already at the table with him.

"When did you get back?" I ask Damiano.

He looks tired as he replies, "Yesterday."

"Everything okay in Sicily?"

He lets out a sigh. "Yeah."

Renzo and I take our seats at the table, then Dario says, "I've filled them in on everything."

"So you've managed to get the attention of Vargo?" Damiano asks as his eyes rest on me.

"Unfortunately. Apparently, the man is after Castro and Diaz. He figures if I'm out of the way he can take over supplying counterfeit notes to South America."

Angelo shakes his head. "Surely the fuckers know if he comes after you, he'll have to deal with all of us?"

"Maybe he's not aware of how close we are," Renzo mutters.

"We've been underestimated before," Damiano grumbles. His eyes lock with mine. "We have to show a united front. We'll send men to guard your companies so the Slovakian fucker sees he has to go through all of us to get to you."

Nodding, I let out a sigh. "Thanks. I appreciate the help." I shake my head. "I just wish Vargo would stop moving around so I can kill him."

"His brother, Miro, is still in Miami," Dario mentions. "Damiano is back, so I suggest we kidnap him."

Damiano's eyebrow lifts. "I can't leave New York right now, but we can assemble a team to kidnap Miro."

"That's a good idea. I'd hate to leave Vittoria," Angelo adds his two cents.

"I'm in," Renzo agrees.

"Then it's settled," Damiano says. "Get the team together to bring Miro to our territory. Once Ivan surfaces, we take out the fucker and call it a day."

"Does anyone else have something to discuss?" Angelo asks.

"I just became the proud owner of a ballet company," Dario says with a grin on his face. "La Rosa Opera Ballet."

"Ah...congrats," Renzo chuckles. "But why?"

Dario gives him an incredulous look. "You clearly haven't seen ballerinas. God's masterpieces."

"Ballerinas or a specific ballerina?" Angelo asks.

Darios's grin widens. "Wouldn't you like to know?"

"Fucker," Angelo mutters before turning his attention to me. "I hear you're finally taken." A mischievous smile curves his mouth. "Mystery man."

My eyes flick to Renzo, and I slap him upside the head. "You fucking told them?"

He holds up his hand in the universal sign for peace. "Of course. I wasn't going to keep that shit to myself."

Even Damiano chuckles, which is rare. "Mystery man. Now I've heard it all."

Just as Big Ricky brings Renzo's food, I climb to my feet and mutter. "Fuck the whole lot of you."

They all laugh at my expense, but I don't mind. We need a bit of light-heartedness in the storm we're facing.

"Are you going to Samantha?" Renzo asks.

I shake my head. "I have a meeting with Paulie. He's been tracking Samantha's ex."

"Is the woman in trouble?" Damiano asks.

"No. I just want to kill the fucker for what he did to her in the past."

"Let us know if you need help," Angelo mentions.

"Thanks." I give the men a chin lift, and leaving the office, I head out of the club to where Marcello and Milo are waiting for me.

Samantha

After work, I joined Jenny for a couple of drinks, and on my way home, I picked up an order of Chinese takeout for dinner.

Jenny is on cloud nine, planning the perfect wedding.

God, I can't imagine having three hundred guests. She's inviting people she's never even spoken to just because they're somehow related to her.

It's insane.

My phone beeps, and I dig it out of my bag as I walk into my apartment building. Seeing a text from Mom, I smile.

Mom: Matt and Wendy had a baby boy. I was right.

Mom: He's so beautiful!!!

I look at the photo of her holding her first grandchild and love how happy she looks.

I type out a reply and press send.

Sammie: He's so adorable. Congratulations, Grandma. Tell Matt I'll call him.

Placing my phone in my handbag, I dig my keys out. When I reach my apartment door, I unlock it, and as I push it open, I'm hit with the smell of flowers.

Thank God Franco stopped leaving the flowers at my window.

I place the takeout bag on the side table, and when I turn around to shut the door, I startle so badly a shriek escapes me.

A man is standing in my doorway, and it takes me a moment to recognize him.

Todd.

Where he used to have dark blonde hair, it's now white. There's a scar across his nose, and it looks like he's aged ten years.

I dart forward, and grabbing hold of the door, I try to close it on him, but he uses a cane to stop me.

"Did you think I wouldn't find you?" Todd sneers.

"Leave me alone!" I shriek.

My breaths explode over my lips, and my heart hammers in my chest as he forces his way into my apartment.

"Why did you run from me, Sam?" Todd asks, his tone that of a deranged man.

Letting go of the door, I spin around and make a run for the fire escape.

The cane wacks me against the side of my head, and I fall over the side of the couch and plow into a side table. The vase with roses falls with me, and as the glass shatters, my palm lands on it.

The broken glass stabs into my hand, and I let out a cry from the sharp pain.

"Now look what you've done!" he chastises me as if I'm a petulant child.

The shock of seeing Todd and having him attack me shudders through my soul, but my body is in flight or fight mode, and I dart back to my feet.

Knowing I won't be able to open the window before Todd gets to me, I rush to the kitchen so I can grab a knife.

"You know we're meant to be together," Todd shouts behind me.

As I reach for the drawer where I keep my cutlery, the cane hits my back, and I slam into the table.

The wooden legs of the chairs and table screech across the floor as they move. The pans hanging from a rack mounted to the ceiling sway, and one falls, knocking against my left shoulder.

Before I can catch my balance, I'm shoved to the floor. I manage to turn around, and as Todd climbs on me, I fight with all my strength.

I slap and claw at him.

My breaths burst in hot puffs over my dry lips.

My heart hammers against my ribs.

My eyes are frozen in horror on the man who's destroyed me once before.

He wraps his hands around my throat, and as he squeezes hard, he shouts, "Look what you've done to me! Because you ran, I had to go after you. I totaled my car because of you. I spent ten months in the hospital because of you."

He leans so close to me I can smell his breath, and his voice is shaking with rage as he says, "Look. What. You've. Done. To. Me."

He tightens his fingers around my neck as if he's trying to crush my windpipe, and I gasp for air.

Todd leans closer, and as I see the deranged look in his eyes, he whispers, "Shhh…shhh… we'll be together soon, Sam. Shhhhh…"

I've heard your life flashes in front of your eyes in your final moments, but as I'm being strangled, I see my future.

Franco kissing me.

Us making love.

Dad walking me down the aisle.

Franco putting his ring on my finger.

Holding our baby.

A strength born from my will to survive courses through my veins, and I slam my fists against Todd. Realizing it's not helping, I frantically search the floor around me for the pan.

My vision goes spotty, and my lungs scream for air.

Todd's deranged face will not be the last thing I see!

My body bucks beneath his, attempting to throw him off, then my fingers touch the handle of the pan, and gripping it tightly, I swing it through the air.

The base of the pan connects with the side of Todd's head, and he sprawls onto the floor beside me.

My throat aches as I suck in desperate breaths of air, and scrambling to my feet, I run for the front door.

It feels as if Todd's right behind me, and it has me sprinting down the stairs. When I burst through the exit of the building, I run up the sidewalk and flag down the first cab I see.

The moment the car pulls over to the curb, I yank the door open and dive into the backseat. "Go!" I shout, the terror of Todd getting to me all I can think of.

The cab pulls away, and the driver keeps glancing over his shoulder at me. "To the hospital?" he asks.

Todd can get to me at the hospital. I won't be safe there.

I shake my head wildly and give him Franco's address.

Chapter 33

Franco

"He was last seen in Seattle," Paulie informs me.

An icy sensation ripples through my body, and I turn to Marcello and order, "Get men to Samantha's apartment. I want her watched twenty-four-seven!"

"On it, boss," he says before hurrying out of the living room.

I turn my attention back to Paulie. "Anything else?"

He shakes his head. "I have men watching all the main airports."

Letting out an angry huff, I pull my phone out of my pocket and dial Samantha's number. When she doesn't answer, and the call goes to voicemail, I say, "I'm coming over."

Just as I walk to the sliding doors, the doorbell starts ringing incessantly.

"Jesus Christ," I mutter before I bark, "Will someone get the fucking door!"

"I'll check who it is." Milo walks out of the living room, and seconds later, I hear him shout, "Boss! Come quickly!"

I rush to the foyer and see Samantha falling into my house. She scrambles to her feet and moves away from Milo and the guards stationed at the door.

Her eyes are wild with terror as she glances around her, and the moment she sees me, she loses all her strength.

I grab her in time, and her body slumps against mine.

Ferocious rage instantly shudders through me as I lift Samantha into my arms, and I see the red and blue marks around her throat.

I hurry to the living room, and placing her on the couch, I ask in a deadly tone, "Was it Todd?"

She nods frantically, and when I crouch in front of her, I see the blood covering her left hand. I take hold of her wrist, and noticing a shard of glass embedded in her skin, I shout, "Milo! Bring the first aid kit and get Marcello."

"Marcello," Milo shouts by the sliding doors. "Boss needs you STAT."

My eyes lock with Samantha's terror-filled ones, and I say, "You're safe now, baby. I'm going to have Marcello fix up your hand. Okay?"

She nods, her face way too fucking pale.

Marcello bursts into the living room, and when he sees Samantha, he asks. "What do you need me to do?"

"When Milo brings the first aid kit, take a look at her left hand."

I lift my hand to the side of her neck and gently brush the pad of my thumb over the darkening bruises.

My rage spirals into chaos, and my body shudders again.

A strangled sob escapes her as her breathing speeds up. Rising to my feet, I take a seat on the couch and position Samantha on my lap.

Cradling my woman against my chest, I press my mouth to the side of her head. "I've got you, baby. You're safe."

Milo comes jogging into the living room and hands the kit to Marcello.

Holding my woman tight, I say, "Marcello is going to touch you. Okay?"

She nods before burying her face in the crook of my neck.

Marcello pulls the coffee table closer, and sitting on it, he carefully takes Samantha's hand.

When he uses tweezers to pull the shard of glass out of her skin, I press kisses to her hair, whispering, "You're going to be okay. I'll take care of you from now on. Okay?"

Her breaths rush over my neck as heartbreaking sobs rip through her.

"She needs stitches," Marcello murmurs. "I'll have to give her an injection to numb her hand."

I nod, then glance at Milo. "Contact the men Marcello sent to Samantha's apartment and tell them to find that fucker."

"On it, boss," Milo says before stepping out of the living room to make the call.

I focus on my woman again and brush my hand over her hair. When Marcello gives her the injection, she doesn't even flinch, which tells me just how fucking traumatized she is.

I pull her face away so I can see her, and the sight of the dark bruises around her slender neck makes a growl rumble from my chest. My body shudders again as the destructive rage fuming in me intensifies tenfold.

"I'm so fucking sorry, baby," I say, my voice hoarse with emotion.

When Marcello is done taking care of her hand, he wraps a bandage around it, then says, "I'll get her some antibiotics in case the wound got infected."

I nod at him. "Thanks."

Milo comes back into the living room and says, "You've got a text message, boss."

I dig my phone out of my pocket and unlock the screen. Seeing a text from Milo, I open it.

Milo: When the men arrived at her apartment, the fucker was unconscious. I told them to bring him to the guesthouse. I'll keep him in the armory until you're ready to deal with him.

He sent the text because he didn't want to talk in front of Samantha and upset her even more.

Franco: Thank you. Make him as uncomfortable as possible.

My gaze flicks to Milo, and he nods before he leaves the room again.

Holding Samantha tightly, I rise to my feet and carry her to my bedroom. I kick the door shut behind us before I walk to the bathroom.

Setting her down on the counter, I frame her face with my hands and capture her eyes with mine. "What happened, baby?"

She swallows hard and sucks in desperate breaths before she whimpers, "W-when I g-got home, he w-was t-there." Her face crumbles and her body jerks with every sob as she cries, "F-Franco."

I press her to my chest and engulf her in my arms. "I'm here, baby."

It takes a while before she manages to calm down again. I let go of her, and turning on a faucet, I wet a washcloth beneath the water and wipe the cool cloth over her face and neck.

Marcello cleaned her hand, but there's blood on her forearm. I clean every inch of her arm before dropping the washcloth in the sink.

Samantha's breathing returns to normal, then she whispers, "I whacked h-him with a p-pan and managed to g-get away."

My eyes lock on hers, and lifting my hands, I brush her hair away from her face. "You're so fucking strong, baby," I murmur with awe in my voice.

"He...he," she gasps. "He t-tried to strangle m-me."

Lowering my hand, I caress the side of her neck with my thumb. "But you stopped him." Amazed by my woman, I say, "You fought the fucker and won."

Her features tighten as she whispers, "I was so scared."

Wrapping my hand around the back of her head, I press a kiss to her forehead. "It's over. You're safe now."

She shakes her head, and her eyes darken with a fresh wave of fear. "I don't know where he is. He can come back. He can try to kill me again. He –"

I capture her eyes with mine and say, "He won't."

"You don't know that," she cries, her fear spiraling out of control.

Fuck, I wanted to wait until she felt better before I told her I have the man imprisoned in my armory.

Keeping my voice gentle, I say, "When my men got to your place, he was still unconscious in your apartment. They are watching him until I'm able to deal with him. He'll never get close to you again."

Her breathing stops, and her eyes widen. She stares at me for a moment then her eyes widen even more. "What?"

"You don't have to worry about him anymore. I'll take care of the fucker."

She nods, but it doesn't look like my words sink in.

Leaning closer to her, I say, "The fucker deserves to die for what he did to you, Samantha."

She nods again, and keeping her eyes locked with mine, she manages to regain some control over her emotions.

Instead of arguing with me about what's right and wrong, she lets out a breath of relief. "Thank you. I don't think I can deal with anything else right now."

Glancing down, she notices the spatters of blood on her pants and blouse, then she whispers, "I need to shower."

"Okay."

When I take a step away from her, she says, "But I don't want to go home."

"You're staying with me." I step into the shower and turn on the faucets.

"But I have nothing to wear."

Moving back to where she's sitting on the counter, I say, "Once you're better, I'll take you to the apartment to pack some of your clothes. In the meantime, you can wear mine."

She nods. "Thank you."

When I begin to walk to the doorway, Samantha hops off the counter and rushes to catch up to me. She follows me to my closet, where I grab one of my dress shirts.

We head back to the bathroom, and I place the shirt on the counter, then say, "I'll be right outside the door. Okay?"

She nods, but as I step away from her, she grabs hold of my arm and keeps her head lowered as if she's ashamed that she needs me.

I turn back to her and tilt my head to meet her eyes. "Do you want me to stay, baby?"

"I'm sorry," she says, and lifting her head, she admits, "I feel safer if I can see you."

"Don't apologize," I murmur while brushing my hand over the side of her head.

She flinches, and it has a frown forming on my forehead.

When she sees my reaction, she lifts her fingers to her ear and carefully touches it. "He hit me with a cane."

Only then do I see the broken skin on the shell of her ear.

My rage comes back in full force, and I clench my jaw as I fight to get the destructive emotion under control.

I'm going to fucking beat him to death.

I suck in a deep breath of air, and once I'm sure my voice won't sound harsh, I say, "Never apologize for needing me."

Her eyes dart over my face. "Okay."

Christ, I hate what happened to her, but I'm so fucking thankful she ran to me.

Chapter 34

Samantha

Right now, I don't care about the decision I have to make about Franco and me. I just can't bear to be alone.

He's the only person I feel safe with.

My nerves are frayed, and I'm so tired I can't deal with anything else.

"How do you want to do this?" Franco asks me.

My eyes drift over his features that look like they're carved from stone. I can see he's struggling to keep his anger at bay so he doesn't upset me.

God. Todd tried to kill me.

As the realization hits me again, my stomach churns, and I feel ill.

Franco tilts his head, and his eyes are filled with concern as he murmurs, "Baby?"

Right. He asked me a question.

I glance at the shower before looking at him again. "I don't know." My chin starts to tremble. "I can't think straight."

Franco wraps his arms around me and presses a kiss to my temple. "I'm going to shower with you. It's nothing sexual. Okay? I just want to clean you up so you can climb into bed and get some rest."

My mind is filled with the trauma I suffered, and I just need Franco to take control until I'm better.

I nod, and the word quivers over my lips as I say, "Okay."

"Stop me if I do anything that makes you uncomfortable."

I nod again, and when he grips the hem of my blouse and lifts the fabric, I raise my arms so he can take it off.

Slowly, I become aware of how badly my body is shivering from the horror I was subjected to. While Franco unbuttons my pants, I focus on calming the shivering.

I step out of my ballet flats, and when he crouches in front of me, I place my hand on his shoulder so I can keep my balance as he pulls my pants off.

Standing in my underwear, I look at the bandage around my left hand before my attention is drawn to Franco.

Raising to his full height, I watch as he unbuttons his dark teal-colored vest. He shrugs it off and drops it on my pile of clothes before he removes his gun from behind his back, setting it down on the counter.

When he works on undoing the buttons of his dress shirt, I get glimpses of his chest.

I don't even realize my mind's growing quiet as I watch him undress.

When he drops his shirt on the floor, my eyes roam his muscled chest. The words 'I will not kneel before anyone' are tattooed across his pecs, and there are two interlinked stars over his heart.

My voice is soft as I ask, "What do the stars mean."

"They're for my parents."

As he pulls down the zipper of his pants, my eyes lower to the six-pack carved into his skin, and even in my shocked and frazzled state, I can't help but admire his body.

He's pure muscle and golden skin.

Franco keeps his boxers on, and after he checks the temperature of the water, he takes my hand and pulls me into the shower.

The warm water quickly wets my hair as it rains down on me, and I let out a sigh of relief as it runs down my body.

"Your hand. The bandage will get wet," Franco says. He takes hold of my hips and positions me so my left arm isn't directly beneath the spray.

Feeling his hands on my skin, my eyes dart to his face and our eyes lock. The connection between us is so strong it forces the trauma to the back of my mind.

As I stare at him, every argument I've had with myself over the past three weeks feels stupid.

Suddenly, it doesn't matter that he's one of the heads of the Cosa Nostra. He's shown me I'm safe with him.

He's proven he loves me by being patient and supportive.

He loves me, and not in a destructive way.

He cares about my feelings.

The list grows longer and longer until the certainty that he's the right man for me fills every part of my heart and soul.

"Are you okay?" he asks when I just keep staring at him.

Nodding, I place my hand on his chest while I push myself up on my tiptoes.

Just as I'm about to kiss him, he says, "You're just been through hell, baby."

"Keep still so I can kiss you," I demand.

The corner of his mouth twitches, but his eyes are still filled with worry.

"I want this," I whisper against his lips.

He lowers his head so I don't have to stand on my toes, and I wrap my right arm around his neck.

With our breaths mingling, I say, "I've made my decision."

His eyes search mine for the answer. "Yeah?"

"I want a relationship with you." Slowly, a smile forms on my face. "I want my mystery man."

Relief fills his eyes, and his arms wrap around me.

"And I want you, Mr. Vitale."

My words make his eyes darken with emotion, and seeing how much my words affect him, I add, "I want all of you."

"Even the mafia part?"

Nodding, I say, "Yes."

The hottest smile I've ever seen forms on his face. "Do you forgive me, baby?"

"Yes."

The word gets smothered by his mouth while he pulls me flush with his chest.

His tongue traces the seam of my lips, and I open for him. As our mouths express our feelings, his hand covers my side where my tattoo is.

The kiss deepens, and I'm swept away to a world where there's only Franco and me.

I lose track of time as our lips knead and our tongues memorize a dance that's only ours.

Only when my mouth is tingling from all the friction does Franco break the kiss. He turns off the faucets before taking hold of my hips and lifting me against his body.

I quickly wrap my legs around his waist, and as he carries me to the bed, I feel his hard cock brush against my butt through his wet boxers.

He places his knee on the bed and gently lowers me to the covers. His eyes drift over my face, and seeing the love he has for me makes my heart feel complete.

It feels as if I was placed on this planet to be his.

"Are you sure, baby?" he asks.

Trailing my fingers over the stubble covering his jaw, I whisper, "I've never been more sure in my life."

"Do I need to use a condom?"

I shake my head. "I'm on the pill."

Franco is so considerate it makes me love him even more.

Pushing his hand behind my back, he unsnaps my bra and tugs it away from my chest.

His gaze lowers to my breasts, and I watch as his irises darken with desire while an expression of awe tightens his features.

He brings a hand to my right breast and softly brushes his thumb over my nipple before his palm covers me.

"You're so beautiful," he murmurs. "So fucking perfect."

Lowering his head, his tongue darts out and swipes over my other nipple before he sucks it into his mouth.

My back arches, and placing my right hand behind his neck, I moan, "Harder."

He sucks and bites my nipple until I'm writhing on the bed.

I'm going to orgasm just from him devouring my breasts.

"Franco," I whimper.

His hand massages my other breast, and his fingers tweak and tug at my nipple.

My abdomen tightens, and tilting my head back, moans and whimpers fall over my lips.

His teeth pull at my sensitive skin, and his eyes flick to my face.

It's the hottest thing I've ever seen, and it sends me over the edge.

My body convulses while my pussy feels neglected and in desperate need of his cock.

Chapter 35

Franco

Making my woman orgasm creates an inferno of need in me.

When Samantha recovers from the pleasure, I smirk with pride.

"Jesus," she breathes, her hand brushing over my shoulder and down my bicep. "That's new."

"You've never orgasmed from having your breasts played with?"

A smile curves her lips. "I didn't know it was a possibility."

"Now you know," I chuckle as I reach for her panties and pull them down her legs. "Move further up the bed, baby."

She does as she's told while my eyes feast on every inch of her.

I've seen works of art but nothing compares to Samantha.

I hook my thumbs into the waistband of my boxers, and as I tug the fabric down, her eyes lock on my painfully hard cock.

When I crawl over Samantha, she wraps her fingers around my cock and swipes her thumb over the precum.

"You're big," she murmurs before stroking me.

It feels so fucking good having her fist around my cock that I groan, "Christ."

"Move higher," she orders. "I want to taste you."

The corner of my mouth lifts as I position myself over her face. I grip hold of the headboard and watch as her tongue darts out to swipe over the precum.

"Hmm."

"Jesus fucking Christ," I growl. "You're so fucking sexy."

Using her right hand, she grips my ass and pulls me closer.

I watch as my cock enters her mouth, and feeling the wet heat has my eyes rolling back in my head. "Fuck, baby."

Her nails dig into my asscheek, then she sucks me so fucking hard I see stars. Unable to control myself, I thrust, and as my cock hits the back of her throat, her gag reflex kicks in.

My eyes snap to her face, and seeing her watering eyes, I almost pull out, but then her cheeks hollow, and she goes to fucking town on my dick.

With the most erotic sight before me and her mouth demanding an orgasm from my cock, my balls tighten and pleasure zaps down my spine.

"I'm going to come," I warn her, but she tightens her hold on my ass and sucks the everloving hell out of me.

"Fuck," I growl as the pleasure makes my cock swell. "Christ, baby." My body jerks, and I can't control myself as I thrust down her throat.

The orgasm hits me so hard my vision goes black, and I lose all my strength. I manage to pull out of her mouth, and a streak of cum lands on her jaw before I fall down beside her on the bed.

"Fuck," I breathe with my hand covering my hammering heart. "Fuck." I glance at Samantha and watch as she swipes her pointer finger through the cum on her face before licking it off. "Fuck."

She lets out a sexy chuckle, and turning onto her side, she gives me a mischievous grin. "Say something else besides fuck."

"Christ."

Samantha pushes herself up, careful not to use her left hand too much, and climbs over me. She straddles my thighs, and leaning down, she presses kisses all over my chest.

Her teeth tug at my nipple, and her palm explores my abs.

She especially pays attention to my abdominal V line running from my hips to my pelvis.

"You like that, baby?"

"Oh yes," she purrs before her teeth sink into my hip.

I'm surprised my cock begins to harden again so soon after my orgasm, but then again, I have a sex goddess on top of me.

Sitting up, I wrap my arm around her, and careful not to jar her left hand, I flip her onto her back while saying, "I'm going to fuck you senseless."

She lets out a soft burst of laughter, and her voice is playful as she murmurs, "Yes, please, Mr. Vitale."

A growl rumbles from my chest, and I force her legs open. My eyes lock on her pussy that's soaked with arousal, and the sight has my mouth watering.

My shoulders push her thighs wider apart, and with her pussy on full display for me, I swipe my tongue over her clit.

Samantha's fingers grip my damp hair, and when I suck her clit hard, her ass lifts off the bed.

I grab her hip with one of my hands while I throw her leg over my shoulder, and then I fucking devour my woman.

Within seconds, she's moaning and rubbing her pussy against my mouth and chin.

I push a finger inside her, and the moment I find her G-spot, she lets out a cry and begins to sob as ecstasy seizes her body.

I keep eating her out, my eyes locked on her face.

Samantha looks at me, and I watch as another orgasm follows closely on the tail of her second one.

Pulling my finger out of her, I lap at her clit and opening, savoring every drop of my woman's arousal. Slowly, I move up her body, pressing kisses on her abdomen and her breasts.

When I reach her neck, I brush my lips over the dark bruises, careful not to hurt her.

Her hand moves up my side and over my shoulder blade, and she pulls me down on top of her.

As my body settles over hers, our eyes lock, and the connection between us feels stronger than ever.

I stare at the woman who's stolen my heart, and I'm so fucking thankful she chose to give us a chance.

I press a kiss to the tip of her nose, then whisper, "Thank you for forgiving me."

A soft smile plays around her lips, and her blonde curls are scattered over my pillow.

"You're welcome."

I press another kiss to the tip of her nose, and with everything I feel for her reflecting in my eyes, I say, "I love you so fucking much, I'd die without you."

Her gaze is soft on me as she teases, "You're too stubborn to die."

"I'm insufferable, remember? You're the stubborn one."

"The perfect pair," she chuckles and hooks one of her legs around my ass.

Lowering my head, I claim her sassy mouth with a deep kiss.

With our bodies pressed tightly together and my tongue tasting hers, she becomes my reason for existing.

For her, I'd wage wars.

For her, I'd kneel.

It feels like my soul becomes one with hers as the kiss becomes more passionate.

She's my twin flame, and together we create an inferno.

Chapter 36

Samantha

I have no idea how much time passes while we kiss, and I don't care.

If I had any doubts about Franco and me, they're all gone.

I've never been kissed like this before. It feels like he's worshiping me.

Just as the thought crosses my mind, he ends the kiss and lifts his head. When he looks at me as if I'm his entire world, it makes me feel emotional.

My eyes start to shine with unshed tears, and my voice trembles as I say, "No one has ever looked at me the way you do."

Franco keeps his left forearm braced beside my head while his right hand brushes down my side.

"That's because no one has loved you as much as I do."

When he reaches my butt, he caresses my skin before moving down to my thigh and hiking my leg higher over his ass. I feel his cock rub over my clit, and it has heat spreading through me.

"You ready, baby?"

I nod, but when I see worry in his eyes, I say, "I'm ready for you." I bring my hand to his jaw and whisper, "Only for you."

Instead of entering me, he continues to rub his cock up and down my slit, creating one hell of a need for more between my legs.

"You said you were going to fuck me senseless," I complain. "Not torture me."

A chuckle rumbles from him as his hand slips between us, and he positions his cock at my entrance.

The anticipation builds, and I can't wait to feel him inside me.

I feel my opening stretch as he pushes against it, and I hold my breath.

Our eyes lock, then he thrusts inside me. We shudder in unison, and he stills for a moment before he pushes another couple of inches into me.

The air wooshes from my lungs, and I grab hold of the covers because he feels too big.

Franco leans over me and braces his forearm beside my head while his other hand grips my outer thigh.

He pulls out then thrusts inside me again, only to be stopped by my body.

Lowering his head, he tugs my bottom lip with his teeth before whispering, "I know you can take all of me."

"I'm trying," I breathe.

His hand moves to my butt, and as he pulls out of me, he only enters me with short strokes.

"Shit," I moan. "That feels good."

"I know," he chuckles arrogantly.

I let go of the covers and place my hand behind his neck. It feels like my heartbeat matches every short stroke from his cock.

Suddenly, he slams into me, and a cry bursts over my lips as he buries himself to the hilt inside me.

I feel stretched to the limits and too full.

"I knew you could take every inch of me," he praises, his voice hoarse.

"Barely," I croak. "I need you to move."

He only pulls out halfway before he fills me with every inch of his hard cock again.

"Jesus," I gasp, my nails digging into his skin.

"You're so fucking tight," the words rumble from him like thunder.

My eyes are still locked on his face that looks like it's carved from stone with the self-control it's taking him to go slow.

He pulls out again and enters me with one hell of a hard thrust that pushes my body higher up the bed.

When he groans, it sounds like it's coming from the deepest part of his soul.

"Fuck me, Franco," I moan. "Fuck me hard, so I'll only remember the feel of you inside me."

I watch as his eyes turn black, then the tension drains from his face, and a predatory expression takes its place.

Jesus.

He pulls all the way out, and when he buries himself deep inside me once more, my back arches from the bed.

I expect him to set a relentless pace, but instead, the thrusts are hard and deep.

By some miracle, I start to grow accustomed to his size, and when I swivel my hips with the next hard stroke of his cock, he lets out a groan.

"That's it, baby. Rub your pussy against me while I fuck you."

My lashes are half-mast over my eyes, and I bite my bottom lip as I look at him. When his pelvis rocks against mine, I rub myself against him and let out a throaty moan.

Pulling my hand away from his neck, I cup my breast, Franco lowers his head and sucks my nipple into his mouth.

I move my hand down my body until my fingers brush against the base of his cock, and feeling where our bodies are connected, fills me with intense satisfaction.

Franco pushes himself up again so he's kneeling between my thighs, and when he pulls out of me, my fingers brush over the length of his hardness.

The moment feels downright erotic and hot, and my abdomen clenches hard.

I move my fingers to my clit, and it has Franco moving my body an inch up with the force of him thrusting inside me.

"Christ, baby," he groans right before his pace speeds up, and he fucks the living hell out of me.

I pull my hand out from between us and claw at his back as he keeps filling me with his cock. My body tenses beneath his, and I tilt my head back and dig my nails into his skin.

The impending pleasure is so intense I can only part my lips, and when the orgasm rips through me, I convulse beneath Franco.

He changes the pace, and every time he trusts deep inside me, he grinds his pelvis against my clit, and it makes another orgasm spasm through me, the pleasure robbing me of my senses.

As I regain my bearings, Franco buries himself to the hilt, and I watch as ecstasy tightens his features.

He falls over me but manages to brace himself on his right forearm, then his mouth claims mine in a forceful kiss, and he slowly continues to plunge into me.

I bring my hand to his jaw and feel how it moves while he devours my mouth.

When he breaks the kiss and lifts his head, our eyes lock, and he fills me one last time before keeping still.

We stare at each other, and caught in a bubble created by our intense connection, I whisper, "I love you."

Franco

Hearing Samantha tell me she loves me fills me with unbelievable happiness.

Staying buried inside her, I stare down at the woman who owns my heart and soul.

She brushes her fingers through my mussed hair, then asks, "What are you thinking about?"

"You." The corner of my mouth lifts.

"What about me?"

I let out a chuckle. "All the hell you gave me."

She pretends to glare at me. "You deserved it."

"I did," I admit.

I don't want to pull out of her, but I have business to take care of. I press a quick kiss to her mouth before pushing myself up and climbing off the bed.

I walk into the bathroom and turn on the faucets in the tub before I clean myself.

When I head back into the bedroom, I say, "While you soak in the tub, I'll get you something to eat."

Samantha stretches her body and covers her mouth as she yawns. "I'm not hungry. I'll just take a bath and get some sleep if that's okay?"

"Of course." I go into the walk-in closet and start to get dressed so I can deal with the fucker who tried to kill my woman.

The rage pours into me so fucking fast, I feel lightheaded for a moment.

"Are you okay?" Samantha asks from where she's standing between the bed and the bathroom door.

"Yes." I pull on a dress shirt and fasten the buttons, my eyes roaming over her naked body. "Baby, I really have to take care of work, and you standing there looking sexy as fuck isn't helping."

She walks closer to me, and wrapping her arms around my neck, she scrunches her nose. "Who needs money? We can survive on love and orgasms."

The corner of my mouth lifts into a smirk. "I like the sound of that, but you need rest." I press a kiss to her mouth. "Get your fuckable ass in the tub."

She steals another kiss before I watch her sexy ass as she heads to the bathroom.

I pull on a vest, and after buttoning it, I roll up the sleeves of my dress shirt. When I've put on my shoes, I walk into the bathroom and grab my gun from the counter.

"I won't be long. There are guards downstairs. If you need something, just text me, and I'll have Milo leave it outside the door for you."

Samantha tilts her head, her eyes filled with love as she stares at me. "Thank you for understanding me so well. Once I've gotten to know your guards, I think I'll be fine with them around me."

I move closer and wrap my hand around the back of her neck. My eyes lower to the aggressive bruises covering her skin.

"You're safe with Milo and Marcello. They will never hurt you."

She nods. "I'll try to get to know them."

"I'd appreciate it." I press a kiss to her forehead, then turn around and leave the room.

Chapter 37

Franco

Taking the stairs down to the foyer, I head into the living room, where I find Milo playing a game on his phone.

"Samantha is in the main bedroom. No one but you can go up to the third floor," I order.

"Got it."

"If she needs something, she'll message me, and I'll let you know. Just leave it outside the bedroom door and knock so she knows it's there."

Milo nods, then asks, "Are you going to deal with the doctor?"

"Yes. Marcello will be with me."

He gets up and goes to sit on a different couch that gives him a view of the stairs.

I leave the living room through the sliding doors, and finding Marcello sitting on a chair out on the veranda, I say, "Let's go."

He darts up and falls in beside me as we head toward the guesthouse. As soon as I walk inside, my men straighten up.

Taking the steps down to the bulletproof door, I place my hand over the biometric scanner. The heavy door unlocks, and Marcello pushes it open.

Stepping into my armory, I stalk past the cabinets holding all my weapons and into the room I reserve for torturing whoever dares cross me.

Santo glances up, and seeing me, he climbs to his feet from where he was sitting while guarding the fucker.

My eyes lock on Todd, where my men strung him up in chains hanging from the roof.

I take in the fucker, from his gray hair to the loafers on his feet.

The rage I suppressed so I could focus on Samantha fills every corner of me until it's all I feel.

I'm glad to see he's conscious. I'd hate to have to wait for him to wake up.

"What do you want?" the fucker asks.

His gaze darts between Marcello and me before it lands on the gun in my hand.

"Don't worry. I'm not going to shoot you," I mutter, then I hand the gun to Marcello.

"Santo, strip him down to his underwear," I order.

"Why am I here? Who are you?" he makes more demands.

I walk to the seat Santo vacated and sit down. Taking a deep breath, I let it out slowly.

My tone is low and deadly as I say, "I'm Franco Vitale."

Todd struggles against the restraints as Santo undresses him.

His eyes keep darting between Marcello, Santo, and me, then he mutters, "I don't know who you are."

I let out a sigh, then say, "Yeah, but I bet you've heard of the Cosa Nostra."

Slowly, the color drains from his face. "I only know what I've seen on the news. I've never been involved with them."

"I know." I cross my legs, resting my ankle on my knee. "I'm one of the five heads of the Cosa Nostra."

He shakes his head. "I don't understand."

As Santo steps away from Todd, my eyes lock on the name carved on his side.

Sam.

"Marcello, bring me a knife," I order, my tone grim. My eyes flick to Todd's worried ones. "Samantha started working for me over a year ago. She's so fucking good at her job, I promoted her to my personal assistant within eight months."

Todd begins to realize why he's here. Honestly, he should've known it involved Samantha, considering where we found him.

When he opens his mouth, I hold up a finger. "I'm still talking."

Marcello returns to the room and holds two knives on display for me. "Which one do you prefer, boss?"

I glance between the large K-Bar and the small pairing knife.

"Maybe we should let Dr. Grant choose. After all, he's going to get well acquainted with the blade."

Marcello nods and walks over to Todd, then I ask, "You work with scalpels, right?"

Todd looks horrified as he stares at the blades in Marcello's hands.

"Choose one," I order.

While he keeps glancing between the knives and me, I continue with my story, "Over the past two and a half months, I've gotten to know Samantha better." A smile curves my lips. "She so fucking strong. Wouldn't you agree?"

He doesn't answer me.

"Marcello, I've changed my mind. Bring me the K-Bar."

"Sure, boss."

When he hands me the knife, I climb to my feet and slowly stalk closer to Todd.

"Leave us alone," I order my men.

"We'll wait in the armory, boss," Marcello says before I hear them exit the room.

When the door shuts, I glance at all the scars on Todd's body. "Christ, you look fucked up. I heard you were in a car accident. It must've hurt like a bitch."

Anger tightens his features, showing me that I'm getting to him.

My voice drops lower, and I let the rage simmer in the words as I murmur, "Samantha told me about you."

He shakes his head. "I…"

I lift the knife and press the tip to where her name is carved into his skin, and it shuts him up.

"I hate being interrupted. Do it again, and I'll remove one of your body parts."

He nods frantically.

"She told me how you drugged her." My eyes narrow on him. "How you raped her repeatedly." I press the tip of the knife into his skin until I draw blood. "How you carved your name on her." I push it deeper, and blood trickles down his side.

I watch as the look in his eyes changes from uncertainty to anger, and it makes me laugh.

I move closer, and when I'm face-to-face with him, I realize he's much shorter than me.

"While you were hanging here, I made Samantha come five times," I say, hitting him where it hurts most.

He's obsessed with her, and to hear that another man took what he considered his property will drive him insane.

A deranged light fills his eyes.

With a chuckle, I add, "She cried my name every time she orgasmed."

With the tip of the knife, I pull the waistband of his briefs back and glance down. "No wonder she came so hard for me. How do you satisfy a woman with such a small dick?"

"Fuck you," he spits.

I turn around and take a couple of steps away from him. "Oh, by the way, she got a tattoo on her side. Shaded brick with a flower growing out of it and the words 'stronger than ever.' Your name has been erased."

"No," he gasps.

Immense pleasure fills me because I've delivered fucking hard blow to the fucker.

"Samantha is mine," I say as I turn around to look at him again. "She loves me."

"No," he shouts, spittle flying from his mouth.

I take a deep breath, and after I exhale, I say, "I'm sure you can understand that I can't have my woman's name on another man."

A frown forms on his forehead. "What are you going to do?

"Marcello," I shout, and a second later, my men come back into the room. "Blindfold and gag Dr. Grant."

"No." The fucker begins to kick his legs, and I know from experience it puts more strain on the shackles around his wrists.

Santo does as instructed, then I order, "Hold him still."

My men grab hold of the man, and when I'm face-to-face with him again, I press the tip of the blade into his skin. "This is what Samantha felt.

Muffled screams are wretched from him as I begin to hack through his skin. I take my sweet fucking time as I flay the skin from his body, his agonizing screams music to my ears.

Samantha couldn't make a sound.

By the time I rip the piece of skin with her name off his body, he trembles from the pain.

I drop Todd's skin on the floor, then say, "Remove the blindfold and gag."

While Santo carries out the order, I glance at Marcello. "I believe he had a cane with him?"

"I'll check with the men."

I turn my attention back to Todd and watch as he looks in horror at the gaping area of raw flesh on his side.

"That's got to hurt," I say, my tone taunting.

Marcello comes back and hands me a light brown cane.

I tap the point against Todd's raw wound, and he wiggles like a worm while letting out a cry.

"You used this to hit my woman, right?" I ask.

His terror-filled eyes dart to me. I use the cane to point at his face. "Samantha had that same look when she got to my house, but don't worry, she's recovered fully."

"Hhh….hhhh," he tries to mumble something.

"I didn't give you permission to speak," I growl before slamming the cane into the raw wound on his side.

I'm rewarded with an excruciating howl, and as I keep swinging the cane, the howls turn to whimpers.

He tried to kill the woman I love.

My rage spirals out of control, and I slam the cane against the side of his head.

Swinging around, my breaths rush over my lips as I toss the cane on the floor and order, "Leave him alone in this room. No food. No water."

Stalking away from the fucker who will soon pray for death, I head back to the main house, where I pour myself a tumbler of whiskey. I down the burning liquid, then focus on getting my breathing under control.

"You okay, boss?" Milo asks from where he's still sitting on the couch.

I nod my head. "I'm fine."

I hear Milo get up. "Is he dead?"

Turning to face him, I answer, "No. I'm not done with him yet."

Chapter 38

Samantha

Even though I'm exhausted, I can't fall asleep.

Lying on Franco's bed, I hug one of his pillows to my chest while I think about my life and everything that's happened.

What will the other employees at work think when they hear I'm dating the CEO?

Probably that I slept my way to the top.

Do I care?

No. Not really.

I have to call Mom and tell her about Franco. She's going to be over the moon.

Is Todd really gone?

How do I feel about that?

Pondering the question, I snuggle into the pillow and take a deep breath of Franco's scent.

I hate that things turned out the way they did. If only Todd had accepted our break up.

Franco is right, though. Todd doesn't deserve to live after everything he's done to me. He's a monster, and God only knows how many women he's already hurt.

Has Franco killed him already?

I wait for the tsunami of emotions to hit, but there's only relief at the thought that Todd won't be able to hurt me again.

I bring my hand to my neck and wrap my fingers around the sore skin.

Todd can't kill me.

I can finally go to Houston, so I can clear out my house and sell it.

Lying in the dark, I find closure to the nightmare that's haunted me for over a year.

As the tears of relief come, I bury my face in the pillow and mourn the loss of everything that was stolen from me.

I hear the bedroom door open and try to rein in the tears as I see Franco come in. He walks to the bathroom, and I hear water run, then there's the rustling of clothes.

Coming back into the room, wearing only his boxers, he climbs on the bed.

He tugs the pillow away from me before lying down and pushing his arm beneath my head. Gathering me against his chest, I hear him take a deep breath.

It feels like his body engulfs mine, and an overwhelming sense of safety surrounds me.

With his mouth near my ear, he whispers, "How are you holding up?"

I wrap my arm around his waist and snuggle as close to him as I can. "Surprisingly good."

He places his hand behind my head, and I've never felt more treasured.

"Then why the tears?"

"It's from the relief of finally having closure," I explain.

Franco presses a kiss to my hair. I tilt my head back, and looking at him, I notice he seems more relaxed than before he left the room to take care of business.

His eyes drift over my face, and the corner of his mouth lifts, making him look way too hot.

"Don't ever smile like that at work," I mutter.

He gives me a confused look. "Why?"

"Every woman at the office is already crushing on you. Seeing you smirk like that will probably start a riot."

He lets out a chuckle, and leaning closer, he kisses me before teasing, "Just admit you're jealous."

I give him a disgruntled look. "No, you're arrogant enough."

He rolls onto his back, a burst of laughter shaking his body.

I crawl over him and straddle his pelvis. I place my hands on his chest, and leaning over him, I say, "I'm not jealous."

I've never seen Franco so relaxed and happy. It's like I'm finally seeing the man beneath the suit.

"You're jealous. There's no shame in admitting it," he continues to tease me.

I shift my butt over his cock, and his expression turns from playful to predatory in a split second.

I rub myself over him again, and watching desire darken his eyes, makes me feel sensual and beautiful.

Lifting his hands, he grips hold of my hips before he moves up the bed so he can lean back against the headboard.

"I love seeing you in my shirt," he murmurs as he cups my breast through the fabric. "It looks sexy on you."

My voice is seductive. "Yeah?" I undo a few buttons. "How about now?"

The smirk on his face makes arousal coat my inner thighs and my abdomen clench with need.

"I love that even more." The words rumble from him as he leans closer to press a kiss between my breasts. He pushes the shirt to the side, then his teeth tug at my nipple. "So much more."

Lifting my butt off him, I reach down and push his boxers out of the way to free his huge cock. Wrapping my fingers around the thick girth, I rub the head of his cock over my pussy and let out a satisfied moan.

"Fuck, baby," he growls. "You're so fucking wet for me."

"Soaked," I complain. "And so achy and needy."

I pull my hand away, and taking hold of the lapels of the shirt, I tug the fabric open and squeeze my breasts while I rub my pussy hard against his cock.

Giving him a hungry look, I purr, "Mmm…your cock is so hard and ready for me."

"Fuck," he breathes, a look of awe warring with his lust for me.

His palms roam my sides, and it looks like it's taking all his willpower to keep still while I give him a show.

I lean forward and tug at his bottom lip with my teeth, then moving lower, I lick and suck at his neck while squashing my breasts to his chest.

I keep rubbing my clit over his cock, and when I feel the first flutters of my orgasm, I reach down and position him at my entrance.

Torturing myself, I take him slowly. I feel every solid inch of him stretch me.

"Jesus fucking Christ, baby. You're going to kill me."

"You're so big," I whimper when it feels like I can't take more. I pull a little back before slamming down on his cock, and it rips a cry from me before I manage to breathe, "Jesus, Franco."

His hands grip my hips, and I feel them tremble. Realizing he's holding back so I can have control has me ignoring the uncomfortable pain, and I start riding him.

"Yes, baby," he groans, then words spill over his lips. "Fuck, your pussy's strangling me...So good...Fuck me harder...show me how badly you want my cock."

With every filthy word, I move faster and harder until my breasts are bouncing.

His eyes feast on them, then he praises me. "So fucking beautiful."

I slow my movements, and swiveling my hips, I ride him slowly while I rub my clit against his pelvis.

He pulls me closer, and his mouth closes around a nipple. While he gives my breasts attention, I keep taking his cock until my body begins to convulse, and a powerful orgasm makes my clit overly sensitive.

It's too intense, and I pull away, trying to stop the orgasm.

Suddenly, Franco throws me onto my back, and he slams hard inside me while growling, "Come, Samantha. Don't fight it."

My hand grips his bicep, and as he hammers into me, I have no choice in the matter, and the orgasm tears through me.

I hear myself scream, and I swear I pass out for a moment.

My body convulses while the overwhelming pleasure keeps crashing over me in waves.

I hear the sounds of our skin slapping and whimper when I can't handle much more.

Franco changes the pace, fucking me slow and deep. I feel his hand push down between us, and when his thumb presses against my clit, my body jerks from how tender I feel.

"Shhh, baby. I'll make it better," Franco murmurs.

He increases the pressure on my clit, and somehow it works, and the tenderness fades away. His thumb begins to rub hard over the bundle of nerves while he continues to thrust inside me.

My eyebrows draw together when I feel my core tightening. "Oh shit," I whisper. "I'm going to come again."

He rubs my clit harder and faster as he begins to hammer into me, and within seconds we orgasm together, making the intimate moment a million times hotter.

As Franco falls over me, I cling to him, and with our bodies suspended in ecstasy, we shudder through our pleasure.

When I regain some strength, I wrap my legs around his ass to keep him locked to me, and I pepper his neck and shoulder with kisses.

His tone is hoarse as he breathlessly says, "You were made for me."

Echoes of pleasure ripple through me while I caress his back, then moving my hand further down, I dig my nails into his asscheek.

"Don't pull away yet," I whisper. "I want to memorize what you feel like on top of me."

He pushes his arms beneath me and holds me so tight it borders on painful.

"Mine." The word is nothing more than a rumble of thunder.

I bury my face against his neck. "Yours."

Chapter 39

Franco

I might not have gotten much sleep, but I feel more rested than I have in a long time.

Where there was a hollow emptiness in my chest, it's now brimming with love and happiness.

Samantha is imprinted in every fiber of my being.

When I walk out of the closet, dressed in a suit, I find my woman sitting on the edge of the bed and staring at her bare legs.

She glances up, and a smile tugs at her mouth as she takes in my suit. "You look handsome."

I grip her chin between my pointer finger and thumb, and nudging her face up, I press a kiss to her lips. "Thank you, baby."

When I pull away, she pouts at me. "Feed me. I'm hungry."

I glance at my dress shirt she's wearing, and the thought of my men seeing her like this fills me with jealousy.

But I can't keep her locked in my room. We need to get some clothes from her apartment.

I stalk back into my closet and finding a pair of sweatpants, I take them to her.

"Stand up," I order as I go down on one knee.

She obeys and places her hand on my shoulder to keep her balance as I pull the sweatpants up her legs. I tighten the drawstring so they stay up.

Looking at the shirt, I fasten the top four buttons so she's completely covered.

Still not happy, I mutter, "That will have to do until we get clothes from your apartment."

"Why are you grumpy?" she asks.

"You look way too fucking sexy in my clothes."

Her eyebrow lifts. "Why is that a problem?"

I narrow my eyes on her. "Because I don't want anyone seeing you like this. Especially not my men."

A mischievous light fills her eyes. "Look who's the jealous one now."

"Damn right, I'm jealous," I grumble. Wrapping my arm around her, I yank her against my body. "You're mine, and mine alone."

Samantha pushes away from me and walks to the door. "No sex. I'm starving."

"Who said anything about sex?" I mutter as I follow her out of the bedroom.

"If you keep talking to me like that and looking like a sex god, it's going to make me strip you out of that suit."

I catch up to her before she can reach the stairs, and grabbing hold of her arm, I pull her back against my chest. Leaning down until I reach her ear, I murmur, "What will you do once you have me out of the suit?"

I cup one of her breasts and squeeze it hard, which earns me a moan.

"I'll shove you onto the bed."

Pushing my other hand down her front, I grip her between her legs and feel the heat coming from her needy pussy.

"Then what?" I growl as I rub her pussy while pinching her nipple through the shirt.

"I'll...I...I..."

"You'll what, baby?"

"Franco," she gasps. "Fuck me."

I push her up against the wall, and unzipping my pants, I free my cock before yanking the sweatpants down her legs. Grabbing hold of her hips, I lift her onto her tiptoes and slam my cock inside her pussy.

I pull her ass back against me with every thrust and fuck her senseless.

Moans and sobs spill from my woman, and within seconds her pussy grips my cock as she orgasms.

I follow right behind her, and squashing her against the wall, I enter her with a few hard thrusts before I bury myself to the hilt inside her.

A growl rumbles from my chest as I come inside her.

It takes a moment before we come down from the pleasure, and when I pull out of her, I watch as my cum trickles down the inside of her thighs.

I swipe some onto the tip of my finger, and pulling Samantha away from the wall so she's leaning back against my chest, I bring my finger to her mouth.

Her lips part, and I groan when she sucks the cum off.

Slapping her bare ass, I say, "I want you eating breakfast with my cum between your legs. Don't dare wipe it off."

"Yes, sir," she replies, her tone obedient as if we're at the office.

Crouching behind her, I pull the sweatpants up her legs.

When I tuck my cock back into my pants and pull up the zipper, Samantha turns around to face me with a playful smile on her face.

"What perks do I get for sleeping with my boss?"

I can't stop a grin from tugging at my lips. "Hmm, we'll have to talk about it once we're back at the office."

Taking her hand, I lead her down the stairs so I can feed her.

Samantha

After I've had my fill of crispy bacon and french toast that Milo apparently prepared, Franco leads me to the living room.

Walking inside, I see Milo and Marcello standing outside on the veranda where they're talking to a woman.

When we near them, the conversation stops, and they all glance at Franco and me.

The woman, who's dressed in the same black combat uniform as the other guards, folds her hands in front of her and straightens her spine.

There's so much respect on her face as she looks at Franco.

"Morning," Franco says, his tone back to being stern.

"Morning," they all reply in unison, then Marcello says, "I've updated Via. She's ready."

"Good." Franco glances at me, then explains, "Via will be your bodyguard. She'll be by your side no matter where you go."

My eyebrows fly up. "Why?"

"To protect you."

"Against?"

Franco narrows his eyes. "Anyone who tries to touch what's mine."

Right.

I turn my attention to Via, who's a couple of inches taller than me. Holding out my hand to her, I say, "It's nice to meet you."

She shakes my hand. "It's an honor protecting you, Miss Blakely."

I give her a friendly smile. "Just call me Samantha."

Her eyes dart to Franco for permission, and when he nods, I glance at Milo. "Thank you for breakfast. It was delicious."

He looks surprised I'm talking to him as he mutters, "You're welcome."

Marcello gestures at my bandaged hand. "Can I take a look at the wound?"

I nod, and walking into the living room, I take a seat on one of the couches. Just like the night before, Marcello sits on the coffee table where the first aid kit is still lying.

Franco comes to stand behind the couch and places his hand on my shoulder.

Marcello is gentle as he removes the bandage. When I see the stitches, I wonder why it doesn't hurt more.

Marcello cleans the wound before he wraps a fresh bandage around my hand. He pulls a small plastic holder from his pocket and says, "Take three a day until you've completed the course."

I take it from him, and seeing it's medication, I ask, "What's it for?"

"It's an antibiotic."

Franco takes it from me, muttering, "I'll make sure she takes them."

I climb to my feet, and say, "Thank you, Marcello."

"Any time," he murmurs.

I turn my attention to Franco and ask, "Did your men, by any chance, lock my apartment last night and bring the keys?"

"Oh. I have them," Milo says, and digging in his pocket, he pulls the keys out and hands them to me.

"Great." Walking to Franco, I stand on my tiptoes and press a kiss to his cheek. "I'll see you later."

His eyebrows fly up, and he shakes his head. "I'm not letting you go to the apartment alone."

"I have Via."

"I'm taking you," Franco says with finality darkening his tone.

"Okay."

He takes my right hand, and I'm tugged out of the house before I'm bundled into the back of the G-Wagon.

When he takes a seat beside me, I roll my eyes at him. "Stop being a caveman."

He sucks in a deep breath, and his features soften. "Sorry. Seeing the stitches pissed me off."

"It doesn't hurt much," I say to make him feel better.

He lifts my left hand and presses a kiss to the bandage as Via and Milo climb into the front of the vehicle.

When we leave the property, I lean my head against Franco's shoulder, wondering how I'll feel when I walk into my apartment.

A while later, Milo parks the G-Wagon in front of the building, and we all get out.

Franco wraps an arm around me as we head up to my apartment, and when I unlock the door, I suck in a deep breath.

Stepping inside my home, I glance at the broken glass and dead flowers on the living room floor before taking in the kitchen table standing askew and the toppled chairs.

There's blood smeared on the tiles from when I struggled against Todd.

A shiver shudders through my body as I remember glimpses of the fight.

Franco pulls me against his chest while he growls, "Via, pack clothes for Samantha."

"Yes, boss," she murmurs before darting into my bedroom.

I move out of Franco's embrace and walk to the kitchen. When I crouch to pick up the pan, I feel him behind me.

Straightening up, I set the pan on the table, saying, "I saw my future while I fought him."

Franco wraps his arm around my waist, and nudging my face up, he asks, "What did you see?"

A smile tugs at my mouth. "Us." Standing on my tiptoes, I press a kiss to his lips. "I saw us."

Chapter 40

Franco

After getting Samantha settled in my place, I head to the armory.

It was a good idea to assign Via to her. I feel a hell of a lot better knowing Samantha has a guard with her when I have to take care of business.

When I walk into the torture room, it's to see Todd's limp body hanging from the shackles.

"Are you still alive?" I ask as I move closer.

He pries his eyes open and lets out a garbled sound.

I glance at Santo and order, "Bring it in." Turning my eyes to Marcello, I say, "Let the doctor down."

While Marcello frees the man's wrists from the shackles, Todd lets out a painful groan.

Santo and Joey carry a wooden box into the room and place it on the floor.

When Todd drops to the floor, he lets out a cry, which makes a smile form on my face.

I gesture at the box and order, "Put him in it."

Santo and Joey gather Todd's broken body off the floor, but when they lower him into the rectangular box, he regains some strength and grabs hold of the sides.

"N-no…N-no," he stammers, his eyes wide with the horror of a man who knows he's about to die.

I move closer and crouch down beside him. "Yes." A satisfied smile curves my lips. "I'm going to bury you alive, but don't worry, I have a parting gift for you."

I pull my phone from my pocket, and looking for the video I took of Samantha packing some of her clothes into my closet, I turn the screen to Todd and press play.

My voice sounds up, saying, "I love you, baby. More than anything."

She lets out a soft burst of laughter. "I love you too. Get over here and help me."

"Or you can join me on the bed," I murmur.

She turns around and with a playful smile on her face, she comes closer. "What are you doing?"

"Recording you so I can watch it whenever I miss you."

She crawls onto the bed, and I have to admit, I got a good shot of her kissing me.

"Who do you belong to?" I ask Samantha.

"You," she murmurs. "Only you."

Pressing stop, I watch as tears stream down Todd's temples.

"I thought you'd like it." Raising to my full height, I look down on the piece of shit, then I order, "Bury him alive."

Todd starts to wail as he tries to pull himself up, but he's too weak. Santo and Joey shift the wooden cover over the box, and I keep eye contact with Todd until the wood slides over his face.

As I listen to Todd's muffled cries for mercy, the men nail it shut.

When the last nail is hammered into the coffin, I stalk out of the room. Marcello's right behind me, saying, "The group we sent to Miami found Miro. They're on their way back."

"Good. Maybe then we can arrange a meeting with Ivan. When they get back with Miro, put him in the torture room."

"Got it."

One down. One to go.

Samantha

Sitting on the veranda with a glass of lemonade, I dial Mom's number and listen as the call connects.

"Hey, sweetie," her voice sounds cheerful over the line.

"Hi, Mom." I smile as I ask, "How does it feel to be a grandma?"

"Amazing. Josh is such a good baby. He hardly cries."

"I'm happy to hear that," I say. "Are you still visiting Matt?"

"No, I got home yesterday." She lowers her voice. "You'd swear I left your father for a year. The man won't let me out of his sight. Oh, here he comes."

I let out a chuckle. "Aww, he missed you."

I watch as the gates open and the G-Wagon comes up the driveway.

"I suppose."

"Who are you talking to?" I hear Dad ask.

"Sammie," Mom answers.

"Put her on speakerphone." Seconds later, Dad says, "Hi, Sammie. How are you?"

"I'm good. Congrats on becoming a grandfather."

"Thanks. You must see how much he's grown already. I'm telling you, he's going to be a football player."

"Hush, Scott. He's not even a month old," Mom chastises Dad.

Franco comes walking toward me, and leaning down, he presses a kiss to my forehead.

"I'm actually calling to tell you I have a boyfriend," I say, and it has Franco's eyebrow lifting.

Too curious for his own good, he pulls a chair right next to mine, and taking a seat, he leans closer to try and hear the conversation.

"You do!" Mom exclaims. "Who? What does he do? When?"

I let out a burst of laughter. "I met him at work." Remembering how I complained to my parents about my asshole boss, a nervous chuckle escapes me. "Ah…it's Mr. Vitale."

"I'm confused," Mom says.

"You're dating your boss?" Dad asks.

"Yes." I glare at the grin on Franco's face. "He wore me down."

"What do you mean he wore you down?" Dad asks with a worried tone.

"I'm kidding, Dad," I say to put him at ease. "He's actually very nice."

"You don't date someone because they're nice to you," Mom mutters.

"Fine. Nice is the wrong word." I take a deep breath, then say, "Franco is amazing. He's been nothing but good to me, and I love him."

"You love him?" Mom asks. "When you were here, it sounded like you hated him. What changed in a month?"

So much. But I can't tell them, because they don't know what Todd did to me.

"It's hard to explain, Mom. I was always attracted to him, and when he told me how he felt about me, I gave him a chance. He's attentive and caring. I promise you'll approve of him once you meet him."

"When are we meeting him?" Dad asks.

I give Franco a mischievous smile, then say, "He's coming with me for Thanksgiving."

Instead of panicking, he looks happy.

Mom sounds less worried when she says, "I'm glad to hear that."

"Does he make you happy, Sammie?" Dad asks.

"Yes, Dad. I've never been so happy before." I take a deep breath, then admit, "He's the one I want to spend my life with."

Franco wraps his arm around my shoulders, and pulling me against his chest, he presses a kiss to my hair.

"Oh, sweetie," Mom mutters with an emotional tone to her voice. "That's all we want for you. If you feel he's the one, we'll accept him with open arms."

"Thank you. I really appreciate it." I clear my throat before I continue, "I have to go. I just wanted to tell you the good news."

"Okay. We'll talk again soon."

I end the call, and rubbing my cheek against Franco's suit jacket, I say, "I can't wait to introduce you to my parents at Thanksgiving."

"I can't wait to meet them."

I tilt my head back to look up at him. "Really?"

"Of course. They have to be incredible people for raising someone as strong, independent, and beautiful as you."

"Aww…" I press a kiss to his jaw.

He rubs his palm up and down my bicep. "You didn't tell them what happened."

I shake my head. "They just think I broke up with Todd. I couldn't break their hearts."

Franco presses a kiss to my hair. "I hate that you had to deal with it on your own."

I look up at him again. "Until you came along."

The corner of his mouth lifts. "I'm glad I could help." His expression grows serious, then he says, "You can't tell them I'm one of the heads of the Cosa Nostra."

I didn't even think about that.

Sitting up straight, I meet Franco's eyes. "They'd freak out."

"That too." He rubs his hand up and down my back. "It's for their safety as well. The less they know, the better."

I nod as I let out a sigh.

Franco's eyes narrow on my face, "Why does your mother think you hated me?"

Giving him a playful look, I say, "Because I told her you were an insufferable asshole."

When I walk toward the sliding doors, Franco grabs my forearm and yanks me backward. I fall onto his lap, and he locks me against his chest with his arms.

"I was an insufferable asshole because you gave me attitude," he grumbles.

I wrap my arms around his neck. "I gave you attitude because you were rude and grumpy."

He presses a kiss to the tip of my nose. "I was grumpy because I was attracted to a woman who tried to drive me insane on a daily basis."

Leaning closer, I smile against his lips. "Yeah? Did you fantasize about spreading me over your desk?"

Fire ignites in his eyes. "I had many fantasies about spanking your ass."

I pull back and scowl at him. "You didn't think about having sex with me? At all?"

He lets out a chuckle. "Baby, I've imagined fucking you in every possible position too many times to count."

A satisfied smile lights up my face. "Good. I like knowing you were sexually frustrated because of me."

I snuggle against his chest and let my eyes drift over the manicured garden.

Franco's tone is soft when he asks, "Am I really the one you want to spend the rest of your life with?"

I nod as I close my eyes, soaking in how good this moment between us feels.

"Move in with me," he murmurs.

"I'll think about it."

He lets out a chuckle. "Don't keep me in suspense for weeks again."

Chapter 41

Franco

When Renzo and the others follow me into the room, Miro's eyes dart between us from where he's tied to a chair.

With Samantha back at the office, I had the guys come over so we could put our plan in motion.

"I can see why he isn't the head of the Slovak mafia," Angelo mutters. "Why did he piss himself?"

Miro might be older than Ivan, but he doesn't have the balls to run a criminal organization.

I let out a sigh. "Because he's shit scared."

"We didn't even slap him around," Renzo mutters.

"Let's do this," Damiano orders.

I hold out my hand, and Marcello passes me Miro's phone. When I move closer to Miro, he starts to breathe faster, his eyes growing wide with fear.

"What's the password for your phone?" I ask.

"T-three, nine, f-five, five, t-t-two," he stammers.

I unlock the device, and checking the contacts, I find Ivan's number and press dial.

I put the call on speakerphone as I move to stand behind Miro.

"*Bál som sa!*" Ivan snaps.

"Your brother is a little preoccupied," I mutter.

"Ivan!" Miro shouts, which earns him a slap against the head from me.

"Quiet until you're permitted to speak," I growl.

There's silence for a moment, then Ivan asks in a thick accent, "Who is this?"

"Really? You don't even want to take a guess?" I say in a mocking tone.

"Vitale?"

"Bingo," Dario chuckles.

"Is my brother alive?" Ivan barks.

"Yes, and he'd like to say hello." Pulling my gun from behind my back, I tap Miro's shoulder with the barrel. "Tell your brother how well we're treating you."

"G-good. T-they treat me w-well."

"What do you want?" Ivan demands.

"A meeting," I inform him. "I think it's time we talk face-to-face."

"I'm not meeting the Cosa Nostra. I'm not that stupid."

"Enough men have died," I mutter. "This is between you and me. We'll fight old-school. No weapons." I press the barrel into Miro's neck, and it has him whimpering, then I continue, "If you win, you get Castro and Diaz. If I win, I kill your brother. I think it's fair."

"What about the others?" Ivan asks.

Damiano steps forward. "A deal is a deal. We won't interfere."

Renzo shakes his head, not happy that I'm going to fight Ivan. He voted that we attack full force, but the others agreed with me.

"Fine, but I say when and where," Ivan spits out.

"Last time I checked, I was the one with the gun to your brother's head," I mutter. "I'll send you the time and place."

I end the call and copy Ivan's number to my phone to send him the message once I'm ready.

We're all quiet as we leave the room, and only when we're out of the armory does Renzo mutter, "I'm going with you."

I shake my head. "No. I'll have Marcello and Milo."

Renzo grabs hold of my shoulder, and I stop walking to lock eyes with him.

"I'm going with," he growls.

"I'll take my sniper rifle," Dario says. "I found a nice spot in the building next to yours that gives me a perfect view inside your warehouse. Just make sure both doors are open."

"Angelo and I will wait nearby with our men in case Ivan brings an army," Damiano informs me.

I glance at them, then shake my head. "You're not going to take no for an answer, right?"

They all mutter some variation of 'fuck no' as we continue to walk out of the guesthouse.

"Give me thirty minutes to scope the warehouse," Dario says. "I'll let you know when I'm ready, then you can notify Ivan of the location. I want to make sure he doesn't send men to take up sniper positions so he can take you out the second you get there."

"Thanks."

"We'll get the men ready," Angelo says.

I nod and watch as they leave, then turn my attention to Renzo, who's still glaring at me.

"Why are you doing this?" he asks. "Why not just hit the fucker hard and call it a day?"

"I don't want to lose half my men going up against the Slovak mafia."

"And?" he pushes.

"They fucking shot at Samantha and traumatized her."
When Renzo opens his mouth to argue, I shake my head
hard. "I'm doing this my way."

"You have no idea how well Ivan can fight," Renzo
argues.

"So? Have you forgotten I've trained with the best?"

Frustrated with me, he shoves a hand through his hair.
"No, I haven't. I just don't want to risk your life."

"Brother." I shake my head. "I'll be risking my life
whether we attack full force or I fight the man old-school."

He stares at me, and realizing I'm right, he lets out a
sigh.

I punch him hard on the shoulder before I walk toward
the mansion.

"What the fuck is that for?"

"For giving me shit," I mutter.

When I enter the house, I pull my phone out of my
pocket and dial the direct number for my line at the office.

"Mr. Vitale's office. Samantha speaking."

"Hi, baby."

"Hmm…who is this?" she teases me.

"Your mystery man."

I hear a loud bark of laughter behind me, and as I glance over my shoulder, I watch as Renzo stumbles out onto the veranda, where he proceeds to die of laughter.

Fucker.

I'm never going to hear the end of that.

"Who's laughing?" Samantha asks.

"Renzo."

"Have I met him?" she asks.

"Yeah, he was with Dario at the office," I remind her.

"Oh, I remember now." She pauses for a moment, then asks, "Why did you call?"

"I wanted to hear your voice," I murmur. "I love you."

"I love you too." I hear her typing on the keyboard, then she says, "I'll see you after work."

"Okay."

I wait for her to hang up, but she doesn't. Instead, her voice is filled with emotion as she says, "I love you with all my heart, Franco."

She ends the call, and I tuck the device back in my pocket before heading to my bedroom to change into my combat gear.

When Milo stops the G-Wagon near the entrance of the warehouse, I take in our surroundings before my eyes lock on Ivan, where he's leaning against the side of his SUV.

"Let's do this," I mutter while shoving the door open and climbing out.

Marcello hauls Miro out of the back while Milo remains in the G-Wagon, so he can alert the others if anything goes wrong.

I unlock the doors and push them open before heading inside and switching on the lights.

For a split-second, my eyes flick to empty crates where Renzo is already hiding.

Marcello pulls Miro to the side and forces him onto his knees while training the barrel of his gun on the back of Miro's head.

Ivan saunters inside with one of his men. He only glances at his brother before locking eyes with me.

"I like New York," Ivan mutters in his thick accent. "Good opportunity for drugs."

I roll my shoulders and slowly move to the right. "Let's do this, Vargo. I want to be home in time for dinner."

He lets out a bark of laughter. "I'm sorry to disappoint you, but you're not going to make dinner."

I'm not just fighting for my territory and the Cosa Nostra.

I'm fighting for a future with Samantha.

I shrug. "We'll see."

"If I kill you, I take my brother, and I supply to Castro and Diaz."

I nod. "*When* I win, you both die."

He lets out a chuckle and tries to taunt me as he darts two steps forward before taking one back.

Fuck this.

I lunge forward, and twisting to the side, I deliver a kick to Ivan's throat. He staggers back while gagging, and with rage tightening his features, he storms me.

His shoulder plows into my chest, and as he lifts me from the ground, I wrap my arm around his neck and knee him in the gut.

I hear the air wooshing from his lungs as he lets go of me and moves away so he can catch his breath.

"Not bad," he mutters before he comes at me again, and as he throws the punch, I duck while sweeping his feet from underneath him.

Ivan falls hard on his back, and before he can try to get up, I'm on top of him, delivering a blow to his face.

He manages to slam his fist into my side, making pain shudder through my ribs.

As my fist connects with his nose and blood spurts from it, Samantha's face flashes through my mind.

Determined to get back to her, I deliver two consecutive blows to his face.

Ivan tries to buck me off him, but I grab hold of his shoulders, and lifting myself up, I slam my knee into his chin, making his head whip back.

Climbing to my feet, I take in his bloody nose and where the skin split over his cheekbone.

He pushes himself up, and when he's back on his feet, he shakes his head and glares at me.

I point to my nose, saying, "You have a bit of blood here."

Letting out a growl, he storms me again, but having had enough, I lunge myself into the air, and twisting, I slam the heel of my boot against the side of Ivan's head.

He staggers to the side and drops to one knee. Again, he shakes his head, but it's game over for him.

I hold my hand up, signaling to Marcello to take out Ivan's man.

The gunshot is loud, and it has Ivan darting to his feet. "You have no honor!" he shouts at me.

I shake my head as I lock eyes with him. "You came into my city and sent your man to kill me. To kill my woman. You took the life of one of my guards. He was like a brother to me." I shake my head again. "No, there's no honor between you and me."

"Marcello," I bark, keeping my eyes locked on Ivan as Marcello shoots Miro in the head.

I drink in the absolute devastation on Ivan's face.

That's for you, Lorenzo.

While Ivan is reeling from the loss of his brother, I hear gunfire erupt outside. I let out a cynical chuckle as I hold out my hand.

When Marcello places the gun in my palm, I train the barrel on Ivan, muttering, "You're one to speak about honor." I pull the trigger, burying a bullet in his gut before moving closer.

He drops down to one knee again, and before he can say anything, I growl, "Say hello to your brother for me."

I pull the trigger and watch as the bullet hits his forehead. His head snaps back, and a second later, he falls dead to the floor.

"Renzo," I shout.

"He ran out the door to help the others," Marcello informs me.

I jog out of the warehouse and find Milo waiting with Uzis. Grabbing the submachine gun, I'm about to head toward the sporadic gunfire when I see Renzo coming back to us.

"What's going on?" I ask.

"Damiano's making the last of Ivan's men tapdance because he's bored. Apparently, killing over twenty men isn't exciting enough for him." He glances into the warehouse then pats my shoulder. "You have to show me how to do that flying kick move."

I glance up to where Dario is watching Damiano and Angelo through the scope of his sniper rifle.

"Marcello, give me my phone."

He places it in my hand, and I dial Dario's number.

"What's up?"

"What are Damiano and Angelo doing?"

"Damiano just shot the last Slovakian. Now they're signaling for our men to head out. Now they're climbing into Angelo's SUV. Now they're driving toward you."

"Christ, Dario, I didn't ask for a play-by-play," I snap. "Get your ass down here."

"Anything for you, mystery man."

I hear the fucker chuckle before I hang up on him.

Glaring at Renzo, I mutter, "I really fucking hate you for telling them about the mystery man thing."

Chapter 42

Samantha

I place the tray with coffee and cookies on the corner of Franco's desk, and leaving his office, I take a seat behind my computer.

Where was I?

I read the last couple of lines, then continue typing the letter I have to send to the bank before ten a.m.

"Morning, Miss Blakely," Franco suddenly mutters before heading into his office.

What the hell?

I get up from my chair, and following him into the chamber of wrath, I place my hands on my hips and scowl at him. "What was that?"

"What?" he asks as he shrugs off his jacket and hangs it over the back of the chair.

"Morning, Miss Blakely," I do my best impersonation of him.

He does something weird with his eyes and gives me a chin lift, which only makes me frown more.

"You don't get to be a grumpy asshole anymore," I say as I walk closer to him, and jabbing my finger in his chest, I continue, "You don't get to fuck m–"

A smile spreads over his face as he interrupts me. "We have company."

"What?"

He gestures to the door, and when I glance over my shoulder, I see Jenny with her jaw practically on the floor.

"Shit," I mutter before turning away from Franco and walking to my friend.

Grabbing her hand, I pull her to the boardroom.

The moment I shut the door, she shrieks before gasping, "What? Ahhh..." She shakes her head. "What did I just see?"

I let out a sigh as I take a seat at the table. "I'm dating Franco."

"Oh, you're on a first-name basis with him?"

"Of course." I shake my head at her. "He's my boyfriend. What else would I call him?"

She slumps down in a chair, looking a little stunned. Giving me an unsure look, she asks, "You're really dating Mr. Vitale and not just hooking up for casual office sex?"

"We're in a committed relationship," I say.

Her jaw drops again, then she asks, "When did this happen? Why didn't you tell me?"

"It's complicated." Not knowing what else to say, I throw Franco under the bus as I lie, "Franco wanted to keep it a secret until we were official, so I couldn't tell you."

"How long have you two been dating?"

"A week."

Her eyebrow lifts. "So it's still pretty new."

"We've been official a week but have been talking about it for a month or so."

She glances through the windows at Franco's office, then looks back to me. "The other women are going to be so freaking jealous when I tell them." Shaking her head, she gives me a confused look. "I thought we hated him?"

"We kinda did," I chuckle. "He's actually very different when you get to know him."

She leans forward as if I'm busy giving her the inside scoop of a lifetime. "Different how?"

"Well, he's kind and caring." I lean forward as well. "He's actually pretty amazing."

Jenny's features soften. "You look smitten with him."

"I am," I chuckle before I admit, "I love him."

"Damn, he must be good in bed if you love him after a week of dating."

Laughter bursts from me. "Like I said, it's complicated. I can't tell you everything."

Her eyes grow bigger. "Oooh, did he make you sign an NDA?"

Taking the out she gives me, I nod. "Yes."

"Shoot." A smile forms on her face again. "Will he be your plus one to my wedding?"

"Definitely."

Her smile widens, then she playfully slaps me on the knee. "Damn, girl, you landed yourself a billionaire."

Shaking my head, I say, "It's not about the money."

"I didn't say it was. I just think it's cool."

I hear the phone ring and tap the button on my earpiece to answer the call. "Mr. Vitale's office. Samantha speaking."

"Do you need me to save you?" Franco asks.

My mouth curves up. "No, I can handle it on my own."

"Okay, baby."

The call ends, and I turn my attention back to Jenny.

"Was that him?" she asks.

"Yes, he says you need to get back to work," I say with a dead-serious expression.

"Shit."

Just as she darts to her feet, I laugh and say, "I'm kidding. Sit down."

She gives me a playful scowl. "You'll give me a heart attack. You might be dating the boss, but the rest of us are still scared of him." She seems to realize something, then says, "I actually came up here to ask whether you'll go to a wedding dress fitting with me on Saturday morning."

"Of course! Just tell me what time and where we're meeting."

She gets up from the chair. "I better get back to my desk. I'll text you the details for Saturday."

"Okay." Then I remember Via. "Oh, Franco gave me a bodyguard. Her name is Via. She'll be with me."

Jenny looks stunned for a second. "A bodyguard? Why?"

I shrug. "Franco's protective of me."

"So freaking lucky," she mutters as she walks to the door. "We'll talk some more later."

When Jenny heads back to the elevator, I walk to Franco's office.

This time I shut the door behind me so we don't get caught by any other employees.

"How did it go?" he asks from where he's sitting behind his desk.

"She's surprised but seems happy for me."

I walk closer and say, "I'm going to a wedding dress fitting with her on Saturday morning."

The corner of his mouth lifts as he asks, "For yourself or Miss Hoffman?"

"Duh, for Jenny. Who am I getting married to?"

"Me."

I raise an eyebrow at him and cross my arms over my chest. "I don't remember you asking me to marry you."

"I'm asking you now."

I give him a have-you-lost-your-mind look. "No."

His smile grows wider. "No, what?"

"No, I won't marry you," I mutter.

"Why?"

I turn around and walk to the door. "Because your proposal sucks."

Leaving his office, I take a seat at my desk and get back to work.

A few seconds later the phone starts ringing, and seeing it's an internal call from Franco's office, I answer, "It's still a no from me."

Hanging up, I work hard to suppress the smile.

My cellphone vibrates, and opening the screen I burst out laughing when I read the message.

Franco: I'm spanking your ass tonight for hanging up on me. Are you finished with the letter?

Samantha: I look forward to it, and yes, give me five minutes, and I'll bring it to you so you can sign it.

———————————

Standing in Franco's state-of-the-art kitchen, I grate cheese because whoever does the shopping apparently doesn't know you buy shredded cheese.

Franco's stirring a tomato-based sauce for the pasta we're having for dinner.

"Who does the grocery shopping?" I ask.

"Milo," Franco murmurs as if he's deep in thought.

I glance over my shoulder. "And the cleaning?"

"I have a cleaning service come in twice a week."

Franco's stirring the sauce slowly, a far away look in his eyes.

I place the cheese on the counter, and going to stand next to him, I ask, "Is everything okay?"

He glances at me. "Yes. Why?"

"You seem preoccupied."

He shakes his head. "It just hit me how good it is to have you here." He lets out a deep breath. "Doing something as simple as preparing dinner with you."

I lift my hand and rub it up and down his back. "I'm enjoying it too."

"I'd like to make a habit of it. Us cooking dinner while talking."

Smiling at him, I murmur, "I'd like that very much."

He leans down to steal a kiss before he checks the sauce and moves the pan from the stove.

We're quiet while we dish up, and when we're sitting at the island with a glass of wine, I mention, "Did I tell you I have a house in Houston?"

He nods and swallows a bite of pasta.

"I want to go back there so I can pack all my belongings and hire a moving company to bring everything here."

"I can send some men to Houston to take care of it for you," he offers.

"Really? You don't mind?"

"Of course not. I'll have them bring your belongings to my house." He reaches across the marble top and gives my hand a squeeze, then he asks, "What are you going to do with the house?"

"As soon as it's cleared out, I'm selling it."

Feeling like a weight is being lifted off my shoulders, I admit, "I actually dreaded going back to Houston."

"It's understandable, baby. If you want, I'll take care of selling the house."

I give him a grateful smile. "I'd appreciate it. I just want it all over with so I can put that chapter of my life behind me."

"Do you have the title deed?" he asks.

I shake my head. "It's at the house. I didn't take anything but a bag of clothes when I ran." Wanting to change the subject, I ask, "You don't mention the mafia much. How are things on that front?"

"Good." A smile tugs at his mouth. "I took care of the person who ordered the attack on us."

My eyebrows lift. "You did? When?"

"Yesterday."

"Did you…" I let the sentence trail away.

Franco's eyes lock with mine. "Yes, I killed him."

"Is it okay if I ask you about things like that?"

He nods. "Of course. I have nothing to hide from you, baby."

I take a sip of my wine, then Franco points at my plate and orders, "You skipped lunch. Eat, baby."

I take a few bites, then ask, "So what kind of mafia business do you do?"

"Counterfeit notes and transporting contraband goods."

"Oh." I tilt my head. "I expected something more...violent."

He lets out a chuckle. "So me killing the head of the Slovak mafia isn't violent enough for you?"

I shake my head. "I was talking about your illegal businesses."

Franco changes the subject by saying, "I've noticed all your clothes are here. Does that mean you've moved in?"

I let out a burst of laughter. "You'd love that, wouldn't you?"

He nods. "If it were up to me, you'd never return to the apartment."

I was going to tell him later, but now is as good a time as any.

"I'm handing the keys back to the landlord tomorrow."

Franco stops eating and locks eyes with me. Slowly, a smile spreads over his face. "So you've moved in with me?"

Giving him a grin, I nod. "Yes. You're officially stuck with me."

Abandoning his food, he gets up, and walking around the island, he frames my face with his hand and kisses me hard. Lifting his head, he says, "You've just made me the happiest man in the world, baby."

Chapter 43

Franco

Watching Samantha open box after box is a sight to behold.

When the men offloaded the truck, she was so happy she actually clapped her hands.

"Ohhhh, this is my grandmother's hand mirror. She got it from her grandmother," she says with nostalgia coating her words.

We're sitting in the middle of the foyer with her belongings scattered around us. From the looks of things, it will take us a couple of days to unpack and find a spot for everything.

She pulls a framed photo from the box and hands it to me so I can see. "This was taken on my first day of school."

I look at the little girl, who's the cutest child I've ever seen. "Why do you have three ponytails?"

She shrugs. "Back then, I thought it looked pretty."

When she takes a shoebox out, she grins at me. "Oooh, all the love letters I received."

"Give that to me." I grab it from her before she can hold it out of my reach, and taking the lid off, I open the first piece of paper. "Your hair looks like candyfloss?" I let out a chuckle.

"Don't laugh. Pete was serious. He even tried putting my pigtail in his mouth."

I open up another one. "If I give you a Hershey's bar, will you go steady with me?"

Samantha grins at me. "I told him I wanted a Hershey's bar once a week. It didn't last long."

I shake my head. "I think it's cute that you kept them all."

"Look at this one." She leans forward and searches through the letters until she finds the right one. Opening it, she points to where the letter ends with the words in dots.

"I'm running out of ink, but I'll write again when I get a new pen."

"That's my favorite."

As we keep working through the boxes, I learn Samantha had a happy childhood.

And, she never throws anything away.

"Time for a break. We can continue tomorrow." Getting up off the floor, I stretch my body before holding my hand out to help Samantha to her feet.

I head to the kitchen and ask, "Want some coffee?"

"Yes, please."

She watches as I pour two cups, and when I hand her one, she asks, "Can we sit on the veranda?"

"Sure."

I follow her past the mess in the foyer, and as we head through the living room toward the sliding doors, I see the men scatter in every direction.

"They don't have to do that," Samantha says. "I'll never get used to them if they keep hiding whenever I come outside."

She sits down on one of the chairs. "Tell them to come back."

I pull my phone out of my pocket and dial Marcello's number.

"Yes, boss?"

"Tell everyone they don't have to clear out when they see Samantha."

"On it."

She sips on her coffee as the men resume their places, and not long after, Marcello walks toward us.

"I thought I'd check your hand while you're out here," he says, placing the first aid kit on the table.

"Sure."

When he removes the bandage, I notice she doesn't cringe.

"I'm going to remove the stitches," he says.

A smile curves her lips. "Today is turning out to be a pretty good day."

I watch as Marcello removes the stitches, and when he's done, she says, "Thank you."

"You're welcome."

I take hold of Samantha's hand and inspect the scars before pressing a kiss to her palm.

"All better," she sighs as she relaxes in the chair.

While her attention is on the garden, I stare at her and whisper, "Christ, you're beautiful."

She turns her head to meet my eyes. "I'm glad you think so."

"I know so."

We're quiet for a moment, then she asks, "What's your favorite memory from your childhood?"

I think for a moment before I answer, "The day I met Renzo. We took one look at each other and decided we were best friends."

A soft smile plays around her mouth. "How old were you?"

"Eleven."

"Wow, twenty-four years is a long time."

I nod, and letting out a chuckle, I say, "The fucker told everyone you called me your mystery man. I'm never going to hear the end of it."

Samantha bursts out laughing. "Why did you tell him?"

"I knew he'd get a kick out of it."

A frown forms on her forehead. "You don't go to *Paradiso* anymore."

"I went there to keep busy, but now that I have you, I don't need to fill my days with work."

She gets up, and taking my hand, she nods to the sliding doors. Rising to my feet, we head into the mansion.

Once we're taking the stairs up to the third floor, and there's no one in hearing distance, she asks, "Want to take a shower with me?"

"You don't have to ask me twice."

When we enter the bathroom, I turn on the faucets before watching my woman strip out of her clothes.

She lifts an eyebrow at me as she unhooks her bra. "Are you going to shower in the suit?"

I pull the gun from behind my back and set it on the counter before I undress.

Stepping beneath the warm spray, I pull Samantha against my body, and enjoy the feel of her naked body against mine.

"This is nice," she sighs.

"It is."

Bringing her hands to my chest, her palms slide over my skin. "I have a confession."

"Yeah?"

She grins up at me. "I'm obsessed with your body."

Gripping her ass, I pull her closer again. I lower my head and brush my lips against hers before saying, "And I'm obsessed with yours. What are we going to do about it?"

Her teeth tug at my bottom lip. "I can think of a couple of things."

Before I can claim her mouth, she kisses her way down my chest. When my woman kneels in front of me, it does something to my heart.

She wraps her fingers around my cock, and with her eyes locked on mine, she sucks me deep into her mouth.

I spread my legs further apart and grip hold of her wet strands.

Samantha keeps the pace slow, her tongue flicking over the swollen head that's already giving her a taste of precum.

"Harder," I demand. "I want to feel your teeth."

My woman obeys, and as her teeth scrape over my cock, I let out a satisfied groan.

She moves her hands to my ass and digs her nails into my skin before she takes me deeper.

"Fuck, baby. Yes," I growl, my eyes locked on her sinful mouth wrapped around my cock. "So fucking sexy."

I bring my other hand to her lips and pull at her bottom lip as she takes me to the back of her throat.

Seeing her eyes tear and hearing her gag, I begin to thrust, and as I feel her throat clamp around the head of my cock, I growl, "Drink every last drop."

My woman obeys as my cock begins to jerk, and I clench my jaw from the pleasure coursing through my body.

Pulling out of her mouth, I wait for her to climb to her feet before I wrap my hand around the back of her neck and slam my mouth to hers.

When I taste myself on her tongue, I lose complete control. I lift her against my body, and she barely has time to wrap her legs around me before I enter her with a hard thrust.

I fucking devour her mouth while I grow harder inside her.

Samantha squirms on my cock, silently begging me to move.

Smirking, I break the kiss and ask, "Do you need me to fuck you, baby?"

"Yes," she moans, squirming again.

I grip her ass with one hand, and bracing my other against the tiled wall, I begin to hammer into her, my pace relentlessly hard.

With her arms wrapped around my neck, and her lips brushing against mine, I inhale her sobs and moans as she takes every punishing thrust.

It doesn't take long before she tilts her head back, and her body begins to convulse in my hold.

"That's it, baby. Come on my cock. Show me how much you love it when I fuck you."

She shatters, and with whimpers falling over her lips, she orgasms so fucking hard, it makes my own release strike like a lightning bolt.

We cling to each other as our pleasure shudders through us, and I swear, it feels as if our souls become one.

Chapter 44

Franco

After my private jet lands in Seattle, Samantha smiles happily as we walk to the SUV. We climb into the back while Milo and Via take the front seats.

I left Marcello in charge of things back home while I take a short vacation to meet Samantha's family.

My fingers tighten around hers, and it has her saying, "They're going to love you. Stop worrying."

"I'm not worried," I mutter. I take a deep breath and let it out slowly. "I'm nervous. It's my first time meeting 'the parents,' and I want things to go well."

"They will." She places her palm on my jaw and nudges my face toward her. When our eyes lock, she says, "And even if everything goes wrong and they hate you, I'll still love you. Nothing will change that. Okay?"

I lean closer and press my mouth to hers, savoring the feel of my woman's lips before I pull back and say, "I want everything to go flawlessly, baby. I know how much your family means to you."

Her fingers brush over my jaw, her eyes soft with love. "It's already perfect."

I press another kiss to her mouth and push the worry back so I won't cause her any stress.

While in Seattle, we'll sleep at a hotel while spending our days with Samantha's family.

When Milo steers the SUV up a short driveway, I take in the suburban house where Samantha grew up.

I recognize her mother from the photos I've seen as she steps onto the porch, and the next second, Samantha's out of the car like a lightning bolt, running to hug her mother.

Via gets out and stays in Samantha's vicinity while Milo murmurs, "Good luck, boss."

"Thanks," I breathe as I shove the door open and get out.

Samantha's father comes out the front door, and he's next to hug his daughter.

Mrs. Blakely glances at me, her smile waning slightly while her eyes widen.

I can't decide whether to shake her hand or hug her, and luckily, I don't have to. As she opens her arms, I place my hand on her waist and lean down so she can give me a motherly hug.

"Welcome to the family, Franco," she says. "It's nice to finally put a face to the name."

I kiss her on both cheeks, then murmur, "Thank you, Mrs. Blakely."

Pulling away from her, I turn my attention to Mr. Blakely, who's looking at me with a scowl.

Here we go.

Samantha playfully slaps her father's arm. "Stop, Dad."

A chuckle escapes him, and as a smile spreads over his face, he holds his hand out to me. "Hello, Franco."

I take it, and while we shake, I say, "Nice to meet you, sir."

"Just call us Vanessa and Scott," Mrs. Blakely interjects.

"Thank you," I say before gesturing at Milo and Via to introduce them to Samantha's parents.

When we walk into the house, and we're busy removing our coats, Vanessa says, "Matt and Wendy will only be here for Thanksgiving day."

"That's a pity," Samantha replies as she takes hold of my hand.

I interlink our fingers and grip her tightly as we follow her parents into the cozy living room.

Milo gives me a silent head gesture, indicating he'll be outside having a cigarette if I need him. Via's still glancing around when Milo takes her arm and nudges her to go with him.

I wait for Samantha to choose a couch before I sit down beside her.

I notice all the framed photos on the mantelpiece, then Scott asks, "How's business? I understand you supply medical equipment to hospitals."

"Yes, I do." I reply as I take Samantha's hand again, and placing it on my thigh, I cover it with my own. "Business is good. Samantha mentioned you're a football coach."

He nods, then asks, "Do you watch sports?"

"Unfortunately, I don't have much spare time," I reply, my shoulders feeling a little tense.

"Okay, this is way too awkward for me," Samantha jumps in to save me. "No talking about sports, politics, business, or religion."

Vanessa smiles at her daughter. "I second that." She gestures at the dress Samantha's wearing. "Is that one of the dresses you got last time you were here?"

Samantha grins wide. "Yes. Franco loves them, so we need to go shopping for more."

Vanessa's face lights up. "We can go tomorrow."

Scott's eyes settle on me again. "While the women are out shopping, we can throw a couple of steaks on the grill."

"Sounds great," I murmur.

Vanessa glances between her daughter and me, then says, "I was a bit surprised when Sammie told us she's dating you. I never got the impression you liked each other."

I let out a chuckle. "Oh, I liked her. She was just too stubborn to notice."

"No, you were too grumpy and insufferable," Samantha argues.

I look at my woman. "Only because you gave me the cold shoulder."

"You deserved my cold shoulder," she chuckles.

Not considering her parents, I place my palm against the side of her head and press a kiss to her forehead. "Luckily, that's all behind us now."

Samantha's eyes lock with mine, her love for me shining from them. "Yeah."

Scott clears his throat, reminding us they're in the living room, and it makes Samantha chuckle.

Vanessa's watching us with a soft smile. "You look happy."

"I am, Mom."

She presses her cheek to my shoulder as the conversation continues, and slowly I relax.

Samantha

While Franco and Dad get to know each other better, I'm walking through the mall with Mom and Via.

Last night, Franco gave me his credit card, ordering me to spoil Mom rotten. When I asked how much I could spend, he said there's no limit.

Just after I moved in with him, Franco and I agreed I would continue to work, but he'd take care of our expenses.

Right now, I have no interest to stop working. Besides, I like giving Franco crap at the office.

Not to mention the hot sex when he bends me over his desk.

"What do you think?" Mom suddenly asks.

"Huh?"

"Where's your mind at?" she asks, holding up a cardigan for me to look at.

"Red's not your color." I dig between the other cardigans and find a light blue one. "This one will go with your eyes."

Mom holds the red and blue cardigans in front of her and turns to Via. "Which one do you like?"

Via instantly agrees with me as she says, "The blue one, ma'am."

Mom drapes it over her forearm, and as we continue to look through the store, she says, "So he's the one, sweetie?"

"Without a doubt," I murmur, glancing at a couple of dresses.

"Have you talked about marriage and children?"

"Yes." I grin at Mom. "We'd like to have two children, but we'll see what the future holds."

"Are you still going to work for him?"

"Yes." Before Mom can throw the follow-up question at me, I say, "Franco is fine with it."

"Really?"

I nod while holding a cute yellow dress in front of me.

"Oooh, I like that one," Mom says.

I glance at Via, and she nods her approval.

When we walk to the counter to pay, Mom mentions, "He comes across as a very intense man."

"It's one of the things I love about him," I reply while I look at some hats and scarves.

"He's quite handsome."

I grin at Mom. "Right?"

"Doesn't it bother you when other women look at him?" she asks.

"No." I place the clothes on the counter and add Mom's items to the pile. "They can drool all they want. He's mine."

When Mom digs in her handbag for her wallet, I say, "Today's shopping spree is sponsored by Franco."

"Are you sure?"

I nod as I tap the credit card on the machine before tucking it back into my wallet.

I grab the bag, and when we continue to walk through the mall, Mom says, "I love how Franco looks at you."

"Yeah? How does he look at me?"

"As if you're his entire world."

I let out a chuckle. "He actually tells me that on a daily basis."

Mom hooks her arm through mine. "I'm really happy you met the one, sweetie."

411

"Me too."

Chapter 45

Franco

Scott sits at the kitchen table, watching as I roast the potatoes with herbs until they're crispy.

"Where did you learn to cook?" he asks.

"My mom." I glance at him from over my shoulder. "She practically lived in the kitchen."

"Do your parents live in New York?"

I shake my head. "They passed away a few years ago."

"I'm sorry to hear that," he murmurs.

"They lived a long life," I mention.

His eyebrows fly up, "How old are you?"

"Thirty-five. My parents had me late in life." I take the pan off the stove and prepare three plates. Walking to the back door, I tell Milo, "Food's ready."

"Coming, boss."

"Let's eat here," Scott says. "If we make a mess in the dining room, my wife won't let me hear the end of it."

I let out a chuckle as I place his plate in front of him. "It sounds like Samantha takes after her mother."

"She does."

Milo grabs his food and heads to the living room while I take a seat across from Scott.

There's a nervous tension in my body as I lock eyes with him. "I need to talk to you about something important."

His features tighten as emotion washes over his face. "I was trying to brace for it."

"What?"

"You asking me for my daughter's hand in marriage," he says.

Nodding, I lift my chin, and after sucking in a deep breath, I murmur, "I love Samantha more than anything. Your daughter is the most amazing person I've ever met. She's vibrant, intelligent, caring, funny, and so stubborn it drives me insane at times. I can't live without her."

He nods. "I know the feeling." The corner of his mouth lifts. "I feel the same way about her mother."

We stare at each other for a moment, then I say, "Your blessing is very important to me."

"It's up to Samantha. She's the one who has to say yes."

414

I nod. "I'd still like your blessing."

He stares at me again. "Treat my daughter right."

"Yes, sir."

"She always bottles up her worries. You have to pry it from her."

I nod. "I'm aware of that."

The corners of Scott's mouth tremble, and it makes me feel emotional. He takes a deep breath, then says, "You have my blessing."

"Thank you, sir. I promise to protect your daughter. I'll do everything in my power to make her happy."

He nods before he cuts a chunk of steak and shoves it into his mouth.

An emotionally loaded silence falls between us as we eat our food.

Samantha

Cradling my baby nephew in my arms, there's an intense need in my soul to have a child of my own.

It totally catches me off guard, and I can't tear my eyes away from his wide blue eyes and chubby cheeks.

"You're so precious," I whisper to Josh, brushing my palm over his white hair. "You're going to be blond like your Aunty Sammie."

Franco's arm rests on the back of my chair, and I can feel his eyes on me.

I want a child with him.

Suddenly, a potent smell drifts from Josh, and I scrunch my nose.

"Christ," Franco mutters before letting out a chuckle.

I stand up and walk to Wendy. "I think he needs a diaper change."

She takes Josh from me and sniffs his butt before she says, "Yep."

I return to my seat and let my eyes drift over my family. We already had Thanksgiving dinner and moved to the living room to relax.

Matt is talking to Dad about the latest sports while Mom watches them with a smile.

Franco leans closer to me and murmurs, "You looked like a natural holding Josh."

A smile stretches around my lips. "He's so cute."

When Wendy returns, she hands Josh to Mom before taking a seat next to Matt.

Franco gets up, and Dad clears his throat and gestures to Matt to stop talking.

I frown at Dad, then my eyes widen as Franco drops to one knee in front of me.

"Oh my God," Wendy gasps.

I lock eyes with Franco as he says, "I didn't know there was a chunk of my soul missing until I met you."

My heart.

"You gave me a chance for which I'm eternally grateful. You've shown me the true meaning of happiness. You've taught me to be patient." He clears his throat, then continues, "I can't live without your sass, your bravery, your strength. I want you to be the mother of my children and my wife."

My chin begins to tremble as I stare deep into Franco's dark eyes.

"Will you marry me?"

I suck in a deep breath and fight to control my emotions as I tease him. "I'll have to think about it."

With a chuckle, he pulls a small blue box from his pocket, and when he opens it, I see an oval diamond with a dainty leaf pattern.

Franco tilts his head, then asks, "How long do you need to think about it?"

"Not long," I whisper. I stare at my man, memorizing everything about this moment. "Yes, I'll marry you."

He lets out a breath of relief as he pushes the engagement ring onto my left hand. Then he mutters, "Thank God you didn't make me wait for weeks again."

Leaning forward, I press my mouth to his in a sweet kiss, and as I pull back, Mom's wiping tears from her cheeks while Dad keeps clearing his throat.

"Congratulations," Matt says, breaking the silence.

Asking me in front of my loved ones shows how well Franco knows me. It was perfect.

We both get up, and while Mom and Wendy admire the ring on my finger, Dad and Matt shake hands with Franco.

Milo comes into the room with a tray of champagne glasses, and as I take one, he says, "Congratulations."

When everybody has a glass of bubbly, Dad toasts, "May you have a long and happy life together."

Franco comes to stand beside me, and wrapping his arm around my lower back, he presses a kiss to my temple. "Do you like the ring?"

I glance down at the diamond and nod. "It's beautiful. Thank you, Franco."

Tilting my head back, I look up at him, and seeing the happiness in his eyes, I feel it flow through my soul.

He lowers his head and brushes a tender kiss against my mouth. "I love you, baby."

I take his glass from him and set it down on the coffee table. Turning back to my man, I wrap my arms around his neck and hug the everloving hell out of him.

His arms engulf me, and with my mouth by his ear, I whisper, "I love you too, my mystery man."

Epilogue

Samantha

Feeling nervous because I know how important tonight's guests are, I check all the platters of food before I walk to the living room where voices are rumbling.

I pause before the entrance and take a deep breath.

Via places her hand on my shoulder. "Are you okay?"

I nod and give her a smile. "Don't leave my side."

"I won't."

When I step forward, she places her hand on my lower back so I can feel her.

The moment I walk into the living room, Franco's eyes lock on me. He comes toward me and gives Via a nod before he wraps his arm around my waist.

"Congratulations on your engagement, Samantha," Dario says.

"Thank you."

My eyes dart to the only other couple, and Franco says, "Meet Angelo and Vittoria."

"It's nice meeting you," I murmur, glad there's another woman here tonight.

While Angelo looks as intimidating as the rest of the men, Vittoria gives me a friendly smile. Seeing her baby bump, the need for my own child increases.

Yep, I officially have baby fever.

I glance at Renzo, and knowing how important he is to Franco, I say, "It's nice to see you again, Renzo."

His features soften as he nods.

When I turn my attention to the last of the men, a shiver creeps down my spine, and I move closer to Franco.

"This is Damiano, *capo dei capi*. He's the boss of bosses."

That explains a lot.

My voice quivers slightly as I say, "Nice to meet you."

"The pleasure is mine," he murmurs.

Franco presses a kiss to my temple, then Renzo holds up a tumbler of whiskey, saying, "To you and your mystery man."

"Shut up," Franco grumbles, which lightens the mood a hell of a lot as everyone chuckles.

When the men return to their various conversations, I look at Franco and say, "Join your friends. I want to get to know Vittoria better."

I pull away from Franco, and as I walk to Vittoria, her smile widens. "Hi."

With Via right behind me, I take in the beautiful woman as I say, "I'm so glad you're here. I'd feel out of place with the men."

She lets out a chuckle. "You'll get used to them."

"So you're married to Angelo?" When she nods, I ask, "How far along are you?"

"Twenty-six weeks."

I scrunch my nose. "And in months?"

She lets out a soft chuckle. "Six months."

"I hope I look as good as you when I'm pregnant," I compliment her.

"You're sweet."

"What are you two whispering about here in the corner?" Franco suddenly asks from behind me.

"Babies." I turn around and grin at him. "I want one."

"Excuse me for a moment," Vittoria says before she walks to Angelo.

"Hmm." Franco pulls me into his arms. "Then stop taking the pill."

My eyes widen and I feel a burst of excitement. "Really? Are you okay with it?"

He presses a kiss to the tip of my nose. "Of course." The corner of his mouth lifts. "What my woman wants, she gets."

Lowering my lashes half-mast, I give him a seductive look. "The more sex we have, the better our chances will be."

His eyes darken. "Baby, I'll fuck you twenty-four-seven if that's what it takes."

"I look forward to it," I say, my tone playful.

Pulling away from Franco, I let out a chuckle when I hear him mutter, "Thanks for the hard-on, baby."

I glance over my shoulder and wink at him. "You're welcome."

Via quickly moves closer to me as I walk to where Milo is standing by the sliding doors.

"Can you have a couple of the men bring the platters to the veranda, please?" I ask him.

"Sure thing."

I've gotten used to Marcello and Milo and can even be alone with them, which I'm taking as a huge win.

When Franco notices the food is being carried to the table out on the veranda, he says, "Let's head outside."

Everyone finds a seat, and I'm glad when Vittoria claims the one to my right.

Franco grabs the chair to my left, and taking hold of my hand, he places it on his thigh.

With the table providing cover, I move my hand until my palm brushes over the outline of his cock.

I squeeze and massage him through his pants, which earns me a grumble by my ear. "If you keep going, I'll throw you over my shoulder, carry you to the restroom, and fuck you raw."

I squeeze him hard before I pull my hand away and grab a salmon puff from the nearest platter.

Soon, everyone is enjoying the food and laughter fills the air as the men joke with each other.

I turn my head, and seeing the smile on Franco's face, I say, "We should make this a regular thing."

"I agree with her," Dario backs me up.

"We can host a dinner next month," Vittoria chimes in. "Right, Angelo?"

"Sure."

Franco rests his arm around my shoulders, and leaning closer, he murmurs, "Thank you, baby."

"Anything for my man."

His eyes roam over my face, then he asks, "How are you holding up?"

"I'm fine." I press a kiss to his jaw before I add, "I have you by my side."

His features soften with a loving look. "Always, baby."

Bonus Epilogue

Franco

(Five years later…)

Augusto barrels past me to where Marcello and Milo are dragging the Christmas tree into the living room before disappearing into the foyer.

"Mommeeee, we're back."

"I'm coming," I hear Samantha answer from the direction of the kitchen.

A second later, our two daughters run into the room with chocolate icing all over their mouths.

"Did Mommy let you lick out the bowl?" I ask as they each grab one of my legs and stand on my shoes.

With my daughters giggling, I keep walking toward the foyer.

Samantha appears in the doorway with Augusto in her arms, and frowning at the girls, she says, "Sienna! Bianca! You're getting icing all over your father's pants. Come wash your hands."

Before Samantha can head to the bathroom with our triplets, I wrap my hand around the back of her neck, and plant a kiss on her mouth.

"Let me just change into comfortable clothes, then I'll take the kids so you can –"

She interrupts me before I can finish my sentence, saying, "We have to decorate the tree."

I give her a no-nonsense look. "Baby, the tree can wait an hour. You've been on your feet all day. Take a nap while we get everything ready."

"You sure?"

"Yes." I take Augusto from her arms. "And stop carrying the kids. You shouldn't be lifting anything heavy."

Suddenly, a smile spreads over her face. "I love how you always fuss about me."

"It's the least I can do."

I brush my palm over her baby bump and give her another kiss.

When I walk away with Augusto in my arms, he asks, "Daddy, why is my brother taking so long to come?"

"He's still growing inside Mommy's tummy," I answer him as I head up to the third floor.

Walking into the bedroom, I drop my boy on the bed, and he lets out a shriek of laughter.

"Again," he demands.

"We'll wrestle as soon as I've changed my clothes."

He stands up on the bed, and making the best angry face he can, he pretends to be the Hulk. "I'm going to win."

I always let him win.

I quickly strip out of the suit while Augusto sounds like a puppy that's learning to growl.

Opening the vault, I place my gun inside before ensuring the door is secure. When I have my sweatpants and a T-shirt on, I dart back into the room and tackle Augusto off his feet.

Before I can tickle him, Samantha comes into the room with Sienna and Bianca. They climb onto the bed and begin to climb all over me.

"Wait. Everyone off the bed so Mommy can sleep," I order.

They quickly scramble off, and in a chorus, they say, "Sweet dreams, Mommy."

"Thank you, my little angels."

"I'm the Hulk," Augusto says, trying to make his voice deeper. "Hulk smash."

"Hulk can go smash downstairs," I chuckle as I herd the kids out of the bedroom.

As I turn to shut the door, Samantha's face is filled with love. "God, I'm glad I married you. Love you."

"Love you too, baby."

I head downstairs with my trio of tornadoes, and walking into the living room, I say, "We have to wrap Mommy's presents before she wakes up."

"Yay!!" They sing with excitement.

"I'll bring everything," Marcello mutters before heading to the guesthouse where I've been hiding the gifts so Samantha doesn't accidentally find them.

I pull the box we keep all the wrapping paper and tape in closer and ask, "Which wrapping paper do you want to use?"

"The one with Santa on," Sienna orders, and her brother and sister don't argue.

She has a take-charge attitude that reminds me a lot of her mother.

When Marcello returns with the gifts, I let the kids pick which ones they want to wrap.

Marcello sits down beside Augusto while Milo and Via join the girls.

Sitting on the floor with everyone, I grab a *Dior* candle and find a gift bag with snowflakes on it.

The kids murmur here and there as they wrap the presents. Some look worse for wear, but I know Samantha will love the effort they put in.

Augusto gives up after wrapping three gifts and crawling onto the couch, he's out cold within seconds.

Bianca yawns, and abandoning the gift Via is helping her with, she crawls onto my lap and snuggles her head against my chest.

Leaning back against the couch, I glance at Via and say, "Switch on the TV so we can watch a Christmas show."

Sienna makes herself comfortable on Milo's lap while Marcello keeps wrapping gifts.

Via scrolls through the movies, then chooses one about Santa Claus.

Fifteen minutes into the movie, the kids are fast asleep, and Marcello places all the presents on the coffee table.

"I'm going to check on Samantha," Via murmurs before leaving the room.

I glance at Milo and grin when I see he's busy drifting off as well.

"Do you want something to drink?" Marcello asks me.

"No, thanks. I'm good."

Not long after Samantha walks into the living room, and I give her a dark frown.

"Oh, hush," she mutters. "I can't sleep."

I get up and carefully pass Bianca to Via so I can join Samantha on one of the couches. Taking a seat by her feet, I lift them onto my lap and gently massage her ankles and calves while we continue to watch the movie.

"You know what's unfair," Samantha grumbles.

"What, baby?"

"Around me, the kids have endless energy, but as soon as they're with you, they're calm."

I grin at her as I say, "It's because you let them get away with murder."

"Hmm…"

I keep massaging her legs, my eyes drifting over her beautiful face.

"What do you want for Christmas?" she asks me for the hundredth time.

"I have everything I want."

"You have to give me a couple of ideas," she complains. "You're impossible to buy for."

"Baby, you've already given me the world. There's nothing else I want."

The End.

Published Books

In Reading Order:

MAFIA ROMANCE

THE KINGS OF MAFIA SERIES

Mafia / Organized Crime / Suspense Romance
(Can be read in this order or as standalones)
This series is not connected to any other series I've written, and there will be no spin-offs.

Tempted By The Devil
Craving Danger

Pre-Order Now…
Hunted By A Shadow

and coming 2024…
Drawn To Darkness
God Of Vengeance

(The Saints, Sinners & Corrupted Royals all take place in the same world)

THE SAINTS SERIES

Mafia / Organized Crime / Suspense Romance
(Can be read in this order or as standalones)

Merciless Saints
Cruel Saints
Ruthless Saints
Tears of Betrayal
Tears of Salvation

THE SINNERS SERIES

Mafia / Organized Crime / Suspense Romance
(Can be read in this order or as standalones)

Taken By A Sinner
Owned By A Sinner
Stolen By A Sinner
Chosen By A Sinner
Captured By A Sinner

CORRUPTED ROYALS

Mafia / Organized Crime / Suspense Romance
(Can be read in this order or as standalones)

Destroy Me
Control Me
Brutalize Me
Restrain Me
Possess Me

CONTEMPORARY ROMANCE

BEAUTIFULLY BROKEN SERIES

Organized Crime / Suspense Romance
(Can be read in this order or as standalones)

Beautifully Broken
Beautifully Hurt
Beautifully Destroyed

ENEMIES TO LOVERS

College Romance / New Adult / Billionaire Romance

Heartless
Reckless
Careless
Ruthless
Shameless

TRINITY ACADEMY

College Romance / New Adult / Billionaire Romance

Falcon
Mason
Lake
Julian

The Epilogue

THE HEIRS

College Romance / New Adult / Billionaire Romance

Coldhearted Heir
Arrogant Heir
Defiant Heir
Loyal Heir
Callous Heir
Sinful Heir
Tempted Heir
Forbidden Heir

Stand Alone Spin-off
Not My Hero
Young Adult / High School Romance

THE SOUTHERN HEROES SERIES

*Suspense Romance / Contemporary Romance /
Police Officers & Detectives*

The Ocean Between Us
The Girl In The Closet
The Lies We Tell Ourselves
All The Wasted Time
We Were Lost

STANDALONES

<u>LIFELINE</u>
(FBI Suspense Romance)

<u>UNFORGETTABLE</u>
Co-written with Tayla Louise
(Contemporary/Billionaire Romance)

Connect with me

Newsletter

FaceBook

Amazon

GoodReads

BookBub

Instagram

Acknowledgments

The support Tempted By The Devil got is out of this world. Thank you so much to my readers for making this girl's dreams come true. I hope you love Franco as much as Angelo, if not more.

My editor, Sheena, has nerves of steel with all the deadlines wooshing past us. Thank you for putting up with me and always being honest with your feedback. I appreciate you so much!

To my alpha and beta readers – Leeann, Brittney, Sherrie, and Sarah thank you for being the godparents of my paper-baby. Thank you for all your time and feedback.

Candi Kane PR - Thank you for being patient with me and my bad habit of missing deadlines. Thank you for being my friend and always being there to calm me down.

Sarah, from *Okay Creations* – I love, love, love the Kings of Mafia covers! Thank you for doing such an amazing job with them.

My street team, thank you for promoting my books. It means the world to me!

A special thank you to every blogger and reader who took the time to participate in the cover reveal and release day.

Love,
Michelle.

Printed in Great Britain
by Amazon

43138951R00245